93

WHEN HELL FREEZES OVER

DARRIEN LEE

WHEN HELL FREEZES OVER

SBI

STREBOR BOOKS

NEW YORK   LONDON   TORONTO   SYDNEY

Strebor Books
P.O. Box 6505
Largo, MD 20792
http://www.streborbooks.com

© 2005 by Darrien Lee

Cover Illustration: André Harris

ISBN-13 978-1-59309-042-5
ISBN-10   1-59309-042-0
LCCN 2004118375

First Strebor Books hardcover edition August 2005

10 9 8 7 6 5 4 3 2 1

Manufactured in the United States of America

For information regarding special discounts for bulk purchases, please contact Simon & Schuster Special Sales at 1-800-456-6798 or business@simonandschuster.com

DEDICATION

I would like to dedicate this novel to all my devoted fans, who have supported me and continue to support my efforts. THANK YOU!

ACKNOWLEDGMENTS

I would like to thank my entire family for continued support, especially my husband and daughters. I appreciate you for giving me the private time I needed to put this novel together. Your love and patience is priceless.

To my fellow sidekicks, V. Anthony Rivers, JDaniels, Tina Brooks McKinney, Harold L. Turley II, Allison Hobbs and Shelley Halima, thanks for the encouragement during the down times and the laughter during the fun times.

I want to thank Cory and Heather Buford for hooking me up with a new website and to André Harris for creating another slamming book cover.

I want to lift up my Pastor, Rev. Vincent Windrow, and the members of Olive Branch Missionary Baptist Church in Antioch, Tennessee for their spiritual guidance and support. I wouldn't have made it without you.

To the rest of my Strebor family members, thank you for pushing my novels even when I'm not around. It means so much to me to know we support each other in our efforts no matter what.

I send more thanks out to the members of The Ties That Bind Book Club for their support and encouraging words. I also have to thank my friend Tiffany Lee for "dogging me" to finish my books when I didn't feel like working. Many thanks also go out to Samantha Green and Rita Rippy for always staying in touch and supporting me.

Many thanks to out to my closest friends, Tracy Dandridge, Brenda Thomas, Buanita Ray, Sharon Nowlin and Monica Baker for the things you've done for me no matter how big or small.

Lastly, I want to thank God for allowing me to have the creative mind to continue to bring these exciting novels to all my readers.

CHAPTER 1

The room was dark and Keaton had listened to Dejá giggle for over an hour. He'd met her at the gym where she worked as an aerobics instructor. She possessed a pair of long, shapely legs, beige skin, and seductive green eyes. She was physically fit with a derriere so firm, you could bounce quarters off it.

"Keaton, why don't you come over here and give me that massage you promised me?" she beckoned him.

She'd been coming on to him for weeks now and had become extremely hard for him to resist; not that he really wanted to. Dejá was very sexy and wasn't the least bit shy about telling him exactly what she wanted.

"I had no idea you was so uninhibited, Dejá," he replied.

She scooted over to him and kissed her way down his body until she made him quiver in ecstasy.

He hissed seductively and moaned, "Damn, girl," while his eyes rolled back in his head.

It had been way too long since he'd been intimate with anyone and Dejá was working him like a magician.

After a few minutes, she giggled childlike. "My turn!"

He grinned as he watched her scoot backwards on the bed. He stood and said, "No problem, but first let me get the ice cream."

"Ice cream? Keaton, you're such an animal."

He left the room and quickly returned with a half-pint of strawberry swirl. Dejá's eyes widened as she watched him dip his finger into the cool mixture. He turned to her, growled, and said, "This may be a little cold."

Dejá took a breath to prepare herself. Keaton smiled, disappeared under the sheets, and happily returned the pleasure.

Keaton's doctor had put him on mandatory medical leave, keeping him from working at his beloved San Antonio restaurant, Lorraine's. It was named in memory of his grandmother, who'd spoiled him to no end as he was growing up. Because of that, it meant everything to him. Now, he wasn't even allowed on the premises, just because his blood pressure had been registering a little high. Everyone in his family had become worried that a stroke was inevitable and vowed to help him regain control of his health before allowing him to return.

Locked out from his restaurant by his parents, he didn't know what he was going to do with himself until his sister, Arnelle, had invited him to come to Philadelphia for some rest and relaxation. He'd be sharing a home with his sister, who was a sports medical doctor at her friend's clinic. Winston, Arnelle's husband and a prominent lawyer, would be spending most of his days in court. Following close behind were their two small children, MaLeah, age four and a half, and Fredrick, age one.

Keaton's parents assured him they'd keep a watchful eye on his restaurant while he was away. He tried to remain positive, knowing he had a dependable staff running the restaurant in his absence.

Leaving Lorraine's in the hands of his trusted assistant manager, Trenton, wasn't something he wanted to do. However, Trenton had done an excellent job running things during a brief absence once before. He'd never been away this long and he couldn't wait until his medical leave was up so he could return.

His father, Judge Herbert Lapahie, was in the process of gearing down his campaign to be San Antonio's next mayor. He was patiently awaiting elections, which would take place within three months. Almost daily, his parents had stressed the importance of following the doctor's orders before he left for Philly. He only hoped his visit to Philly would be a short one.

CHAPTER 2

Keaton was awakened by his energetic niece, MaLeah. She found it amusing to sit on his back and bounce up and down like she was riding a horse. He'd had a long night with Dejá and had returned home a few hours earlier.

MaLeah tugged on his T-shirt and yelled, "Uncie Key, wake up!"

Keaton thought he was dreaming at first.

"Uncie Key, I'm hungry! Wake up!"

Keaton turned over, causing MaLeah to roll off his back. She giggled as she tried to pry his eyes open with her fingers. Keaton suddenly grabbed her and started tickling her. MaLeah screamed with laughter as her uncle playfully wrestled with her. Her long pigtails swung wildly as she kicked and screamed for mercy. He finally stopped allowing her to catch her breath. She looked adorable, dressed in her Philadelphia Eagles football jersey.

"Shorty, what are you doing in here waking me up so early? Where are your mom and dad?"

"Mommie's feeding Freddie," she announced as she poked his dimples.

Freddie was MaLeah's one-year-old brother, Winston Fredrick Carter IV. Keaton threw the covers back and climbed out of bed. MaLeah stood and started jumping up and down on the bed, turning it into her personal trampoline.

He turned and said, "Stop before you fall and break your neck."

"K!"

He sat her on the side of the bed. "Sit right there until I come out of the bathroom. Then we'll go make breakfast."

MaLeah giggled and clapped. Her uncle couldn't do anything but laugh as he entered the bathroom.

Dressed in sweatpants and a T-shirt, Keaton returned to the room, slid into his slippers and took MaLeah by the hand. Walking out, he noticed the time: seven-fifteen. He sighed and figured this was the first of many rituals he'd have to perform while visiting his sister and her family.

Downstairs, Keaton and MaLeah found Arnelle finishing up breakfast with Fredrick.

Arnelle looked up and smiled. "You had a late night last night, Keaton. Why are you up so early this morning?"

He nodded toward MaLeah as he raised his coffee cup up to his mouth.

She laughed. "You know she can't help herself. You created that monster. That's why she stays up late with you, and she's your alarm clock in the morning."

"I'm going to start locking my door," he proclaimed.

"You know that won't stop her. She'll sit outside the door, calling for you until you open it. Accept the fact, dear brother, that MaLeah Carter is going to continue to be your little shadow. At least until her daddy comes home. Only then will you get a temporary break."

They laughed together.

Keaton added more cream to his coffee, then asked, "Where's Perry Mason?"

Arnelle threw Fredrick's toy at him. "Winston had to go into the office early this morning, and stop calling him Perry Mason."

Keaton grinned. "He'll always be Perry Mason to me."

She smiled and walked over and poured herself a cup of coffee. "Whatever, Keaton. You and Winston are always teasing each other about one thing or another."

He defended himself. "He starts it most of the time."

Leaning closer, she whispered, "Look, Keaton, I hope you're being careful with those women you've been going out with."

"Of course I am," he answered with a frown. "Do you think I'm crazy?"

"You'd better be," she argued. "You know your history with women."

Without responding to her last comment, he walked over and kissed Fredrick on the cheek before adding pancakes to MaLeah's plate. He didn't need Arnelle playing momma to him. If that was going to be the case, he'd find somewhere else to chill until he could return to Texas.

MaLeah tried to follow in her uncle's footsteps by walking over to her brother. She glanced up at Fredrick as he sung and made other baby noises. She leaned in and planted a kiss on his tiny hand. As she turned to walk away, he grabbed one of her pigtails with a kung fu grip. It took only seconds for her to let out a bloodcurdling scream. Both Arnelle and Keaton turned at the same time to find Fredrick trying to put MaLeah's hair into his mouth. Arnelle quickly went to them and popped Fredrick's hand so he'd release his grip. Startled, he closed his eyes briefly, but continued to hold on to her hair.

"Fredrick! Turn your sister's hair loose!"

Fredrick was big for his age and he wasn't easing up on his grip at all. She popped his hand again as MaLeah continued to scream. Arnelle couldn't believe that she'd popped his tiny hand twice and he'd neither cried nor turned MaLeah's hair loose. Keaton watched this go on for a few more seconds. He shook his head, then walked over with his plate in his hand.

He stood in front of Fredrick and yelled, "Fredrick! Let go!"

Fredrick's eyes quickly filled with tears as he looked up at his uncle who was frowning at him. He slowly released MaLeah's pigtail as he looked at his momma and burst out crying. Keaton turned around and casually sat down at the table to eat his breakfast.

Arnelle hugged MaLeah. "Don't even try it, Fredrick! You hurt your sister!"

MaLeah clung to her momma's neck for comfort. Looking over Arnelle's shoulder at her uncle, she saw him wink at her and smile. A few sobs later, she kissed Arnelle on the cheek and walked over to Keaton.

He smiled and asked, "Are you okay, Shorty?"

"Freddie hurt my head," she said as she pointed to her hair.

"I know, but he's sorry. Aren't you, Fredrick?"

Fredrick was still crying as Arnelle hurriedly cleaned up the kitchen. She had no sympathy for her crying toddler.

up MaLeah and took her back over to her brother. He knelt

, stop crying and give your sister a kiss so she'll know you

his bottom lip and looked at his uncle. He was only one but seemed to understand.

Keaton said again, "Kiss, Fredrick!"

Fredrick leaned over and kissed MaLeah on the cheek.

"Now, MaLeah, you kiss your brother," he instructed her.

MaLeah reluctantly kissed her brother, then quickly jumped back into Keaton's arms. When all was finished, he sat her in her chair with her plate of pancakes in front of her. Arnelle watched him be the peacemaker with her children. She thought to herself, realizing he'd make a great father one day.

"Why did Winston have to go in so early this morning?" Keaton inquired.

Giving the kitchen another look, she replied, "I don't know, but I need to hurry up and get out of here myself."

Keaton laughed. "Are you guys ready for tonight?"

He was talking about the Professional African-American Awards banquet. Winston was up for Man-of-the-Year.

Arnelle turned on the dishwasher. "As ready as we're going to be. Winston's so excited, but if he doesn't get it, he's okay. He enjoys working with those young boys over at the youth center. Since he's taken over, the attendance has risen."

"Dang, Sis, those kids must really like old Winston."

She smiled with pride. "They love him and so do I."

Keaton watched his sister's eyes brighten when she spoke of her husband. They'd had a rocky start, but neither of them could fight off the inevitable. With what they'd shared, they were destined to be together. He couldn't imagine having that kind of love and connection with one woman for the rest of his life. Besides, marriage wasn't for everyone.

Looking around the kitchen once more, Arnelle said, "Okay, I'm out of here. We should be home by four so we can get ready for the banquet. Are you sure you're going to be all right with these two rugrats tonight? Camille said she'd watch them for us."

Keaton frowned at his sister. "You act like I'm the babysitter from hell or something. I told you, I got it. We'll be fine!"

Arnelle threw up her hands in surrender. "Okay, okay. I didn't mean for you to get all bent out of shape."

"I'm cool. I have a lot of fun and games planned for these two."

MaLeah was smiling at her uncle as she sat eating her pancakes. She'd heard the words "fun" and "games" in the same sentence. When her uncle said "fun" he meant *fun*.

On that statement, Arnelle grabbed her jacket and said, "Well, it seems you have everything under control so let me get out of your way."

Before walking out the door, she kissed Fredrick, MaLeah, and lastly Keaton.

"See you guys later," she said as she pulled on Keaton's ear playfully like he was a little boy. Even though he was her younger brother, he looked older than his thirty-two years.

"Bye, Mommie!" MaLeah loudly shouted.

CHAPTER 3

Later that evening, Keaton helped MaLeah with her bath while Arnelle and Winston dressed for the banquet. As MaLeah splashed and tossed her duck at Keaton, he sat on the toilet seat and tried to read his *Sports Illustrated* in peace.

"Uncie Key!"

Without looking up, he answered, "Yes, Shorty?"

"Look! My ducky can fly!"

Keaton glanced over and watched her throw the duck against the wall and giggle loudly.

He shook his head. "Are you almost done?"

"Nope!"

About that time, Winston walked in looking debonair in his suit.

"Daddy!"

Keaton eyed him up and down. "Dang, Bro, you look like you stepped off the cover of *GQ*."

"Thanks. So how did it go with Dejá last night?" Keaton smiled mischievously. Winston laughed. "Say no more. Are you sure about being the nanny tonight? I mean, you don't have another date or something?"

Keaton chuckled. "Get the hell out of here. I have everything under control and no, I don't have a date. You just make sure you win tonight."

"Oooo! Uncie Key said a bad word!" MaLeah screamed.

Keaton rolled his eyes while Winston laughed.

Winston folded his arms. "You do know she watches and listens to everything you say and do?"

"Yeah, I know. I hope I don't leave any bad habits with her when I leave."

Winston looked over at his daughter. "MaLeah, you make sure you behave tonight and help take care of your brother with your uncle. Now blow me a kiss 'cause you're not about to get me wet."

Keaton stood up. "Hold up, Bro. That'll never work with her, and you know it."

Keaton grabbed the towel and pulled MaLeah's naked, slippery body out of the suds. He wrapped the towel around her body, pinning her arms to her side so she couldn't move.

"Now, give your daddy a kiss."

She smiled and gave her dad a welcomed kiss.

Afterwards, Winston yelled, "Arnelle, you'd better get in here so you can give your daughter a goodnight kiss while she's retrained!"

MaLeah saw this entire scene as a game. She giggled as she looked up at her daddy. "Daddy, kiss, kiss!"

"You're greedy, just like your momma," he said with a smile.

Arnelle walked in looking stunning in her ivory beaded gown. "I heard that, counselor," she warned him. He turned to kiss Arnelle on the cheek. "Hurry up, woman, so we won't be late." She looked at her brother, standing there holding her daughter imprisoned in the towel.

"What have you done to my baby?"

Keaton laughed. "I'm attempting to keep you and Winston dry. Hurry up before she figures out this towel is a restraint and not a game."

Arnelle kissed her daughter. "MaLeah, we'll be back later, so make sure you don't drive your Uncle Keaton crazy tonight. Okay?"

"K!"

Keaton looked at his sister. "You clean up real good, Sis. You look beautiful."

"Thanks. Now make sure you call if you need us, and all the important numbers are by the telephone in the kitchen. Fredrick is sleeping right now, but he'll probably wake up in a few hours for some milk and a diaper change."

Keaton dried MaLeah's body. "Arnelle, I got this! Go! Get out of here with your Man-of-the-Year."

Kissing him on the cheek, she smiled. "Okay. We're out of here."

MaLeah yelled, "Bye, Mommie!"

CHAPTER 4

K eaton and MaLeah had been watching TV for almost two hours. Dejá had called his cell phone three times, but he'd let his voicemail catch her calls. He'd been out with her several times, and it seemed like she was starting to get too attached to him, demanding more of his time.

MaLeah sat next to him, sharing popcorn and Pepsi. Fredrick's monitor had been silent for a while, so Keaton said, "Come on, Shorty. Let's go check on your brother. He should've been up by now."

"K!"

"You're supposed to say 'okay,' Shorty; not just 'K.'"

She giggled as Keaton took her hand and led her up the stairs. When they reached the landing, he knelt down. "Now you have to be quiet so you won't wake your brother."

"K! Uncie Key."

Hearing her say "K" again made him shake his head and laugh. It would be a while before she got it right.

They pushed open Fredrick's door and walked over to his bed. Keaton looked down on him and ran his hand across his back. It felt unusually warm. Frowning, he picked him up and cradled his head against his neck.

"Whoa! MaLeah, your brother feels kind of warm. We'd better take his temperature."

Keaton moved Fredrick over to the changing table, with MaLeah following closely behind. When he laid him down, he woke up crying.

"Hold on, little man. I'm getting ready to take care of you."

He removed the footie pajamas from his chubby body. Fredrick screamed louder as MaLeah looked on.

She watched her uncle fumble with the pajamas, then yelled, "Be quiet, Freddie!!"

Keaton softly said, "MaLeah, your brother doesn't feel well so be nice."

"K!!"

After removing the soaked diaper from Fredrick's bottom, he immediately released a stream of urine directly in Keaton's face.

"Oh shit!!"

He tried to duck, but it was too late.

MaLeah giggled out loud. "Ooooo! You said another bad word, Uncie Key!"

"I know, Shorty. I'm sorry and I better not hear you say it either," he explained as he wiped the urine from his face with a baby wipe.

She nodded in agreement, then said, "Freddie tee-teed in your face, Uncie Key!"

He placed a cloth diaper over Fredrick's naked body and continued to wipe his face.

"Yeah, he got me, Shorty. Man! I don't see how people do this every day!"

When he finished cleaning his face, he cautiously removed the cloth diaper and cleaned Fredrick's body. MaLeah watched with curiosity as she handed him the powder and fresh diaper. Fredrick had calmed down a little, until Keaton put the thermometer in his ear. While waiting for the results, he rubbed his round tummy in a soothing manner.

"Hold on, little man. I'm just taking your temperature," Keaton said as he tried to remain calm.

About that time a beep sounded and Keaton looked at the digital reading.

"Damn…103 degrees! Not good, Fredrick!"

Keaton now took on a serious tone. "MaLeah! Go get the telephone," he instructed, trying not to panic. He hardly ever called her MaLeah so she looked at him as if he was talking to someone else.

He raised his voice slightly this time. "Shorty! Go get the phone!"

MaLeah sprinted out of the room and brought back the cordless phone. Fredrick continued to cry as Keaton put a fresh diaper on him. He gently put his pajamas on him and picked him up.

"Let's go get your brother some milk. I have to get his temperature down. Shh, Fredrick! I'm going to take care of you."

When they walked into the kitchen, he removed a bottle from the refrigerator.

"MaLeah, hand me that piece of paper on the table."

"K!"

MaLeah handed the piece of paper to him as she watched him balance Fredrick and the telephone on his shoulder. Keaton dialed Arnelle's cell phone, but got an out-of-area message.

"Damn it!!"

MaLeah covered her mouth. "Oooo! You said another bad word, Uncie K!"

"Not now, MaLeah, and stop being the bad word police. Okay?"

She smiled. "K!"

Keaton tried to dial the number again and once more, got the out-of-area message.

Fredrick's bottle was almost empty and Keaton sat there trying to figure out what to do next. He knew Craig and Venice were also at the awards banquet so he couldn't call them for help. As Fredrick continued to suck on his bottle, it soothed him temporarily.

"MaLeah, I can't get your parents on the phone."

She patted him on the leg. "I'm sowwy, Uncie Key."

"I know. Oh! I can call your Ms. Camille," he remembered.

Keaton dialed Camille's number, trying to stay calm. Within seconds, a female voice answered.

"Hello?"

"Ms. Camille. This is Arnelle's brother, Keaton."

"Oh yes! How are you?"

"Fine, but Fredrick's not doing so well. Arnelle and Winston are out for the evening and I can't get either of them on their cell phones."

Ms. Camille asked, with worry in her voice, "What's wrong?"

"Fredrick's crying and has a fever of 103 degrees. He's drinking his milk right now, but I don't know what to do."

"The best thing is to get him to the hospital right away. I'm sure he'll be fine. If I didn't have the Bennett children, I could meet you there. Look, I'll keep trying to get in touch with Arnelle and Winston. Call me from the hospital and let me know what's going on. Do you have MaLeah with you?"

"Yes, Ma'am."

"Well, wrap her up good. It's cool outside. I'm sure it's nothing, but we're better off safe than sorry."

Keaton stood. "Thank you. I'll call you back later." He hung up the phone. "Let's go get some clothes on, Shorty. We have to take Fredrick to the doctor."

"K!"

CHAPTER 5

Keaton was getting frustrated at the nurse asking him all sorts of questions regarding Fredrick. Another nurse had taken Fredrick to an examining room and Keaton was unable to see what was going on.

"Look, Ma'am! He's my nephew. I can't get in touch with his parents and I need to get back there to see what's going on!"

The nurse stood up. "I'm sorry, Sir, but I need this information to make sure your nephew gets the proper treatment."

Keaton ran his hand over his face in frustration. "I don't know any more than I've already told you!" he yelled.

MaLeah sat on the counter in front of her uncle, singing. She entertained herself by sticking her Barbie doll inside his jacket pocket. She looked over his shoulder and yelled, "Doctor MeMe!!"

Keaton turned and was face to face with Dr. Meridan St. John. He hadn't seen her since the day Arnelle had given birth to Fredrick, but there hadn't been a day he hadn't thought about her. Her natural beauty and tall athletic body had caused him to have many sleepless nights. Her skin was cocoa brown and her smile was as bright as the sun. Her hair was short and brown with blond highlights and today she wore it curly.

Meridan walked over. "Well, hello, MaLeah. What are you doing here? This is your uncle…right?"

Giggling, MaLeah said, "Uncie Key!"

Meridan pretended not to remember his name. In reality, his name, face and other important attributes had been etched in her brain since she'd met him.

"It's Keaton, right?"

Keaton blushed. "You remembered my name?"

"I wasn't sure," she answered as she blushed. She was lying. She hugged MaLeah and asked, "What brings you guys here? MaLeah, are you sick? Where are Arnelle and Winston?"

MaLeah yelled, "Freddie's sick!"

She frowned. "What's wrong with him, Keaton?"

Frustrated, he answered, "I don't know. When I went to check on him, I could tell he was running a high fever. I couldn't get in touch with Winston and Arnelle on their cell phones so his sitter told me to bring him here. Arnelle and Winston are at a banquet at one of the hotels in the city, and I don't know the answer to all the questions this lady is asking me."

Meridan turned to the nurse. "Tamera, Fredrick Carter is one of my patients. Look up his records in my files. Everything you should need will be there."

The nurse listened attentively. "Thank you, Dr. St. John."

Meridan then turned to Keaton. "Don't worry. I'll go see what's going on with my little patient. I'll be right back. Tamera, when you're done, please get Mr. Lapahie something to drink and MaLeah a snack."

"You got it."

Keaton watched as Meridan exited through the double doors leading to the examining room. She'd taken a lot of worry off him because he knew Fredrick was in good hands. Now, if he could only get in touch with Arnelle and Winston. Finding a seat in the waiting room, Keaton pulled out his cell phone and tried Arnelle's number again. The nurse walked in with a hot cup of coffee for Keaton and a fruit roll-up for MaLeah.

Inside the examining room Meridan assisted the emergency room doctor as he worked on Fredrick. Once Meridan informed him that Fredrick was her patient, he let her take over while he left to treat another patient. Meridan talked to Fredrick in a soothing voice while caressing his chubby cheeks. His temperature was still around 103, but at least it wasn't climbing. Once she completed the examinations, she instructed the nurse to prepare a syringe of medicine. She gave Fredrick the shot, then immediately picked him up to comfort him.

"Shh. I know it hurt, but this will make you feel all better. I promise." She turned to the nurse. "Heather, go ahead and get this medicine so little Fredrick can get home to his warm bed."

"Okay, Dr. St. John."

Meridan put Fredrick's pajamas back on him and kissed him on the forehead. She looked in his eyes. "Your Uncle Keaton did the right thing bringing you here. I'll have to tell you how worried he was about you when you get a little older. Now, let's go show him you're much better. Your uncle and your sister are very concerned about you."

When Meridan walked out the door with Fredrick, Winston and Arnelle were coming around the corner with fearful expressions on their faces. She waved at them, smiling. "He's okay. Calm down, guys. It's only an ear infection."

Arnelle grabbed her heart and, with tears in her eyes, took Fredrick into her arms. She could see the relief in Winston's eyes also as he seemed to slowly let out a breath. Arnelle planted kisses all over Fredrick, then said, "Thank you, Meridan."

"That's what I'm here for, but the credit goes to Keaton. He's the one who noticed Fredrick had a high fever and brought him here."

Winston patted Keaton on the shoulder. "Thanks, Man! You just don't know..."

"Yes, I do. These guys are my blood and I love them like they're my own."

Tears were flowing down Arnelle's cheeks as she walked over and kissed Keaton. "Thank you, little brother," she said as she hugged him.

MaLeah was hugging Meridan's leg and from nowhere shouted, "Freddie tee-teed in Uncie Key's face!"

Keaton lowered his face in embarrassment. "Thank you for the reminder, Shorty."

Everyone laughed together.

Winston said, "Well, I guess we'd better get this little guy home. Thanks again, Meridan, and don't work too hard. Goodnight."

She blushed and folded her arms.

"Goodnight, guys, and don't forget to follow the directions on Fredrick's medicine. Oh, by the way, you two, you look great. What's the occasion?"

Arnelle smiled and proudly announced, "Winston won Man-of-the-Year tonight."

Meridan smiled. "Well, congratulations, Winston!"

Keaton shook his hand and hugged him. "Yeah, Man, congratulations. You deserve it."

MaLeah jumped up and down and yelled, "Yeah, Daddy!"

Winston scooped her up in his arms. "Thanks, everyone. It was a great feeling. Now, we'd better get home and get these little people into bed. Keaton, are you coming?"

He turned away to look at Meridan before answering. "What time do you get off work? I'd like to treat you to breakfast, lunch, or something for taking care of Fredrick."

Meridan blushed. "It's my job and I'm so sorry, Keaton, but I'm covering for someone tonight. I just came on and I'm on duty until tomorrow afternoon."

Winston and Arnelle smiled as they started walking out of the hospital, leaving them to their conversation.

MaLeah yelled, "Wait, Daddy! Uncie Key!"

He smiled at Meridan. "Excuse me for a second. Duty calls."

Keaton walked over and knelt down, giving MaLeah a hug and kiss.

"I'll see you in the morning, Shorty. It's way past your bedtime and you need to get some sleep. I love you, and thank you for helping me with Fredrick tonight."

She hugged his neck and yelled, "K!"

Keaton watched as his sister and her family exited the hospital doors together. When he turned back around, Meridan was gone. Confused, he walked over to the nurse's station.

"Excuse me. Which way did Dr. St. John go?"

The nurse smiled and handed him a note.

"Thank you," he said as opened the note and slowly walked toward the door.

Keaton,

Sorry I had to run. Dinner sounds very nice. Call me at 555-8458 and tell me where and the time. It was nice seeing you again.

Meridan

Pleased, he smiled, folded the note, and slid it inside his jacket before walking out into the cool night air.

CHAPTER 6

Saturday morning Keaton was awakened once again by MaLeah trying to pry open his eyelids. He was startled awake and when he saw who was staring down at him, he sighed.

"MaLeah, baby, you're going to have to stop doing your uncle like this. What are you doing up so early?"

She pouted. "I wanna play, Uncie Key."

Keaton picked her up and put her in bed beside him, covering them both with the comforter.

She cuddled against his chest. "Can I watch TV, Uncie Key?"

Closing his eyes and turning onto his stomach, he responded, "Knock yourself out."

She crawled over his body and grabbed the remote off the nightstand. She sat on his back and proceeded to watch the Nickelodeon channel. Keaton tried to go back to sleep, but it was difficult with MaLeah laughing and bouncing on his back. Just when he thought all hope was gone, Winston walked into the room.

"Baby girl, I should've known you'd be in here bothering your uncle. Get off his back and come on so you can get your clothes on," he said, laughing.

Pointing toward the TV, she yelled, "Daddy, look! Rugrats!"

Winston walked over to the bed and picked her up. As he turned and walked out, he looked back at Keaton. "Sorry, Bro. We'll try to keep better tabs on her. You can go back to sleep now."

Keaton turned over. "She's all right, Man. Don't worry about it. How's Fredrick doing?"

"He's much better. His temp is down, thank God. You really came through for him last night. Speaking of which…What happened between you and the beautiful doctor last night?"

MaLeah heard the word "doctor" and yelled, "Dr. MeMe!"

Winston looked at her in frustration and sat her down. He playfully patted her on the bottom. "Go find your momma and stop being so nosey."

MaLeah giggled and ran from the room. Winston folded his arms and said, "Now back to you. What's up?"

Keaton sat on the side of the bed, smiling. He stood and said, "Nothing's up. I only asked her out."

"Tonight?"

"That's what I'm hoping for." He grinned mischievously. "I have to call her and see if we're on."

Winston watched as Keaton blushed simply from talking about Meridan. It was obvious he'd been very interested in Meridan every since he'd laid eyes on her. As long as Winston had known Keaton, he'd vowed he would never, ever, marry. As Keaton would tell his family…he'd get married "when hell freezes over." He'd never allowed himself to get serious with any one woman because of the demands of his restaurant and his loyalty to bachelorhood.

Winston laughed again. "I'm surprised she has time for you, or any man. Her medical career is very demanding and stressful. She has her private practice and covers at the hospital when needed. I assume that's why she was there last night."

Keaton curiously asked, "I wonder why she works so hard?"

Winston flicked some lint off his sleeve. "I'm not sure. Maybe she loves her job."

Keaton stood and started making up his bed. He turned and said, "I'm sure as fine as she is, she takes the time to wind down and go out every now and then."

Winston picked up a CD case off the nightstand and scanned the titles. "I don't know when she has time for much of a social life. I'm surprised she even considered your invitation."

Keaton flexed his muscles in the mirror. "She accepted because she likes what she sees and I'm a true gentleman."

Keaton was a handsome man, all six feet six inches of him. His bronze complexion, dark eyes and heated passion gave away the Indian heritage he'd obtained from his father. His African-American mother passed on to him unbelievable dimples, a fiery temper and his unique culinary skills. He had other talents he was proud of but found cooking to be not only relaxing, but rewarding.

Winston laughed. "Don't think for one second she's going to be what you're used to, Bro. Meridan might surprise you. Actually, you too are a lot alike. Number one, you're both single. Second, you're both passionate about your careers and third...never mind, I'll let you find what number three is."

This bit of information got Keaton's attention. When Winston turned to walk out of the room, Keaton asked, "What's number three?"

"Have a nice dinner, Keaton," he said as he walked away laughing.

Keaton hurriedly put on his robe. "Yo, Winston, hold up! What were you about to tell me?"

He found Winston in his bedroom retrieving his jacket. "I'll let you find out for yourself," he said, still grinning.

"Okay! Hey, don't make a big deal out of this dinner with Meridan. I don't want Arnelle telling Momma and Daddy, for them to start acting crazy. I still stand by my vow of remaining single."

Winston laughed out loud, making Keaton look in his direction. "Keaton, my brotha, Dr. Meridan St. John is going to turn your world upside-down. You're already on your way, and it shows all over your face every time you get within a mile of her. I'll put money down on this and I know you don't like losing money."

He folded his arms and yelled, "Winston, you're crazy! Okay! Name your price. I'm up for this little game of yours. How much do you want to lose? I'm in Philly for a short time and I'm going to enjoy taking your hard-earned money. Besides, she seems like she'd be cool to hang out with while I'm here; that's all."

"Okay, Keaton. If I win, at your wedding reception you have to get up in front of everyone and tell them how you vowed you'd be single for life until you met Meridan. Then you have to serenade her with a song of my choosing in front of everyone."

Keaton stood there in silence, staring at Keaton as if he was weighing his options.

"Okay, but if I win, I want that Ninja motorcycle in the garage," he negotiated as he paced the floor.

Winston glared at him as if Keaton had asked for his firstborn. Now it was his turn to stare his brother-in-law down. After a few seconds, he said, "Aight! You've got yourself a deal."

"Deal!"

The two sealed the deal with a brotherly handshake. Winston walked out of the room, saying, "You need to start practicing on your song."

"No, you need to get that motorcycle tuned up for me, my brotha! This is going to be so easy."

"Whatever!"

Winston disappeared down the stairs, laughing.

It wasn't until Keaton was alone that fear tried to sneak in on him. After a series of deep breaths, he laughed and said to himself, "Calm down, Playa. It's only dinner. Winston must be crazy if he thinks I'd let any woman get me to the altar."

Before he could enter the bathroom, he heard MaLeah coming back up the stairs. "Uncie Key!"

"I'll be down in a minute, Shorty. Pour me some orange juice."

"K!"

CHAPTER 7

Meridan was exhausted by the time she got home from the hospital. She didn't know why she'd accepted Keaton's dinner invitation for that night. Maybe it was the sexy tone of his voice over the phone when he'd called earlier or it could've been those unbelievable dimples. Whatever it was, it made her unsure about the evening. He'd called her earlier and told her the name of the restaurant so she could meet him there at seven o'clock. It was now three o'clock and she desperately needed a bath and a nap. She'd been on duty for over twenty-four hours; now she was off for the next four days. Her plan was to get plenty of rest and finally give her house that spring cleaning it needed.

When she entered her house, she sifted through the mail and tossed it on the kitchen table. Opening the refrigerator, she pulled out some bottled water and kicked off her shoes. There were two messages on her answering machine: one from her nosy, older sister, Gwendolyn; and the other from her father, who still lived on a farm in Mississippi. It had been months since she'd had a chance to go visit her family, but her father's upcoming sixtieth birthday was approaching in about three weeks. The family had planned a huge party for him; one that she'd missed out on helping to plan. Her father had been everything to her since losing her mother when she was eight years old. Getting something very special for his birthday was something she planned to do on her week off.

Stepping into the hot sudsy water induced her fatigue. Meridan figured she'd take a catnap in hopes of gaining an energy boost for her dinner with

Keaton. She quickly applied lotion to her skin, crawled under covers of her soft linens, and fell fast asleep.

Keaton hurried about his room getting dressed. He'd checked his watch several times to make sure he wasn't running late. He'd chosen some brown dress slacks, a beige collarless shirt, and a matching jacket.

Arnelle walked by his room, then backed up to take a second look. She'd grown accustomed to him going out since he'd been in Philly but, for some reason, tonight he had a different vibe.

Walking into his room, she asked, "Hey, Little Brother! Where are you headed?"

"To dinner," he said without looking directly at her.

Arnelle walked further into the room, approaching him. She played with the lapel on his jacket. "Who are you going to dinner with?"

Keaton didn't want to get into a big discussion with his sister. "Meridan."

"Meridan?" Arnelle started pacing the floor, ranting. "Keaton! Don't you go playing around with Meridan like you do those other women you go out with! She's not the one!"

Keaton picked up his keys and glared at her. "I love you, Arnelle, but stay out of my business! I'm only having dinner with her. Damn! You act like I'm going to hurt her or something."

Folding her arms, she yelled back, "Well, aren't you? You've made it an art form, mistreating all the others when you're done with them."

"I don't mistreat them. I make it plain and clear in the beginning that I'm not looking for love. It's just that some of them have a hard time accepting it."

"Keaton, please don't…"

Keaton kissed her on the forehead and softly said, "It's only dinner, Sis. Goodnight."

Arnelle gnawed on her nail as she turned to watch her brother walk out of the room. She hurriedly walked into her bedroom where she found Winston in bed reading. "Winston! Did you know Keaton was going out with Meridan tonight?"

Without looking up, he calmly replied, "Yes, I did."

"Why didn't you tell me? I don't think this is a good idea. You know how Keaton is with women. He's never been serious with any of them and most of them end up stalking him out of anger. One of these days…"

Winston looked up at his wife, who was talking a mile a minute. She was clearly upset and worried about Keaton hooking up with Meridan.

He took a deep breath, closed his book, and firmly said, "Sweetheart, calm down! Meridan and Keaton are grown. Stay out of it!"

She put her hands on her hips and saw she wasn't getting any help from her husband. Maybe he was right. If anything went wrong, it would be on Keaton's head, not hers. She let out a breath and crawled into bed next to him. She took the book out of his hands and straddled his lap.

He looked up at her and smiled. "Are you okay, now?"

She cupped his face, kissed him tenderly on the lips, and said, "I'm sorry, sweetheart. You're right; it's none of my business."

He caressed her thigh. "Good."

She winked at him. "Have you noticed we have the house to ourselves tonight and your children are sound asleep?"

"I was wondering when you were going to notice it," he said in a challenging tone.

"So, what are you going to do, Counselor?"

Without any warning, Winston flipped her over on her back and covered her body with his. Arnelle moaned as he sprinkled her neck with soft kisses.

"Mrs. Carter, you're in for a long, long night," he whispered as he caressed her curves.

"Bring it on, Mr. Carter."

CHAPTER 8

Keaton was on time at the restaurant, but an hour had passed and Meridan still hadn't shown up. He was starting to get worried so he called her. After about four rings, he heard the telephone pick up.

A sleepy voice answered, "Hello?"

"Meridan? It's Keaton. Where are you? Are you okay?"

Startled awake, she asked, "Oh, Keaton! What time is it?"

Keaton felt relieved that she was safe, but also a little upset that she'd stood him up.

"It's almost eight o'clock. Look, maybe we should do this another time. I realize you just got off work today."

Sitting up in bed, Meridan tried to clear her head. She squinted her eyes and looked at the clock. "Keaton, I'm sorry. I really am exhausted and I never should've accepted your invitation for tonight. Can we do this some other time?"

Keaton tossed some cash on the table as he stood to leave. With disappointment in his voice, he said, "Sure, Meridan. Get some rest and I'll call you tomorrow."

Biting her nail, she asked, "Are you sure you're not mad?"

"I'm not mad. Go back to sleep," he solemnly answered.

Meridan sat on the side of the bed and answered, "Thank you, Keaton. Goodnight."

Keaton hung up the telephone and walked out to the car feeling defeated.

Meridan really did feel bad that she'd stood Keaton up. She was relieved a little that she didn't have to look into those dark, sensual eyes. He was about as sexy as they came and knew he was a lot more than she could handle. She crawled back into bed and her telephone rang once again.

"Hello?"

"Girl! Get your tired ass out of bed so we can go downtown and check out that new jazz club!"

Meridan didn't have the energy for her best friend, Nichole, tonight. She was the total opposite of her, but they'd been friends throughout college. She was a manager at a Fortune 500 company and when she wanted to wind down, she'd wind down.

"Nikki, I don't have the strength tonight. I just got off work this evening. Call me later in the week."

Pouting, Nichole said, "Now you know I'm going out of town this week. I'll be gone for two weeks. Come on, Dee! I want to have a good time before I head off to those boring meetings in Atlanta."

Nichole had given Meridan the nickname, Dee, when they'd met as freshmen and Meridan started calling her Nikki.

"You know you're going to miss me when I'm gone," she teased playfully. Meridan fought Nichole as hard as she could, but the truth was, she was right. She'd miss her.

"Nikki, I turned down a dinner date tonight. I really don't feel like going out."

Nikki laughed. "Hold up! Who did you have a dinner date with? Is he fine?"

Putting her hand over her eyes, she said, "You don't know him. He's just a friend."

Nichole listened, then said, "You left something out, Dee."

"What?"

Teasing, she asked, "Is he fine?"

"Nikki, you're impossible. Besides, every man's fine to you."

Snapping her finger, she said, "You got that right!!"

Nichole turned up her CD player and started dancing around the room. "Dee, are you going to hang out with your girl or not?"

Defeated, Meridan yelled, "Okay! Okay! But I'm only going for one drink and I'm out of there."

Excited, she yelled, "Thank you, Dee!"

"I guess you're welcome," Meridan said as she threw the comforter off her body.

Pleased, Nikki turned the music down and sat down, out of breath from her dancing. "With that settled, how have you been feeling lately? Your nightmares haven't started back up, have they?"

Sighing, Meridan said, "No, and I'm trying my best to bury the entire ordeal forever. You know?"

Smiling, Nichole said, "Now that's a good thing, Dee. You've got to put this thing behind you for good and start living."

"I know," she said with commitment.

"With that said, when are you going to stop dragging your feet and have those cobwebs cleaned out?"

As if she didn't hear Nichole, Meridan said, "You know Sam's getting out of jail in a few weeks."

"Yes, I'm aware of that, but Sam knows not to mess with you anymore," Nikki added. "I mean, I admire you for your courage but you're not getting any younger and it's not like you're sweating on anybody right now. The nightmares have stopped. Dee, it's time. Okay?"

Silence engulfed the phone.

Nichole sighed. "Meridan! You know you're my girl. I don't want you to mess around and let Mr. Right get away from you. Are you hearing me?"

"I know you care about me, Nikki, and I hope to meet Mr. Right one day. But for now, I'm simply going to take it one day at a time. If and when I decide to hook up with anyone, I *might* let you know. You know you're a trip."

Nichole laughed. "Honey, you know I've got your back like I had it when Sam hurt you. If I could've prevented what happened, I would've; you know that."

"It's because of you that I'm here today, Nikki, and I'll forever love you for that."

Tears welled up in Nichole's eyes briefly before saying, "Like I said, I'll always have your back, Sam or no Sam."

Ready to change the subject, Meridan said, "I know and thanks. So, what time are you picking me up, Nikki?"

All Meridan could hear was screaming on the other end of the phone. It was obvious she'd made Nichole very happy by going out with her. She'd become accustomed to discussing the terrible thing that had happened to her in college with her best friend. In a way, it had helped her heal, but she wasn't completely healed yet.

"I love you, Girl! Thank you so much for hanging with me tonight! We're going to have some f-u-n!"

Meridan hated the fact that she couldn't call Keaton and ask him to meet her there. She'd given him her number, but she'd failed to get his and she didn't have any of her patients' home numbers at her house. Tomorrow, if he called her, she'd remember to ask him for his number.

CHAPTER 9

Keaton drove around Philly trying to find something to do. His dinner date was a bust, so now what? He thought about calling Dejá, then realized he didn't have the energy for her that night. Instead, he picked up the flyer that was on the windshield of the car when he left the restaurant. It was the grand opening at a new jazz club called Sax's. He didn't have anything else to do, so he thought he'd go check it out.

Meridan was getting sleepy again as she sat at the bar sipping on her soda. Nichole was getting her dance on with some brotha with fake gold hanging around his neck. An hour or so had already passed and she'd turned more than her share of brothas away. As she sat there, she kept pulling on the short black skirt Nichole had convinced her to wear. Her red silk blouse accented her red lipstick and cinnamon skin. As she twirled lazily from side to side on the bar stool, she felt hands steadying it from behind.

"Nikki, quit playing. I'm ready to go! I'm tired!"

The seat was twirled around and she came face to face with Keaton. Startled, she yelled, "Keaton! What are you doing here?"

She could tell he was upset to see her out partying after she'd cancelled their dinner date.

With hurt in his voice, he calmly said, "I thought my eyes were playing tricks on me when I saw you from across the room. I know we really haven't gotten the chance to get to know each other, but if you didn't want to have dinner with me, you should've declined my offer."

Meridan opened her mouth to respond. At the same moment, Nichole returned to the bar. She looked up into Keaton's handsome face and said, "Well, hello there."

"Hello," he said, without looking away from Meridan.

Nichole extended her hand to Keaton and politely shook it. She turned back to Meridan. "Dee, you've been holding out on me. Aren't you going to introduce me to your friend?"

Meridan stared at Nichole. "Keaton, this is my best friend, Nichole Adams. Nikki, this is Keaton Lapahie."

Wanting to get Meridan alone, he said, "It's nice to meet you, Nichole. Would you excuse us for a second?"

Nichole smiled and sipped her drink. "Sure."

He took Meridan by the hand and led her out onto the dance floor.

"Keaton Lapahie, I don't remember you asking me to dance," she said, trying to redeem herself.

He looked her in the eyes. "Okay, I'm giving you another chance to decline one of my offers. Dr. Meridan St. John, would you like to dance?"

Meridan stared at him, to make him sweat a little. She could tell he was trying to be cool.

He shoved his hands in his pockets. "Well, what's it going to be?"

She looked around and noticed couples slow dancing around them. Finally, she said, "Yes, I accept."

He pulled her close to his body and it felt wonderful. For Meridan it was like static electricity, catching her off guard. She jumped back.

"Are you okay?"

Meridan cleared her throat. "I'm fine."

They began to dance to the music, making her feel like she was on cloud nine. Keaton was tall, handsome, and so smooth.

She glanced up at him. "I really am sorry about tonight. I truly am tired and sleepy, but Nikki's my friend and she's going out of town for two weeks so she begged me to hang with her tonight."

"If you had other plans, all you had to do was tell me."

"Oh, no! She called after I talked to you. I told her I'd have one drink with her and I'm out of here."

Swaying to the music, he asked, "Well, have you had your one drink?"

Meridan looked at her watch, smiled, and said, "I sure have."

"Are you ready to go?"

"Yes."

"Did you drive?"

"No, I rode here with Nikki."

He continued to dance with her in silence and began noticing how well she fit to his tall frame. He caressed her back, then said, "You know you're very tall."

Smiling, she looked up at him, and answered, "So are you."

He blushed. "Exactly how tall are you?"

"That's for me to know and you to find out."

They laughed together.

He pulled her even closer, then whispered, "My ego's still bruised, Doctor, but I'll be a gentleman and ask if you'd like a ride home?"

"I was hoping you'd offer," she responded with a smile.

Before leaving, Meridan hugged her friend and told her she'd call her tomorrow. She was a little reluctant to leave Nikki alone until her boyfriend showed up to keep her company.

Keaton was hypnotized by the fragrance Meridan wore. Once out in the bright lights in front of the club, he realized just how sexy she looked in her attire. All the other times he'd seen her she was in her medical uniforms. The short skirt revealed muscular legs and very sexy thighs. Her full hips left plenty to his imagination of the woman underneath the clothing. He opened the car door for her and tried not to stare when her skirt rose high on her thighs as she sat down. Closing the door, he walked around to the driver's side and mumbled, "Mercy."

As he climbed into the car next to her, she said, "Keaton, thanks again for the ride home. If you'd given me your number, I could've called you back to reschedule our dinner."

He smiled at her. "Don't stress out over it, Meridan, but this is the first time I've been stood up by a woman only to catch her out partying."

Laughing, she said, "I said I was sorry. Now stop making me feel worse than I already do."

"I'm only teasing and you look beautiful tonight," he admitted before pulling away from the curb.

Surprised, she tilted her head. "Thank you. You don't look so bad yourself."

They smiled at each other in silence until Meridan blushed and looked away. Keaton felt his stomach flutter momentarily. He reached into his jacket pocket and handed her a business card.

"Don't lose this card. It has all my numbers on it so you can't use that as an excuse anymore. Now, buckle up. Have you eaten?"

"No I haven't," she admitted.

"Well, let me take you somewhere so I can get some food in your stomach, then I'll tuck you into bed."

As soon as he said it, he realized how intimate his words must have sounded.

Meridan tilted her head again, looking over at him in silence. She studied his features for a few seconds, then said, "Thank you, Keaton, and I won't lose your number."

"Good, now that's settled. So, what do you have a taste for?"

"I like everything," she admitted.

Keaton pulled out of the parking lot and listened as Meridan told him of various restaurants in the area. They finally settled on an Italian restaurant.

Dinner and the conversation were wonderful, Keaton thought as he drove Meridan home. He couldn't believe he'd told her the reason he was in Philly visiting and about his high blood pressure. She was so easy to talk to and he felt like he'd known her for years. Once he started talking, he started spilling his guts about his personal life. It was so unlike him to talk so much about himself to a woman on the first date. Meridan made him feel so comfortable, he couldn't help himself.

Meridan told him that she was born and raised on a farm in Mississippi and that she'd gotten her unique name from her deceased mother. Meridan, Mississippi happened to be the city where her parents had met and fallen in love. He was in awe of her wholesome and sweet personality, and it was obvious she was a Southern girl. They came to a point when he realized it was time to cut their dinner short. Meridan had practically fallen asleep in her plate as the evening wore on. He eventually convinced her to get a doggy bag and they left the restaurant.

As he drove down the expressway, he looked over at Meridan as she slept. He was glad she'd given him directions before she fell asleep. It didn't take long for him to reach her home, which he noticed was a modest style home. His heart accelerated as he wondered how he'd wake her up. He didn't know where to touch her because he was afraid what it would do to him. He looked down at her shapely legs, sighed, then decided to take her hand into his gently. He caressed the back of her hand, waking her. She slowly opened her eyes and smiled.

"We made it, huh?"

Releasing her hand, he said, "Yes, now let me help you to the door so you can get to bed."

Keaton unbuckled and exited the car. He walked around and opened the car door so she could step out. He extended his hand to assist her and she took it without hesitating. They made it to the front door and Meridan opened it, then walked over to deactivate the alarm. She turned and found Keaton still standing outside.

"Don't just stand there, silly. Come on in," she said with a smile.

Keaton looked around. "Thanks, but I'd better get home so you can get some sleep."

She walked over to him. "Are you willing to let me make tonight up to you?"

He kissed her on the cheek. "You already have. Goodnight, Meridan."

"Goodnight, Keaton."

She watched him drive off and, at that moment, she realized she'd been holding her breath.

CHAPTER 10

The next morning, Keaton finally came to the conclusion that he'd never need an alarm clock as long as he stayed with his sister and her family. On this morning MaLeah sat on the pillow next to him singing the theme song to the *That's So Raven* show. Keaton slowly opened his eyes and watched her nibble on a Pop Tart. He studied her as the crumbs fell onto the sheet and realized he'd spoiled her to no end.

"Good Morning, Shorty."

Smiling, she said, "Hi, Uncie Key."

He pulled her gently by one of her long ponytails and said, "Give me a kiss."

MaLeah gave her uncle a kiss, crumbs and all.

"Where's your momma and daddy?"

MaLeah offered him her half-eaten Pop Tart.

"Gone to work," she sung.

Keaton jumped up and asked, "Where's Fredrick?"

"Gone with Daddy," she announced.

Keaton hurried out of the bed to check out her story for himself, with MaLeah close on his heels. He quickly checked all the bedrooms, then walked downstairs. On the refrigerator was a note from Winston.

Hey, Bro,

I hope everything went well for you and the doctor last night. I took Fredrick over to Camille's house. I figured you and the princess would like to hang out together but, if you have plans, just drop MaLeah off over there also. Oh yeah...keep on practicing your song.

Peace!
"*W*"

Keaton crumpled the note. "What he needs to be doing is getting my bike tuned up."

"Uncie Key? Who are you talking to?"

Turning to MaLeah, he smiled. "Nobody, Shorty. Do you want some breakfast?"

Jumping up and down clapping, she yelled, "Yay!"

She knew her uncle loved to cook; especially for her and he always let her help.

About an hour or so later, their stomachs were full and the kitchen was clean. In MaLeah's room, he picked out an outfit for her to wear because today, he wanted to work out. He knew there was a possibility that he'd run into Dejá, but the fact was he really didn't want to go out with her anymore. Friends…fine, but anything more was out of the question. Dejá had taken care of his sexual appetite over the past several weeks, since his arrival in Philly. Now, like with all the others, he'd lost interest.

There was an inner-city basketball tournament for charity coming up and he had promised Winston he'd be in top shape to play on his team. Working out several days a week at the gym had helped him stay in shape. Arnelle had been checking his blood pressure regularly and it was doing very well. He'd be back to his restaurant in Texas in no time.

"Uncie Key! I don't want to wear those pants! I want to wear this!" MaLeah pulled out a red, chiffon Sunday dress.

He laughed. "Shorty, you can't wear a dress. We're going back to the gym."

"K!"

Arriving at the gym, Keaton took MaLeah to the playroom she'd grown accustomed to. She'd been there with her daddy and her uncle before and was quite familiar with it.

Squatting down eye-level with her, Keaton reminded her of the rules.

"Now I want you to be a good girl, Shorty. I'm going to work out and I'll be back in a little while. You have a lot of friends to play with and try not to be so bossy this time. Okay?"

She threw her arms around his neck and gave him a big kiss, saying, "K!"

About thirty minutes into his workout, Keaton couldn't help but replay the previous night in his head. Meridan was a stunning woman and during their conversation, he'd discovered she had a sister and a lot of cousins. He'd also found out that her father farmed one of the largest tracts of land in his area. He still couldn't believe he'd revealed so much about his life to her so soon. He'd told her that his dad was running for mayor and told her about his mom's catering business. Meridan seemed very impressed with all his family's accomplishments. Keaton expressed how much he admired her father for raising her and her sister alone while running a farm and a business. He still couldn't get over how tall Meridan was. She had to be at least six-two; a true-to-life Amazon.

In the gym, he continued to lift weights and work out. He noticed several attractive women working out alongside him but, for some strange reason, he wasn't interested in any of them. Thinking to himself, he wondered, *What the hell is wrong with me?*

Moments later, one woman in particular approached him and asked if he'd spot her on the bench press. He accepted and stood over her to spot her. She was physically fit, attractive and appeared to be well into her forties but still trying to dress like she was in her twenties.

"So, what's your name?"

"Keaton."

"It's nice to meet you, Keaton. My name's China. Do you live around here?"

In a friendly tone, he replied, "No, I'm visiting from Texas."

The woman continued lifting the barbell as she questioned him.

"You should let me show you around sometime," she volunteered.

Keaton was starting to feel disgusted, for some reason. The woman was clearly flirting.

In a dry tone, he said, "I have family here so I know my way around pretty good, but thanks for the offer."

The woman lifted the weights and said, "Last one." Keaton placed the barbell back in its stand. The woman stood. "That's too bad. Well, I guess I'll see you around."

"Likewise," he said as he wiped the sweat from his brow.

The woman walked over into a different part of the room and started talking to another man. It became obvious she was out looking for men. Keaton also realized how it made some women feel when they were being hit on by men. There was a time he would've pursued a woman like her. Why he wasn't up to it that day, he couldn't understand.

He decided to take a break on one of the benches. As he wiped the sweat from his face, from behind, he felt ice cold water against his back. He jumped up and turned around, seeing Dejá standing there thoroughly upset and holding an empty cup.

"What the hell did you do that for?"

Dejá walked over to him and put her finger in his face. "I don't know who you think you are, but you're not going to use me anymore!"

He moved her finger away from his face, trying to avoid a public scene. Looking around, he said, "Dejá, calm down."

"I will not calm down!"

He pulled her over to the side. "Look, Dejá, I laid my cards on the table up front, when we first started going out. I told you, I only wanted to hang out. Now here you stand trying to lay demands on me? I don't think so."

Tearing up, she said, "Don't think I'm going to let you get away with this, Keaton!"

"Get away with what, Dejá? You had as much fun as I did, so let's just end it."

Dejá didn't have a response for him because everything he'd said was right. But, she hadn't expected to fall so hard for him. Now it was hard for her to accept what he was saying. She stood there staring at him and said, "You could've told me, Keaton, instead of avoiding me."

"You're right and I'm sorry about that. I did plan on talking to you about it, but I guess now is as good a time as any. Look, we enjoyed each other's company and had a great time. I'm only in Philly visiting and there's no reason for us to leave each other like this."

Dejá folded her arms and tapped her foot as she stared at him. She was gorgeous and a man would have to be a fool to walk away, but he was.

Hurt, she said, "Goodbye, Keaton."

As she walked away, he softly said, "Goodbye, Dejá. Take care of yourself."

CHAPTER 11

Meridan didn't wake up until around eleven o'clock. She probably would've slept longer if her dad hadn't called. She was happy to hear his voice and she promised she was eating right and getting plenty of rest. She couldn't wait to see her family at the birthday party. She hoped the gathering would be without incident. It wasn't unusual for a family member to have too much to drink and end up embarrassing the entire family. The award usually went to her father's sister, Aunt Glo, which was short for Gloria. She'd seemed bitter with everyone since her husband had left her for a younger woman over ten years earlier, leaving her to raise their five children alone. She really didn't raise them alone because Meridan's father and other siblings made sure they had everything they needed. Her bitterness stemmed from the adultery. In any case, the birthday party for her father was going to be the event of the year and she'd do her best to make sure Aunt Glo didn't ruin it.

"Okay, Meridan, it's time for you to start your spring cleaning," she said, talking to herself.

She slid into her sweats and started pulling winter clothes out of her closet.

Hours later, she'd completely rearranged her closet and drawers. Looking at her watch, she realized it was almost four o'clock. She sat on the edge of her bed and thought about Keaton. Then she thought about her conversation with Nichole. Was she really ready to move on with her life? According to Nikki, it was past time, but it's easier said than done. She remembered the girls in the dorm whispering as she passed them in the hallway and the stares as she walked across campus. After that horrible night, she'd thrown herself into her studies and never looked back. Anybody else would've transferred to another college, but she wasn't about to let anyone run her off campus; no matter what.

She sighed and ran her hand across her scar on her abdomen. Tears formed in her eyes momentarily before saying out loud, "Maybe Nikki's right. Maybe it is time."

Smiling, she wondered what Keaton might be doing. She hoped he would call, if for nothing else, just so she could hear his voice.

Keaton and MaLeah drove to Mrs. Camille's house to pick up Fredrick. As expected she wouldn't let them leave until they'd eaten dinner and he wasn't one to turn down a home-cooked meal. After they finished, he thanked Mrs. Camille, gathered up the kids, and loaded them into the car. He was glad to help out his sister and brother-in-law. Even though he knew he wouldn't have children of his own, he enjoyed his niece and nephew very much.

"Uncie Key! I want some ice cream!"

"Later, Shorty. I need to get you guys home."

Fredrick was drooling and babbling in the carseat.

"Hush, Freddie!!"

Keaton looked in the rear-view mirror and yelled, "Chill, MaLeah!"

When she started crying, he knew she was sleepy. He'd kept her out all day without a nap. What Keaton didn't realize was that he'd called her "MaLeah." He only called her that when she was in trouble or something serious was going on. What MaLeah didn't realize was that her uncle's mind was on another woman…Meridan St. John.

"Shhh, Shorty! I'm going to have you guys home in a sec. Then you can get your bath and go to bed. Okay?"

MaLeah continued to sob and rub her eyes. Within minutes, both she and Fredrick were sound asleep. Keaton welcomed the peace and quiet for the final fifteen-minute drive home. He pulled into the garage and let out a sigh.

"I don't see how people do this every day," he said out loud.

He exited the vehicle and unlocked the door so he could take the children into the house at the same time. He laid both of the sleeping children across his bed, then jumped in the shower.

Meridan looked over at the telephone for the fourth time without picking it up. The business card Keaton had given her was sitting on the nightstand.

"Oh! What the hell!"

She dialed the number and gnawed on her nails as she listened to it ring on the other end.

"Hello?"

Startled, she stuttered, "Keaton, it's Meridan. Did I wake you?"

"No, you didn't. What a nice surprise. How are you?"

She nervously paced the floor. "I'm well and you?"

"Better, now that you've called. Have you caught up on your rest yet?"

"I guess you can say that. I've been spring cleaning and sleeping in. I didn't know how tired I was."

Keaton ran his hand across MaLeah's dark hair and said, "You were kind of wiped out the last time I saw you. I'm glad you're getting some rest."

"Thank you."

Silence engulfed the telephone for what seemed like an eternity. Meridan began to sweat and her heart was beating loudly.

"Meridan?"

"I'm here," she whispered.

"Do you want to catch a movie tonight?"

Smiling, she said, "That would be nice, but it's my treat."

"I don't think so. How does seven o'clock sound?"

"It sounds like a plan to me. Shall I meet you somewhere?"

Keaton softly answered, "I'll pick you up, so be ready."

Laughing, she said, "I will and I promise not to fall asleep on you."

"That doesn't sound so bad, if you ask me," he said mischievously.

She giggled. "I'll see you at seven. Goodbye, Keaton."

"Goodbye, Meridan."

Keaton couldn't help but smile as he hung up the telephone.

Meridan, on the other hand, hung up and went into a panic. It took a minute to calm herself. The last thing she wanted to do was have a panic attack. She couldn't believe she'd called Keaton in the first place, but she still felt she owed him the date since she'd stood him up. Then again, maybe she simply wanted someone like Keaton Lapahie to hang out with. The fact was, Nikki's comments were starting to make her think. Keaton was cute and seemed to be nice, so why not? She remembered, just like it was yesterday, the way he'd gone from nurse to nurse, holding conversations on the day they'd first met. From the way the nurses were blushing, it was obvious their conversations were on the seductive side. This was something she was beginning to feel she needed to do…no…had to do.

Winston arrived home before Arnelle and found Keaton, MaLeah, and Fredrick all asleep. As he turned and walked out of Keaton's room, Fredrick woke up.

"Da Da!"

Winston quickly picked him up and exited the room so the other two could continue their naps.

Minutes later, Keaton walked into the family room and greeted Winston. "Hey, Bro."

Keaton sat down and leaned back in the chair. "What's up?"

Winston sat there playing with Fredrick and watching TV. "You act like you're exhausted. What did you guys do today?"

"You don't want to know, but I can tell you that Dejá is crazy."

Laughing, Winston asked, "What did she do?"

"I was at the gym and she walked up behind me and threw cold water on my back. Then she started going off about me using her and that she wasn't going to let me get away with it."

"You'd better stop playing with that girl."

Keaton grabbed the remote. "It's over with Dejá. She seems cool with it now. By the way, I'm taking Meridan to the movies tonight."

Winston picked up one of Fredrick's toys and started laughing.

Keaton frowned. "What's so funny?"

"Oh, nothing. Have fun."

"You can have your laugh right now, but you won't be laughing when I ride your motorcycle out of the garage."

"You're dreaming, Keaton. I already have this bet won, so I'm not worried."

Keaton looked at his watch. "When hell freezes over! Meridan's cool people. I'm going to kick it with her until I go back to Texas."

"Keaton, my man, I wish you luck. I will say that Meridan has talents you might be surprised about."

It was at that moment that MaLeah walked into the family room, completely naked, and yelled, "Daddy's home!"

She walked over to him and climbed up into his lap. Startled at her appearance, he kissed her and calmly asked, "MaLeah, sweetheart, where are your clothes?"

"I don't know, Daddy. I like being naked," she answered as she swung her ponytails over her shoulders.

He picked up MaLeah, shook his head, and said, "Come with me, lil' girl, so we can find your clothes. You're so much like your mother. Oh! Keaton, we're practicing for the tournament in a few weeks and there's a possibility that Byron might have to drop out. His baby's due around that same time but I'm working on his replacement. Are you sure you're in shape?"

Keaton laughed. "I'm as ready as I'm going to be. Now, I guess I'd better start getting ready. Oh yeah, we ate over at Mrs. Camille's house, so the kids might not be hungry."

"Thanks, Keaton, and make sure you practice your song when you get in the shower."

Keaton followed them up the stairs and on the way up, he said, "Varoom! Varoom!"

"My bike's not going anywhere, Keaton."

"Winston, it's already gone," he teased.

MaLeah broke up their conversation, saying, "Daddy, I have to boo boo."

Winston laughed and hurried his naked daughter up the stairs.

CHAPTER 12

A couple of weeks passed and Meridan and Keaton were spending more and more time together. The kisses they shared were becoming more intimate as each date ended. Keaton found himself thinking about her much more since he'd been spending quality time with her. They'd been meeting for lunch and dinner, working out at the gym together, and snuggling in front of the TV. She fit him so well—too well—and it was getting a little scary for Keaton. Something was happening, but he couldn't quite put his finger on it.

On this movie date, Keaton found himself loving the way Meridan giggled. They'd chosen a comedy to watch instead of a drama. He was mesmerized as he continued to stare at her.

Blushing, she asked, "Keaton, why are you staring at me?"

He replied, "You're very beautiful when you laugh."

"Thank you."

She turned and continued to watch the movie. When it was over, they walked hand in hand down the sidewalk to a coffee shop.

Once seated, Keaton said, "I couldn't have asked for better company tonight."

"I agree. Tonight has been the most fun I've had in a long time. Thank you for hanging out with me over the past few weeks."

"It's my pleasure," he answered as he leaned back in his chair.

They sat together enjoying coffee and pastries. Meridan revealed more about her family; including her father's upcoming birthday celebration. She felt herself being pulled under the spell of Keaton Lapahie. Each time he kissed her, it left her breathless. It would only be a matter of time before she wanted to explore more of him.

As Meridan talked about her father, Keaton could see she missed him very much.

"I'm sure your father will be happy to see you. How long will you be there?"

She answered, "I'm taking a four-day weekend. Would you like to go?"

Before she realized it, she'd invited him. She hadn't known Keaton for very long, but in the short time they'd spent together, she felt like she'd known him for years. Keaton was surprised at her invitation and didn't really know how to respond; except to smile. Usually when a woman invited a man home to meet the family, things were serious between them. Looking into her amazing eyes, he realized that it wasn't such a bad thought.

"Meridan, I appreciate your invitation, but I don't know what your father would have to say about it."

"Relax, Keaton," she said, laughing. "My father would love to meet you. Look, I know we haven't known each other for very long, but I thought it would do you some good to get back to the South for some R & R. So do you want to go? I promise I'll be a perfect lady."

Keaton took a sip of his coffee. "Does your father have any horses?"

"He sure does," she said as she bit into her pastry.

He sat his cup down, smiled, and said, "In that case, count me in."

Meridan clapped and said, "This is going to be fun!"

"When do we leave?"

She sipped her coffee and said, "We leave next weekend and Keaton... thank you for going with me. I'll take care of all the arrangements."

He waved her off. "Thanks for the offer, but I'll pay for my own ticket. Okay?"

"You're my guest, so I'm paying," she strongly objected. "I insist."

"Forget it, Doc. I'm looking forward to breathing some fresh, country air. You're not buying my ticket, Meridan, and that's final."

She stared at him in amazement. He was so adorable.

"Fine, Keaton, but we're staying at Daddy's so there's no need for a hotel. Besides, the closest hotel is forty miles away."

He smiled. "I can live with that, as long as you don't try to sneak into my room."

"You're so bad. I'll behave. Now, are you ready to go?"

Standing, he said, "After you, Miss St. John."

CHAPTER 13

S everal days later the guys met at the gym to practice for the basketball tournament. Everyone was there, except Winston and Byron. Keaton, Craig and Malik and a couple of other guys played around while they were waiting on the other two to arrive.

Keaton threw up a three-pointer and said, "I can't believe Winston lectured me about not being late and he's the one late."

The guys laughed at his comment. About that time, his cell phone rang.

He ran over to the bleachers and answered, "Hello?"

"Keaton, it's Winston. Byron's wife went into labor so he's out. We're one person short, but I'm bringing someone to take his place."

Keaton shook his head and relayed the information back to the other teammates. Putting the telephone back up to his ear, he asked, "Who's the replacement?"

"Don't worry. I'm bringing someone with a lot of experience." He laughed mischievously.

"Whatever, Winston! Just hurry up!"

While Keaton and the guys continued to mess around on the basketball court, Winston walked in moments later with none other than Meridan St. John.

Keaton turned around and openly mumbled, "What the hell?"

Malik threw up a three-point shot and whispered, "Who's the babe?"

Craig laughed. "That's Dr. Meridan St. John, former All-American point guard for the University of Tennessee."

Keaton's head spun around again in shock.

All-American!

He stared as Winston and Meridan slowly approached. The guys could see Winston grinning as they got closer and it was obvious Meridan was nervous.

He sat his gym bag down and said, "For those of you who don't already know, this is Dr. Meridan St. John. She's going to play in Byron's place until we get his replacement. I don't have to tell you guys that Meridan's credentials speak for themselves since she's played on a National Championship Team. So, if there's nothing else, let me introduce everyone. Meridan, this is Malik. You already know Craig and Keaton. Over there are Jonathan and Quinton."

Meridan nodded toward them. "Nice to meet everyone."

Keaton stood there in shock. Meridan was an All-American. He finally snapped back to reality and walked over to her.

He dribbled the ball and said, "Nice shorts, Doc."

"Thank you, Keaton," she responded shyly. "Look, I know this is a shock to you. I hardly ever mention my days on the basketball court to people. I guess I look at that as my past life or something. When Winston called me, I told him this might not be a good idea. If this is going to be a problem for you, just say the word and I'll back off."

He stopped dribbling the ball and took her hand into his. "No, it's okay. I'm just surprised, that's all. I am a little anxious to see if you got game."

She playfully punched him in the arm. "You just try to keep up."

At that time, Winston called all of them together to go over their strategy. Keaton couldn't take his eyes off Meridan as she stretched; neither could Malik. He frowned and couldn't wait to tell Winston to call his boy off or he would, and he wouldn't be nice about it. When they got into their positions, he heard Malik tell Craig, "Man, that is one fine woman."

Craig looked over at Meridan. She was sporting a beautiful red short set that enhanced her athletic legs. Before starting, she pulled her hair into a neat ponytail and laced up her shoes. Keaton overheard Malik and Craig talking.

Malik whispered, "Is she seeing anyone?"

Keaton walked over to them and angrily said, "Yes…me, so back off!"

Malik threw his hands up in the air. "Sorry, man, I didn't know."

"Well, now you do. Let's play ball."

Winston smiled when he heard Keaton stand up for Meridan. He laced up his shoes and laughed to himself, knowing Keaton was falling slowly in love with Meridan.

After practice, as everyone was gathering their belongings, the guys complimented Meridan on her precise passes and dribbling skills. Keaton was still in complete awe. She zipped up her warm-up suit and grabbed her duffle bag.

Before leaving, she softly said, "Thanks, guys, for letting me practice with you. It was fun. I'll see you all later."

In unison, they said, "Thanks, Meridan!"

Keaton walked over to her and pulled her bag off her shoulder. He looked down at her and asked, "Need a lift?"

With a smile, she answered, "Only if you're offering."

Keaton grabbed his bag. "Winston, I'll take Meridan home. See you later, guys!"

With his arm around her waist, he possessively escorted Meridan out of the gym.

Once they were out of sight, Winston said, "Guys, dust off your tuxedos because my brother-in-law, the Playa-of-the-Century, is finished."

They all laughed loudly together in agreement.

As he drove down the street, he couldn't help but look over at her and laugh.

"Keaton, will you please let me in on the joke?"

He smiled. "I'm sorry, Meridan. I'm still trying to come out of my shock. You are one hell of a ball player. How many of the National Championship teams were you on at UT?"

"I was on two of them. Those were some great times. I was pretty good because I've played all my life. It wasn't until I was recruited and given a scholarship that it really sunk in that I was even better than I imagined. Everyone in my family told me, but I thought they were just supporting me."

Keaton adjusted the CD player. "Well, UT has always produced championship talent. You were at the right university. Did you ever consider the WNBA?"

"I played one year; just so I could pay for medical school. Surprisingly, they agreed. After the season, they tried to get me to sign another contract for three years. I told them thanks, but no thanks."

Keaton came to a stop at a traffic light. "You're kidding. You turned down a lot of money."

She gazed into his starstruck eyes. "I wanted to be a pediatrician; nothing else."

The light turned green and Keaton was speechless. This woman had mesmerized him once again. She was as unique as any woman he'd ever met. Not only was she gorgeous, but she possessed a spectacular business mind.

"Are you hungry?"

"Just a little bit. You want to grab something?"

With a gleam in his eyes, he said, "Hot Wing Heaven is right around the corner."

"I don't think so, Keaton. Those wings are too salty and you're not supposed to be eating that type of food. Let's go get a giant salad and split it."

Grumbling, Keaton jokingly said, "Yes, Dear."

Back at Meridan's, Keaton walked her to the door. He had to admit, he was a little worn out from practice, but being in Meridan's company gave him a boost of energy.

She turned and asked, "What kind of dressings do you like?"

"It doesn't matter. What do you have?"

Opening the refrigerator, she pulled out ranch and Italian dressings.

He took the Italian out of her hand. "This will do just right."

They sat at her bar and split the salad. Their conversation consisted of basketball strategy and the upcoming tournament.

When they finished, Meridan asked, "You are staying for dinner, aren't you?"

Grinning, he said, "I would like to, Miss All-American, but I could use a shower first. Look, I'll go pick up some movies, take a shower, and come back so I can help you with dinner."

"That'll work perfectly. So, I guess I'll see you in an hour or so?"

"Sooner, if I can help it."

Giggling, she leaned in and kissed him on the cheek.

"Do we need to synchronize our watches?"

He pulled her into his arms and kissed her unexpectedly on the lips. He released her and casually said, "It's not necessary. I guarantee you, I won't be long."

"Drive carefully, Keaton," she said as she let out a breath.

"I will. Be back shortly," he answered as he jogged down her steps.

Meridan closed the door and leaned against it. His kiss left her lightheaded and wanting more.

Back at the house, Keaton walked in singing. Arnelle was in the kitchen warming Fredrick's food.

"What are you singing about?"

He hugged her. "Did you know Meridan was an All-American in college?"

"Yes, why?"

He headed out of the kitchen. "Ask your husband. He's on my list for a serious ass kicking."

"What happened?"

Keaton stopped and said, "One of our teammates had to drop off the team because his wife had a baby today. Your husband brought Meridan to the gym in his place. You should've seen my face."

"Do you have a problem with Meridan playing on the team?"

Sighing, he said, "Not at all. She was awesome. It's just that Winston seemed to enjoy messing with me, but I've got a surprise for him."

Arnelle laughed. "You two are always going at it."

At that time, Winston and MaLeah walked in the door. Winston laughed and asked, "What's up, Bro?"

"You're very funny, Winston. What you did today was foul. You could've told me you were bringing Meridan to the gym over the phone."

Laughing, he said, "It wouldn't have been as much fun if I had done that; now, would it?"

"Uncie Key!"

MaLeah ran over and outstretched out her arms for him to pick her up. He bent down to be eye level with her and said, "Hey, Shorty. Where have you been?"

She giggled and held out her sticky tootsie pop for him to get a taste.

"I don't think so. I'll see you when I get out of the shower."

"K!"

Keaton stood and walked out the room.

"Payback is hell, Brother-in-law."

Winston yelled, "You just go practice on your song!"

Arnelle looked at him and asked, "What song? What are you two up to?"

He kissed her. "Just a private joke between us; that's all. I'm going to take your sticky daughter upstairs for her bath. I love you."

"I love you, too, Counselor."

CHAPTER 14

M eridan let the hot, steamy water hit her brown skin. It was soothing as it caressed her tired muscles. She didn't want to admit it to herself, but it felt good back out on the court. After entering medical school, she didn't have much time for playing basketball anymore. She would catch a pick-up game every now and then, but her studies required too much of her time. She basically left her basketball days behind her, as well as the bad memories of college. All her hard work paid off because she graduated from medical school with honors. When Winston called her to join him at the gym, she was a little nervous, not knowing what Keaton's reaction would be. She was thrilled he was supportive and amazed to see her do her thing.

Noticing Keaton was still trying to eat meals he shouldn't be, she was glad she had convinced him to share the giant salad. She also decided she would give him a lecture on his blood pressure and diet; whether he liked it or not. As a doctor, she knew it was definitely nothing to play with. She had some paperwork to finish up, but decided she would do it after Keaton left. She had been spending a lot of time with him lately and she was starting to get more and more comfortable with him.

It only took Keaton about an hour and a half to get back over to Meridan's house. When he arrived, she had changed into some navy Capri pants and a white button-down shirt.

"You smell wonderful. What do you have on?"

She blushed. "It's only scented soap, but thank you."

Keaton, dressed in jeans and a long-sleeved shirt, handed her the movies and a bottle of wine.

He removed his jacked, rubbed his hands together, and asked, "What is that delicious smell?"

"It's something that will go great with this wine. Dinner is served."

"I was supposed to help you," he reminded her

She waved him off. "It didn't take long. Plus, I wanted it finished by the time you returned because I knew you'd be starving."

He followed her into the kitchen. "What do we have here?"

Meridan proudly revealed her dishes.

"I have baked chicken, steamed vegetables, and yeast rolls."

Rubbing his stomach, he said, "Yummy."

"Keaton, do me a favor and move the items off the coffee table. I'll bring the plates in."

Meridan walked back into the room with two steaming hot plates. Keaton took the plates from her and smiled. The aroma was mouth-watering.

"Everything looks delicious, Meridan."

"Thank you."

She threw the pillows on the floor. "I'll get the wine while you set up the movie."

Keaton sat the plates down and adjusted the DVD player. Meridan returned with two glasses and the bottle of wine Keaton had graciously brought. She couldn't help but admire his physical attributes. He was a very sexy man. She sat the glasses down and asked, "Ready?"

"Most definitely! Are you sure you want to eat here, on your table?"

"Keaton, unless you're terribly messy, we'll be fine. Now let's eat."

He helped her down on her pillow before sitting himself. They pulled the table back toward the sofa so they could use it as a backrest. After saying grace, Keaton started the movie and poured the wine. The chicken Meridan cooked was delicious and filling. He'd served dishes similar to this at his restaurant, but had never tried them. There were a lot of dishes he hadn't tried, but he knew the staff of chefs he had were some of the best in the country, so he let them do their thing. Keaton volunteered to clear the dishes from the table after Meridan protested to no avail.

The movie was now halfway over and Meridan was starting to feel the effects of the wine. Keaton hadn't showed any signs as he watched the movie diligently. Keaton's body warmed hers as he sat next to her. Feeling his jean-clad leg brushing up against hers was driving her crazy. His arm rested behind her shoulders securely, making her skin feel like it was on fire. Before she knew it, she had dozed off.

From what seemed like hours later, Meridan woke up to find Keaton cleaning up the room.

His eyes met hers. "I was trying not to wake you," he softly whispered.

She sat up, yawned, and said, "You didn't wake me. I can't believe I fell asleep on you."

He smiled back at her. "It wasn't too bad. I actually got a chance to hear you snore," he teased.

She giggled at his comment. "I hope I didn't get too loud."

"I'm only teasing you. You didn't snore."

She smiled as he disappeared into the kitchen with their empty dinnerware. Meridan stood and stretched. Keaton walked back into the room and moved the table back into position.

"Keaton, you don't have to do that right now."

"I know, but I want to," he replied as he placed the pillows back on the sofa.

Meridan picked up the remote control and turned it to the news. "What time is it?"

He looked at his watch. "Late. It's about one o'clock in the morning."

Meridan walked over to him and watched as he placed the movies back into the bag. She took the bag out of his hand. "Could you stop straightening up for a second?"

Curiously, he looked down at her. "Sure. What's up?"

Meridan moved in closer and wrapped her arms around his waist. As she laid her head against his chest, his heart skipped a beat. Embracing her in silence, they just stood there holding each other. The rhythm of their breathing was soothing and relaxing to both of them. He looked down at her and their eyes met. Without the slightest hesitation, he kissed her. Meridan closed her eyes and savored his lips as they moved over hers. He pulled her even closer to him, deepening their kiss. She now felt like she was on cloud nine as they slowly made their way back over to the sofa. He lowered her body onto it, without breaking contact. He positioned himself over her as he continued to sample her soft lips. Meridan started hearing strange noises, then realized they were coming from her. Keaton kissed his way down her neck to her cleavage. She moaned even louder as his hands roamed ever so slowly over her body. He couldn't believe what he was doing or hearing. He'd been waiting to get closer to Meridan St. John for some time now. The fact that she was allowing him access to her voluptuous body was about to send him into overdrive. The question of the day was just how far was she willing to let him go?

He continued his exploration of her lips and neck. Feeling a little daring, he slowly unbuttoned her blouse, exposing a white lace bra covering very full breasts. Her breathing had become erratic and she was even panting when he traced the outline of her bra with his moist tongue.

A breathless voice pierced the silence. "Keaton…please."

He continued his exploration, asking, "Please what, Meridan?"

She couldn't answer him. She was so confused that she didn't know if she wanted him to stop or continue. She was utterly speechless and wanted to scream, feeling his lower region pressing against her body. What she did know was that Keaton Lapahie was driving her crazy. She had no idea she would respond to him in a way to make her feel like this. Keaton himself felt delirious so he became even more daring as he slid his hand inside the waistband of her pants and stroked her. Meridan bit down on her lower lip, closed her eyes, and prayed very hard. She was beginning to have flashbacks of that horrible night with Sam.

You can get through this. Don't let Sam win. Sam will never break your spirit.

"Meridan?"

Their eyes met and she relaxed. Even though she was speechless, she had an idea what he was asking, but she didn't know the answer. She was a little afraid to open her mouth, in fear that she would scream. Keaton's hand slid down even further as he found her to be moist and ready for him. He slid his finger inside her, causing her to scream out his name.

"Keaton!"

Overwhelmed at the moment himself, he breathlessly answered, "I'm here, Baby."

He kissed her harder, knowing if she didn't stop him now, he wouldn't be able to stop later. Then like a bomb going off in his head, it dawned on him… he didn't bring any protection and it was so unlike him. He normally carried it like an American Express card but, for some reason, he was totally unprepared tonight. The reason being this was the last thing he thought he'd be doing with Meridan; even though he'd dreamed about it countless times.

He removed his hand. "Meridan, sweetheart, we have to stop. I don't want to, but I have to. I don't have anything to protect you. Do you have anything?"

Still somewhat dazed, she shook her head to let him know that she didn't. He kissed her and rested his head on her breasts.

"I'm sorry," he sadly admitted.

She gently stroked his head and neck.

"Don't be, Keaton. It was beautiful. Thank you."

He was silent as he absorbed her words. It seemed he'd pleased her just by his touch. God knows what their experience would be like when they finally made love.

As Meridan lay there trembling, she prayed he'd never find out her past before he returned to Texas. She wouldn't be able to look him in the eyes again. A man like Keaton would never be able to understand.

Later that night, Keaton tossed and turned in his bed after returning from Meridan's house. For some reason, he couldn't get comfortable. He stared at the clock, which read three forty-five a.m. As he lay there in the darkness, he realized it was the encounter with Meridan that was causing his sleeplessness. He knew she had to get up early for work, but he needed to hear her voice; just to make sure she was okay. Turning to pick up the telephone, he dialed her number. He could hear his heart pounding, which was so unlike him. A sexy sounding voice answered on the second ring.

"Hello?"

"Meridan, it's Keaton. I'm sorry to call you so late," he said apologetically.

Breathing a sigh of relief, she answered, "That's okay. I wasn't asleep anyway. Is anything wrong?"

He rolled over. "Nah, I couldn't sleep."

"Me either, so I decided to get a little work done."

Keaton sat up against his pillows and softly said, "I guess you know what's causing my sleeplessness."

Smiling, she said, "I don't have a clue. Fill me in."

"Oh, I don't know, maybe a particular All-American beauty and what she did to me tonight."

Laughing, Meridan playfully asked, "Really? Ah, Keaton, that's so sweet and the feeling's mutual."

Humbly, he said, "I'd better let you get some rest. I realize you have to go to work in the morning."

She laid her paperwork down. "I'm used to late hours. There are nights I can't sleep. Besides, I don't have to be in the office until nine o'clock. I'm going to try and catch a few winks in a sec. You should try to go back to sleep, too."

"I'm going to try," he said, sighing.

"For the record, I had a great time tonight, Keaton."

"I wished I could've made it better for you," he admitted.

Meridan smiled. "Believe me…you made my day, in more ways than one. I'm still tingling."

Silence gripped the conversation as Keaton silently punished himself for not having protection.

"Keaton?"

"I'm here," he said seductively.

She sighed. "You'd better get to sleep. You're going to need your rest before we get to Mississippi. One, my dad is going to talk your head off from sunup to sundown. Two, my Aunt Glo will probably try to make passes at you the entire time. I'll do whatever I can to keep her under control."

Keaton laughed out loud. "Is she fine?"

"Keaton Lapahie!"

"I'm kidding. I'm sure if she's anything like her niece, she's very beautiful. Don't worry. I'm sure I'll be well-rested by the time we leave."

Yawning, she said, "On that note, I guess I'd better turn in. You, too, Keaton."

"I guess you're right. Goodnight, Meridan."

"Goodnight, Keaton. Sweet dreams."

With a smile in his voice, he answered, "Oh, that I'm sure of. I'll talk to you in a few hours."

"I'll be waiting."

They hung up together and, at the same time, let out a loud sigh. Meridan reached over and turned out the light on her nightstand before settling under her comforter. She wasn't lying to him when she said her body was still tingling. Their encounter left her anticipating the moment he would make her complete.

On the other end of town, Keaton fluffed his pillows and turned over for hopefully more dreams of an angel. He couldn't wait to see her after she got off work. If given another chance, he'd make sure he was prepared for Meridan St. John.

CHAPTER 15

The next morning, Keaton got up bright and early. He wanted to show Meridan how much fun he'd had last night. The two stops he made were unusual and he had to laugh about it himself.

Meridan had already seen two kids with strep throat and three others with ear infections. She had a few minutes before her next appointment and took the time to make a few calls. When she sat down at her desk, her receptionist called her office.

"Meridan? You have a delivery up front. Do you want me to bring it to your office?"

Meridan looked confused, since she wasn't expecting a delivery.

"Sure, Ashley. Thanks."

She hung up the telephone and picked up her appointment book. About that time Ashley walked in with a basket full of inflated latex gloves. They were arranged in the basket like a bouquet of flowers. Meridan burst out laughing as soon as she saw it because she knew only one person could've sent them.

Ashley sat the basket on Meridan's desk. "Do you know who sent this?"

Meridan removed the card. "I have a good idea. It's from a very good friend."

"From the way you're smiling, I take it you mean a male friend?"

"Yes. Thanks for bringing it in for me."

"You're welcome. Enjoy!"

Ashley gave Meridan her privacy. Once alone, Meridan sat down and opened the card.

Meridan,

This is just a little something to let you know that you could never have too much latex. Hehehe! For the record, I'll never be caught without my latex again. Hope I made you laugh and I can't wait to see you.

Keaton

Meridan laughed again and picked up the telephone. She dialed Keaton's cell phone.

"Hello?"

"You're so bad, Keaton" she said, laughing.

He chuckled. "I take it you got my delivery?"

Twirling in her chair, she said, "Yes, I did. You're so crazy and your little note was even funnier."

"I'm glad you like it. So are you going to let me cook dinner for you tonight?"

She stood, playing with the latex gloves.

"I guess that could be arranged."

Keaton smiled.

"Great! You're coming over for dinner. Is it okay if I pick you up around five-thirty?"

"That'll be fine. Thanks again, Keaton."

"The pleasure was all mine. I'll see you at five-thirty."

Meridan hung up the telephone and left her office to attend to more patients.

Hours later, Keaton worked diligently in the kitchen preparing dinner. Winston arrived home first with MaLeah and Fredrick.

She danced around the room, yelling, "Uncie Key!"

He looked down at her. "Hey, Shorty. What you know, Fredrick?"

MaLeah ran over and hugged her uncle's leg. Keaton stood at the sink, rinsing off vegetables.

Winston put Fredrick in his highchair. "What's for dinner, Bro?"

Since Keaton had been in Philly, he volunteered to be the cook since he was at home all day.

"Just a little sumptin' sumptin'. Meridan's coming over for dinner tonight." Winston gave him a sneaky grin.

"Oh really? That's so sweet. You guys must've really had a good time the other night. You got in kind of late. Is there anything you want to tell me?"

Keaton wouldn't give Winston the satisfaction.

"Yeah, Man, we had a good time. I told you I like hanging out with her." Winston gave Fredrick his milk.

"That's good. How's your throat?"

"What do you mean?"

He took his jacket off. "I don't want you to strain your voice before the wedding."

Keaton put a dish in the oven. "Forget you, Winston! I told you, my name is all over your motorcycle. You have the wrong guy."

"How would you like to sweeten the deal?"

Throwing the dish towel over his shoulder, Keaton folded his arms. "What do you have in mind?"

"I'll tell you what. If I'm wrong, I'll go in with you on that Sports Bar and Grill you've been talking about opening. If I'm right, you'll have to go in with me on that summer house in Florida Arnelle has been eyeing."

Rubbing his hands together, Keaton yelled, "Damn, Winston! This is going to be so easy. You're on!"

As Winston walked out of the room, he said, "By the way, Craig, Venice and the kids are coming over for dinner, so make sure we have enough."

"I've got this," he assured Winston.

CHAPTER 16

When Keaton arrived later with Meridan, MaLeah was in the process of pushing her brother full speed down the hallway in his walker. As usual, she was going too fast, causing Fredrick to hold on for dear life. Winston and Arnelle were nowhere to be found but he knew they weren't far away from the kids. More than likely they were somewhere tangled up in each other's arms.

Keaton frowned and yelled, "Shorty! Slow down before you kill your brother!"

She giggled and yelled, "K!"

Noticing Meridan standing beside him, she yelled, "Doctor MeMe!"

Meridan leaned down, stroked MaLeah's ponytails, and said, "Well, hello, MaLeah. How are you this evening?"

She put her hand over her mouth and giggled. Keaton stood, watching two of his favorite women.

He asked, "Where are your mom and dad, Shorty?"

"In the kitchen," she answered, while hugging his leg.

He swung her up in his arms, kissed her on the cheek, and said, "Go tell them we're here."

He sat her back down, then without hesitation, he leaned over and kissed Meridan slowly on the lips.

MaLeah squealed out loud, "Ooooo! Uncie Key kissed Doctor MeMe! Mommie! Daddy! Uncie Key kissed Doctor MeMe!"

She ran toward the kitchen to broadcast the news. He looked at Meridan and said, "Sorry!"

"It's okay, Keaton. You know how children are."

"I guess we'd better go face the music, huh?"

"Lead the way."

Keaton took her hand into his and led her toward the kitchen to join the others.

Dinner went off without any problems. After MaLeah finished giggling over Keaton kissing Meridan, they were able to enjoy the delicious meal he'd prepared. As they ate, Arnelle complimented Meridan on the pink cashmere sweater she wore with her black leather pants. Her black boots put about three more inches on her height, bringing her even closer to Keaton. He couldn't help but admire the way the leather fit to her shapely backside. It was hard for him not to stare as they sat side by side. Winston and Craig smiled throughout dinner as they observed Keaton's obvious weakness around Meridan. They continued to talk about the upcoming Mississippi trip and, before long, it was time for the children to go to bed. MaLeah cried because she wanted Meridan to help her with her bath. When Winston and Arnelle protested, she cried even louder.

Meridan stood. "Arnelle, it's okay. I don't mind helping MaLeah with her bath."

"Are you sure?"

MaLeah ran over and hugged Meridan's leg.

"It's not a problem at all. Come on, MaLeah. Let's get you ready for bed."

Keaton stood also. "I'll go so I can show you where everything is."

As Winston, Craig, Venice and Arnelle cleaned up the kitchen, they couldn't help but discreetly discuss how soft Keaton had become since he'd become involved with Meridan.

Winston said, "Arnelle, I guess you know, your brother's halfway to the altar."

Craig wiped off the table. "I agree. He's like a different person."

Venice put the leftovers in the refrigerator. "Don't ya'll think you're jumping the gun a little?"

"Hell no!" Winston loudly answered. "You guys must not have eyes."

Arnelle said, "We have eyes. It's just that my brother doesn't seem like the marrying type."

"It's different, now that he's hooked up with Meridan," Craig explained.

Turning, Arnelle asked, "What do you mean?"

Venice said, "Don't pay Craig and Winston any attention, Arnelle. If it's meant for Meridan and Keaton to be together, they will be. I think they're a cute couple."

Winston gathered the trash bag. "I don't care what ya'll say; I think his playa days are over."

Arnelle opened the garage door for him. "You don't think he's getting serious about her, do you?"

"I guess time will tell, huh?"

At that time, Keaton walked in and noticed the surprised look on everyone's face. Sensing that he had walked in unexpectedly, he asked, "What?"

Arnelle turned her back to him to place a plate in the cabinet.

Winston smiled and asked, "What do you mean...what?"

"You all look like you're up to something," he said with a frown.

Venice and Craig tried to keep busy with the dishes so they wouldn't give away the fact that Keaton was the topic of their conversation.

Arnelle walked over to him. "You're imagining things. Is Meridan doing okay with MaLeah?"

"Yes, and I gave Fredrick his bath. Is his bottle ready?"

Arnelle pointed over to the bottle warmer. "Keaton, you'd make a great daddy."

He hissed, "Please!"

He turned and walked out of the kitchen. As he climbed the stairs, he felt chills run over his body. *Daddy? Arnelle has lost her damn mind.*

After he walked out, everyone burst out laughing.

Venice walked across the room. "Ya'll are so wrong to do Keaton like that.

Skeeter, you don't need to be messing with him; you were the same way about Arnelle."

Craig said, "She got you there, Bro!"

Winston said, "Oh! Ya'll teaming up on me now, huh? Anyway, that was different. I wasn't going around talking about never getting married."

Craig laughed. "No, you were just trying to be the Playa-of-the-Century."

Arnelle waved them off. "Please! Don't remind me."

They all laughed together.

Venice responded, "Well, we'd better get the kids and get out of here. It's getting late and they've been asleep for a while. Brandon had a good time playing with MaLeah."

Winston said, "So did MaLeah. It would be wild if they end up married one day, huh?"

Everyone froze and looked at him.

Craig hugged and kissed Arnelle. "Tell your husband to slow his roll."

Venice hugged Winston. "Well, I would be honored to have MaLeah as a daughter-in-law."

"The same here, Venice." Craig shook hands with Winston and said, "Skeeter…Arnelle, thanks for dinner."

"You're welcome," they answered in unison.

"Keep us posted on the love birds," Venice requested.

Winston smiled. "We will. Let me help you guys get the kids to the car."

Before returning to Fredrick's room, Keaton stopped by the bathroom to check on the ladies.

Leaning against the door frame, he asked, "How's everything going in here?"

Meridan was in the process of drying MaLeah's body. She looked up at him with sparkling eyes. "We're almost done. What are you doing?"

In a daze, he responded, "Getting ready to give Fredrick his bottle."

"Okay…and Keaton?"

"Yes?"

"Thanks!"

He curiously asked, "For what?"

"Everything," she whispered.

"You're welcome, Meridan." He blushed.

Smiling, he grabbed MaLeah's ponytail. "Kiss."

MaLeah puckered her lips for her uncle to kiss her. After the kiss, she giggled loudly.

"Uncie Key! You have to kiss Dr. MeMe, too!"

Meridan blushed as she looked up at Keaton.

He smiled. "You heard her. Kiss, Meridan St. John."

Meridan blushed one last time as Keaton leaned down and kissed her, lingering to taste her soft lips. MaLeah put her hand over her mouth and screamed with laughter.

Keaton finally pulled away and said, "Jesus."

Breathless, she answered, "Ditto that and I'll meet you in Fredrick's room in a couple of minutes so I can tell him goodnight."

Turning back to MaLeah, he took a breath and said, "Okay. MaLeah, give me a goodnight hug."

MaLeah now had on her pajamas as she jumped into her uncle's arms, giving him a big hug. Afterwards, Meridan took her by the hand and led her back downstairs to her parents.

After coffee, dessert and a yawn or two from Meridan, Keaton knew it was time to take her home.

He stood and said, "Well, guys, I'd better get Meridan home." Looking in her direction, he asked, "Are you ready?"

"Yes, it's been a great night. I had fun with the kids. Winston, Arnelle, it was so nice to see you guys again. It was also good to see the Bennetts and the kids, too."

They all stood together and Winston said, "Same here, and we hope to see more of you. The kids really love you."

Winston looked over at Keaton and winked. He went on to say, "And I must say, Keaton is a changed man since you two have been hanging out."

Keaton took Meridan's hand. "Don't listen to him. Let me get your jacket."

Keaton walked out of the room. Arnelle hugged Meridan and whispered, "Winston's right. Whatever you did to my brother, I want to thank you."

Meridan felt a little awkward, not realizing exactly what they were giving her credit for. She said, "Well, I'll see you guys later and I'll make sure to take good care of him in Mississippi."

"I'm sure you will," Winston said, grinning.

"Goodnight. Keaton, are you ready?"

Glaring at his sister and brother-in-law, he said, "Yes, I am."

Walking them to the door, Arnelle said, "Keaton, drive carefully and, Meridan, have a wonderful time visiting your family."

"I'll try. Goodnight."

In unison, Winston and Arnelle said, "Goodnight."

CHAPTER 17

Meridan and Keaton arrived at the Jackson Airport early Friday morning. When they stepped off the plane, Keaton could immediately tell he was back in the South. It was a welcomed feeling and the humidity was no joke. Meridan had on some faded jeans, a white, button-down blouse and brown suede boots. Before coming home, she got some microbraids that hung a few inches past her shoulders to keep her hair more manageable during the trip home. Keaton, also dressed in jeans, adorned a white T-shirt and leather jacket.

On the plane ride there, Keaton occasionally played in her hair, causing chills to run down her arms. Meridan, on the other hand, was starting to get a little nervous about bringing Keaton home. She'd never taken a man home to meet her family before.

As soon as they exited the plane she heard a familiar voice call out her name.

"Meridan! Over here!"

"Daddy!"

Meridan ran over to her father, who stood at least six-feet four-inches. He smiled as his youngest daughter jumped into his arms. Keaton followed close behind her and watched the loving exchange.

A few tears fell from Meridan's eyes as her dad whispered, "Welcome home, sweetheart."

She kissed him and wiped her tears away.

"Daddy, I'd like you to meet—"

Extending his hand, he said, "This man needs no introduction. Why didn't you tell me you were bringing home the Chief?"

"Chief? Daddy, this is Keaton Lapahie," she announced.

Keaton laughed. "Nice to finally meet you, Mr. St. John."

"Chief, you can call me William. I can't believe you're the friend Meridan was talking about bringing home."

Confused, Meridan asked, "Daddy, why do you keep calling him the Chief and how do you know him?"

Mr. St. John put his arm around his daughter. "You mean to tell me you don't know?"

Keaton helped by saying, "Mr. St. John, Meridan doesn't know. I really hadn't got around to telling her yet."

"Got around to telling me what?" she asked in confusion. "What's going on?"

Keaton turned to Meridan. "Meridan, people nicknamed me the Chief when I played in the NBA with the San Antonio Spurs."

Her eyes bulged out in shock as she listened to him. She punched him on the arm. "You mean to tell me you played in the NBA? Why didn't you tell me? You were going on and on about me and you didn't say a word."

Mr. St. John stepped between them. "Now, now. Meridan, I'm sure Keaton didn't mean to keep that info from you on purpose. Did you, Son?"

He turned and winked at Keaton, then went on to say, "That was a few years ago anyway. You busted your knee right, Keaton?"

"Yes, Sir."

He turned to her again. "Meridan, I was going to tell you, but I wanted to surprise you like you surprised me. I didn't know your father was going to recognize me right away."

Mr. St. John intervened again. "Who wouldn't recognize the Chief? Well, my daughter didn't, but I digress. You'd think she would've, being a basketball star herself."

"Daddy! I couldn't help it that I was a recluse while I was in medical school. Besides, I don't have time to keep up with all that stuff anymore." She eyed Keaton again. "So, Keaton, you're one of them."

He held her hand. "I used to be one of them. I'm sorry. Do you forgive me?"

She gave his hand a little squeeze. "I'll take care of you later. For now, I temporarily forgive you."

Mr. St. John clapped his hands together. "With that settled, let's hit the road. I have a nice dinner waiting on you two."

"Thank you, Daddy."

Keaton and Meridan followed Mr. St. John to the baggage claim area, then out the door to his awaiting car.

It felt good to Meridan to be back at home in her room. Her dad had put Keaton in her sister's old room across the hallway. Her parents' room was on the first floor near the kitchen, which made it hard for them to sneak in after curfew when they were teens.

Falling down on her bed, she let out a loud sigh. She could hear her dad across the hall, holding a conversation with Keaton. She lay there listening to their muffled voices through the door. Thinking back to basketball practice in the gym, she remembered how much he was skilled, but the NBA? At that moment, her dad knocked on her door.

"Meridan, hurry up and come on down so you can eat."

Standing, she yelled back, "Okay, Daddy!" She looked at her suitcase and said, "I guess I'll have to unpack later."

Once downstairs, Meridan found him standing over the stove telling Keaton God knows what about her. Keaton was laughing so hard, he was in tears. When she stepped into the kitchen, Keaton tried to stifle his laughter.

"Daddy, what are you down here telling him?"

"Nothing, baby girl. Grab a plate so you can eat. How's that friend of yours from college, Nikki?"

"She's fine, Daddy."

"Well, tell her hello and that she doesn't have to stop coming down for a visit just because you guys aren't in college anymore."

"I'll tell her, Daddy. Now stop trying to change the subject. What were you telling Keaton?"

Keaton didn't want to make eye contact with her, in fear that he'd start laughing again. What her father had told him was that Meridan never thought she was good at anything. When she didn't think she was pretty enough, she tried to change her looks by allowing her best friend to dye her hair. Sadly, it turned out green. He went on to tell Keaton that she also never thought she measured up in basketball, until college scouts started calling the house. Only then did she take it seriously. He warned Keaton that Meridan was very hard on herself, causing her to always challenge her abilities.

Meridan sat down and noticed that her father had gone all out in the kitchen.

He was an excellent cook, preparing meatloaf, macaroni and cheese, and green beans.

Of course, no meal was complete without hot water cornbread.

"Daddy, when did you cook all this?"

He sat down at the head of the table. "Oh, about an hour or two before you got here. Now eat up. You look like you've lost weight since the last time I saw you."

"I told you I was dieting," she reminded him.

Her dad looked at her sternly. "For what? You look fine. Doesn't she, Keaton?"

Keaton froze with his fork halfway to his mouth.

"Daddy! Keaton's not in this conversation."

Keaton put his fork down and looked directly at Meridan.

"Meridan, your father asked me a question, and I'm going to answer it. Mr. St. John, I think Meridan is perfect just like she is. I don't understand why she's trying to lose weight either."

Mr. St. John poured a glass of tea. "You need to eat! A man likes a woman with a little meat on her bones. It's your heart you need to keep healthy."

"Daddy, I understand what you're saying, but for me, I want to lose some weight. Okay? I want to get my college figure back."

Grumbling under his breath, he said, "Whatever you say, Meridan. So Keaton, did you see the horses when we came in? If you like, I'm sure Meridan would love to show you the farm."

"Yes, Sir. We sort of talked about riding before we came. Thank you."

Mr. St. John turned to Meridan. "Your Aunt Glo has been pretty quiet lately. I hope she's not waiting until my party to cut loose."

"Me, too, Daddy," Meridan agreed.

Mr. St. John looked at Keaton. "Keaton, my sister's a little eccentric so you'll have to excuse her if she starts acting strange."

"That's okay, William. Meridan already warned me that her aunt can be a little colorful at times."

Mr. St. John continued to eat. "Brother Jones is coming out to set up the tent and tables in a little while. Keaton, I'd appreciate it if you'd ride in with me to pick up the meat from the butcher. Is that all right with you, Meridan?"

"Sure, Daddy. That'll give me a chance to go pick up a few things."

He stood and said, "Oh! Your cousins, Devon and Keyshaun, are home from college for the weekend. If you don't mind, go by your Aunt Elizabeth's house and pick up the pies she baked. Your Uncle Conrad and family will be in early in the morning. Your sister and her crew are staying at Elizabeth's house and they'll be getting in tonight."

"I'm glad of that. I'm not for any of her drama this weekend."

Her father sternly said, "I don't want you two going at it this weekend. Do you hear me?"

"I won't start, if she doesn't," Meridan told him honestly.

Meridan left them alone in the kitchen to retrieve her purse.

Her father looked at Keaton. "Some things never change in this family. I hope it won't give you a bad impression of us."

"Don't worry about me. Every family has its share of sibling rivalry."

Meridan took mental notes of all her father's instructions as she pulled her purse upon her shoulder. One meeting she wasn't looking forward to was with her older sister. She was bitter with her, for some reason, and every chance she got, she'd pick a fight or try to hurt her feelings. Meridan thought that after they'd gone their separate ways, her sister would've mellowed out, but she hadn't. Gwendolyn St. John-Monroe was hell on wheels every chance she got. Meridan had observed that her husband, Thomas, seemed to take the bitter with the sweet, but it was obvious he wasn't as passive as he appeared. She liked him and their relationship had always been a good one.

She couldn't wait to see her two nieces whom she enjoyed spoiling.

Back downstairs she found Keaton in the den looking at a wall full of family photos.

Embarrassed, she shouted, "Oh my goodness! I look a mess, huh?"

He turned and frowned.

"No, you don't look a mess. You were beautiful then and you're still beautiful. Stop being so critical of yourself, Meridan! You're the only one who seems to have a problem with your appearance."

As soon as he'd said it, he knew his words may have been a little harsh, but he wanted to reassure her in some way that she was a desirable woman.

Meridan tilted her head, surprised at Keaton's outburst, but flattered nonetheless. She walked over closer to him. "Come here."

He turned and she pulled his face close to hers and softly said, "Thank you."

He showed her his incredible dimples. "You're welcome."

She kissed his lips. "Beware of my sister this weekend. As you heard, we don't see eye-to-eye sometimes so she'll try to get in my business. Okay?"

He pecked her on the lips once more. "Okay."

"I'll see you guys later. You're in for a treat here in my little town. Daddy's going to want to show you off to everyone, so I hope it won't get on your nerves."

He hugged her. "Actually, I'm looking forward to it."

CHAPTER 18

The morning sun woke Keaton up the next day. He hadn't enjoyed himself like he did last night in a long time. He could hear voices outside, but didn't know what was going on. They all had sat up late last night talking and catching up on things. It was way past midnight before everyone went to bed. Slowly, he made his way to the bathroom and into the shower. He'd actually had a restful night, even though Meridan was only a few feet away from him. He could smell her scented cologne all night, and it was welcomed aromatherapy circulated by the ceiling fan.

Once dressed, in his jeans and shirt, he wandered downstairs to find a young man in the kitchen making a sandwich.

Keaton said, "Good morning."

The young man turned. "Dang! Unc was right! You really are here!"

Keaton extended his hand. "I'm Keaton Lapahie, a friend of Meridan's."

"Nah, Man, you're the Chief! I can't believe it!"

"What's your name?"

He took a bite of his sandwich, then said, "I'm sorry. I'm Devon, Meridan's cousin."

Keaton smiled. "You're home from school, right?"

Devon took another bite of his sandwich. "Yeah, I'm a freshman at Morehouse."

Keaton crossed his arms and asked, "How old are you?"

With crumbs falling onto his shirt, he answered, "Eighteen."

"You look older than eighteen."

"I hear that all the time," he said, bragging.

Laughing, Keaton responded, "William said you were home from school. What are you studying?"

He proudly answered, "Electrical Engineering."

"That's a great field. Good luck," he wished him before turning to look down the hallway. "Where is everyone?"

While putting the sandwich up to his mouth, he said, "Thanks, Chief. Oh! Uncle William's out in the barn. Meridan rode out to check on the fences and I'm here to get some of this home-cooked food that I've been missing."

Laughing, Keaton said, "I understand. What are you eating?"

"It's a pork chop sandwich. Do you want one?"

He walked over to the cabinet and poured himself a cup of coffee.

"No, but thanks anyway. It was nice meeting you, Devon."

"Same here, Man!"

Keaton stepped out onto the back porch and sipped his coffee. He took in a deep breath and closed his eyes. The smell of the South was like none other. While leaning again the railing, two large, hybrid dogs ran up on the porch and growled.

Devon stepped out onto the porch and yelled, "Cut out all that noise! Keaton, don't make any quick movements. Reach out and let them smell your hand."

Keaton looked at him, surprisingly, and asked, "Are you sure?"

"Yeah. They're okay, once they get used to your smell."

Keaton was worried about trusting this eighteen-year-old, but he knew the dogs better than he did, so he did as he was told. The dogs immediately took in Keaton's scent and ran out to the barn playfully.

Devon laughed. "Told you."

Keaton chuckled. "Yes, you did."

Devon continued to chew on his sandwich.

Keaton turned and said, "If you don't mind, put this cup in the kitchen for me. I'm going over to talk to William."

"No problem."

In the barn, Keaton watched William go about his daily routine. He looked up and saw Keaton enter.

"Well, you're finally up. Did you meet Devon?"

It was only nine o'clock but he was sure Mr. St. John had been up for hours. He picked up a pitchfork, ready to help him. "Yes, and I slept very well. Devon said Meridan was out checking the fences."

"I thought you might want to join her. I have your horse saddled up and ready to go."

Keaton looked over his shoulder, eyeing the horse. He walked over and patted him. William led the horse outside and pointed over the hill behind the house. Then he handed him a two-way radio.

"Take this radio and when you get to the top of the hill, radio her so she can tell you where she is. We always use these when we go out on the property. You never know when you might get lost or hurt."

"I understand, Mr. St. John."

Keaton mounted the horse and tucked the radio in the saddle.

"Keaton, this is the last time I'm going to tell you to stop calling me Mr. St. John. It's William...okay?"

Keaton put on his sunglasses. "Okay, William. Well, I'm off. I'll radio back to let you know I found her."

William patted the horse. "I'll be waiting."

Keaton rode off to find Meridan.

Meridan had found another section of the fence that needed mending so she tied a red ribbon around the post to mark the spot. She looked up at the hot sun and sighed. She decided to take a little break under her favorite shade tree, a long way from everything. Dismounting her horse, she pulled out a blanket and a bottle of cold water. Settling down on the blanket, she closed her eyes and leaned back against the tree. Moments later, a familiar voice radiated over the airwaves.

"Ms. Meridan St. John, where are you?"

Meridan grabbed her radio and answered, "Keaton?"

"The one and only, and I'm trying to find you. Where are you?"

She stood and asked, "What are you near?"

"I see what looks like a lake ahead of me. To my right is a cornfield."

She laughed. "Keep riding toward the lake. You should see a row of trees. Ride through the row of trees and you'll find me on the other side of the lake."

Laughing, he said, "I'm on my way."

It didn't take Keaton long to find Meridan resting against the tree. He got off his horse and walked over to where she was.

He smiled and asked, "May I join you?"

Meridan patted the space on the blanket next to her and took another sip of cold water.

"What brings you out here, Keaton?"

"I was looking for you. I didn't expect you to leave without me."

Setting her water down, she said, "I was just helping Daddy by checking the fences."

She walked over to her horse and pulled out another bottle of water. She returned to the blanket and sat down, handing him the water.

"Thank you."

Meridan finished drinking her water. "You're welcome. Now if you'd like, I can make this your official tour. I really just got started."

"That works for me. Your farm is beautiful. William has his hands full, keeping it up to these standards."

Meridan played with a blade of grass and said, "My uncles and cousins help him. There's no way he could do this by himself. I used to help when I was here."

"Somehow I knew that. You never cease to amaze me, Meridan."

"Thank you, Keaton, but I've never been afraid to get my hands dirty. As a matter of fact, I enjoyed working on the farm with my family."

She could see Keaton's eyes gleaming at her in a strange way.

He gulped his water down. "I'm going to be leaving Philly in about two weeks. This time off was exactly what I needed, but I need to get back to my restaurant. I'm so glad I got the chance to get to know you better."

Meridan closed her eyes briefly. Her heart skipped a beat, hearing the word "leaving."

She solemnly responded, "Thank you and I'm glad I met you, too. I'm going to miss you, Keaton, but I understand you have to get back to your business, and life, in Texas."

He smiled at her. "I'm going to miss you also, but I'll be back. Hopefully, I can get you to come down to visit me."

"We'll see."

Silence surrounded them for a moment. He noticed her reaction to his news. He wasn't sure if what he saw was relief, or disappointment. He hoped it was the latter of the two.

"Thanks for the drink," he said as he played with one of her braids.

"It was my pleasure," she whispered.

Meridan was about to stand to dispose of their bottles when Keaton reached over and grabbed her arm.

She looked at him and asked, "What is it, Keaton?"

He shook his head. "I don't know. I can't explain it, but I do know that you're a unique woman."

"I don't know about unique, but I am a woman," she said with a smile.

He reached up and cupped her face, pulling her toward him.

"Oh, that's without a doubt," he said, staring at her.

He leaned forward in silence and kissed her very, very slowly. Meridan felt like she was about to hyperventilate as Keaton's lips moved over hers. His seduction was extremely powerful. Meridan wrapped her arms around his neck and found herself straddling his lap. His kisses were hot and sweet. There was no doubt in her mind that Keaton wanted her right then and there. They'd come close once and his seduction had become even more intense each time their lips joined. Her body had also become very responsive; even when he came within a few feet of her. Keaton lay back onto the blanket, taking her down with him. Keaton grabbed her hips, pulling her body closer to him. Their hearts were beating wildly as they both tried to maneuver to get even closer to each other. He was fully aroused and feeling as if he was going to explode.

Breathlessly, she panted, "Oh, Keaton. I... I... My God!"

Rolling over to change positions, he unbuttoned her shirt, removed her bra, and buried his face in her chest. Meridan's body jerked as soon as his lips came in contact with her breasts. He took his time as he gave her body his undivided attention.

"Damn, Meridan." He moaned as he ran his tongue over her nipples.

At that moment, Mr. St. John's voice boomed over the two-way radio, startling them.

"Keaton! Meridan! Did you two find each other?"

If he only knew.

Meridan picked up her radio with trembling fingers and stuttered, "Uh, yeah... I mean yes, Daddy, he found me. We're going to...uh...finish checking the fences and then head home."

"Okay, you two be careful out there," he warned her. "A storm is brewing."

She stared at Keaton and answered, "We will."

Keaton rolled off her body and gazed at her. He was a little shaken himself.

"Meridan, if I didn't think that we'd get caught, I'd pick up where I left off. But I'd hate for someone in your family, especially your dad, to ride up on us."

Meridan buttoned her blouse in silence. She couldn't look at him right now because her emotions were too raw.

She stood. "We wouldn't get caught, but I do need to finish checking the fences. There's a lot of work to do before the party tonight. I hope the rain holds off."

Keaton stood and folded the blanket for her. He pulled her into his arms and said, "I'm sure it will." Silently they packed up the blankets. Keaton touched her arm and said, "Look at me." She turned toward him shyly. "Are you really going to miss me when I leave?"

"Without a doubt, Keaton. I only hope you don't forget about me."

He wrinkled his brow and firmly said, "I could never forget about you."

She slowly looked up into his eyes. "Keaton, I don't know what it is you're doing to me. I feel so...so...."

He put his finger over her lips. "What I'm doing to you is showing you how I feel about you. You do realize this little encounter was strike two, sweetheart?" He leaned down closer to her ear and whispered, "Third time's the charm."

Blushing, and without responding, she took the blanket from him and put it in her saddle. As a matter of fact, she was anxiously awaiting the moment when she'd give herself to him.

Climbing up on her horse, she asked, "Are you ready to ride?"

"More than you can imagine," he said as he mounted his horse.

Within moments, they rode off across the meadow.

CHAPTER 19

It looked like more than two hundred people had graced the St. John farm for the birthday party. All the family and friends were there to help celebrate William's sixtieth birthday. Meridan was working frantically alongside other family members to make sure all the food was in place. She wanted to dress light tonight because of the humidity. She chose a long, halter dress with matching sandals. Keaton was busy making sure there were enough drinks for the guests as well as seats. Cousins Devon and Keyshaun served as the DJs. Meridan made sure they brought a variety of music so they wouldn't have to dance to rap music all night. Several times, Meridan caught Keaton staring at her as she worked. One time he even snuck over and kissed her lovingly on the cheek in front of some family members. Her aunts made it a point to react loudly to the loving exchange.

As usual, Meridan's sister Gwendolyn showed up after all the work had been completed. Her two daughters, Jaresa and Kennedy, saw Meridan and ran over, giving her a hug. They were six and eight years old and had always been close to her. Even though she'd had differences with their mom, it didn't stop her from spoiling them with love and gifts all the time.

Gwendolyn walked over to Meridan. "Well, Little Sis, I'm surprised you took off from your job to come home to see Daddy."

"It's good to see you, too, Gwendolyn. I have one thing to say to you...

Don't start with me tonight. I won't let you and Aunt Glo ruin this night for Daddy. Can't you be civil with me for one night? Damn! I don't know what's up your ass!"

Gwendolyn's husband laughed. He was used to this sisterly bickering. Meridan turned to him. "Hello, Thomas, how are you?"

Her brother-in-law gave her a hug and kiss. "Fine, how are you? It's so nice to see you again, Meridan. You need to come for a visit soon. The girls would love to see you and so would Gwen. Wouldn't you, Honey?"

Gwendolyn gave Thomas a fake smile.

Thomas laughed. "I'm going over to say hello to William. You girls behave. Okay?"

Meridan liked Thomas. He could see right through Gwendolyn, but stayed neutral most of the time.

Gwendolyn waited for him to walk off, then sarcastically said, "You know Thomas is right, Meridan. You should come and visit us, but we'll talk about it later. So is Daddy still dating that woman? What's her name?"

"Gwendolyn, Daddy's in love with her, so stop tripping. Ms. Leona is a very nice woman and she makes him happy."

Gwendolyn turned up her nose. "She's probably after Daddy's money."

"She doesn't need Daddy's money. Unless you've forgotten, Ms. Leona has her own. She's run that store by herself for the past ten years and I admire her. It wasn't easy for her to keep it going after Mr. Gilbert passed away and you know it."

Gwendolyn snarled. "Well, I don't like it. Daddy acts like the world revolves around her. Is she here?"

Meridan grabbed Gwendolyn's arm firmly. "Yes, and you'd better be nice to her, Gwen. I'm not playing with you. Unless you've forgotten, Daddy pursued her; not the other way around. Remember?"

Yanking her arm away, she said, "Okay, Meridan, chill out. Damn! I'm going to find Daddy. I'll catch up with you later, Little Sis."

"I look forward to it, Gwendolyn."

Meridan watched her sister work the crowd as she made her way over to their father. She was going to do her best not to let her get under her skin; especially not tonight.

CHAPTER 20

I t had been about two hours since dinner had started and now the dancing had begun. So far everyone seemed to be enjoying themselves. The menu consisted of barbecue in several varieties, fried chicken, baked beans, potato salad, slaw, turnip greens, and so on. The dessert table wasn't much different. There was a sea of drinks ranging from iced tea to soft drinks. The tent was decorated beautifully with plenty of greenery and flowers. A huge three-tier cake adorned a special table near the guest of honor's table. He'd share his table with his daughters and escorts for the evening. Gwendolyn tried to act startled that Meridan had brought a man home to meet her family. She tried her best to quiz Keaton about his relationship with Meridan, but he only revealed what he wanted her to know. It was going to be a long night.

As he turned in his seat to look for Meridan, he noticed a gentleman hugging her intimately.

Gwendolyn saw his reaction. "Keaton, do you want to know who has Meridan all locked up?"

He sipped his drink. "Not particularly. I'm sure she knows most of the people here."

"I'll tell you anyway. That's Jacob Richardson, Meridan's high school sweetheart. He's a doctor in Atlanta and very handsome, don't you think?"

Gwendolyn didn't lie. Jacob was quite handsome. He was built like a male model and radiated a warm and loving personality as well. The suit he wore was custom-made to his muscular frame and his dimples were embedded in dark chocolate skin.

Keaton wasn't going to let Gwendolyn's comments get to him, but in a way they did. He was having a hard time watching this man put his hands all over Meridan. He stood and said, "Excuse me for a moment, Gwendolyn. Can I get you anything?"

"No, thank you," she replied.

Meridan was surprised to see Jacob there. It had been a while since she'd seen him, and he looked very nice.

"Jacob, how's Hotlanta treating you?"

Sliding his hands inside his pockets, he leaned in and whispered, "I can't complain, but it would be so much nicer if you'd come with me."

Meridan put her hands on her hips. "Jacob, tell the truth. You couldn't wait to get to Atlanta to chase all those fast women."

Solemnly, he said, "You were the only woman I ever wanted. I had plans for us to practice together."

She was speechless and thought maybe Jacob had gotten over his so-called crush. She knew he wasn't the one for her, but he was a nice man nevertheless.

A warm breeze blew over her body and, with all the people there, she was able to pick up Keaton's heavenly scent even before she saw him. Keaton was heading in her direction with an unreadable expression on his face. He approached slowly, then smiled as he made eye contact with her.

Looking Jacob in the eyes, he said, "Excuse me, Bro. Meridan, do you have anything for a headache?"

With concern, Meridan said, "Sure, Keaton, but first I want you to meet a dear friend of mine. This is Jacob Richardson; we grew up together. Jacob, this is Keaton Lapahie, a dear friend from San Antonio."

Keaton extended his hand. "Nice to meet you, Jacob. I've met so many friends of Meridan's tonight."

Laughing, Jacob shoved his hands in his pockets, looked around, and said, "Yeah, Meridan has a lot of friends here who love her."

Love her? What the hell?

Playfully smacking Jacob on the hand, she grabbed Keaton's arm and said, "Keaton, don't listen to him. Jacob's laying it on a little thick because I haven't been able to hang out with him in a long time. Jacob, would you excuse us for a moment? I need to get Keaton something for his headache."

Jacob hugged and kissed her on the cheek. "Go right ahead. I want to say hello to the rest of your family anyway."

Shaking Keaton's hand again, he said, "Nice to meet you, Keaton."

"Same here, Jacob."

Jacob watched as Meridan held Keaton's hand as they walked through the crowd together and, in that instant, it angered him. He had no idea he would have any serious competition for Meridan's heart... Until now.

Meridan led Keaton through the crowd, but before they could get out of the tent, her cousin Devon yelled over the microphone, "Yo, Cuz! Don't hurt him!"

Everyone laughed as they noticed Keaton and Meridan leaving the tent together. She put her fist up at him, signaling that she was going to give him a serious beat down when she got back.

Entering through the back door of the house in silence, Meridan went to the cabinet and retrieved some pain reliever. She held it out to him, then said, "Before I give this to you, I want to check your blood pressure. Okay?"

He played with one of her braids. "You're always the worry wart, huh?"

"Don't make fun of me, Keaton. I'm serious. There's a lot of food out here tonight that you shouldn't be eating."

He walked over and looked down at her angelic face. "Meridan, seriously, I've behaved myself tonight and eaten only the nutritious food with the pork in it."

Meridan didn't find his comment funny. "Keaton, I'm trying to be serious here and you're playing," she scolded him.

He walked closer, pinning her in the corner with his body. "I'm just having a little fun with you, Doc. Do you really care that much about me?"

She could feel his hot, sweet breath on her face. It seemed that all the air had been sucked out of the room, making breathing difficult.

"Yes, I do," she said in a whisper.

Keaton ran his finger gently down the side of her face, until he tilted her chin with the tip of his finger. Inches away from her lips, it only took two words to turn her knees to jelly.

"Meridan.... Kiss."

They embraced each other and gave each other a deep, passionate kiss until they were interrupted by Devon bursting through the back door. Keaton pulled away from Meridan slowly and smiled.

"Whoa, Cuz! I see you and the Chief have started your own party up in here!"

Meridan walked over to him. "I'm gonna beat your little freshman ass, if you try to embarrass me again."

Laughing, he tried to hug her. "You know I was just kidding. You're my favorite cousin!"

Pushing him away, she said, "Don't try to kiss up to me now."

Laughing, he said, "Yo, Chief, you make sure you take care of Meridan. Aight?"

Giving each other a handshake, Keaton answered, "No doubt."

After grabbing another pack of paper plates, he headed toward the back door. "Oh, Meridan, Aunt Glo has got her drink on and she's over there shaking her booty to some Johnny Taylor."

Meridan put her hands over her head. "I was hoping she wouldn't show her tail tonight. Is Daddy upset?"

Laughing, he said, "You know Unc is used to her. As long as she's not causing a disruption, he'll leave her alone to enjoy herself. After this is over tonight, I'm not driving her home, so don't even think of looking my way."

"I'll make sure she gets home. You're a lot of help."

Putting a homemade roll in his mouth, he said, "Yo! Keyshaun and I are spending the night, so I hope you two don't keep us up all night."

"Devon!"

Keaton laughed. "We'll try not to."

"Keaton, don't play into his infantile little games."

Devon left out the back door, laughing. Meridan closed her eyes and shook her head. Once again, Devon had embarrassed her and Keaton hadn't help matters.

He noticed her embarrassment. "Meridan, he's eighteen. What do you expect?"

She looked at him, unable to respond. Her cousins were a handful.

He hugged her and jokingly said, "I won't make noise, if you won't."

"Keaton!"

He released her. "Sweetheart, I'm just teasing. Come on so I can make you happy and let you take my blood pressure."

Nodding, she said, "Okay."

They went into the den and sat down. They could hear the music booming from outside.

He smiled and said, "You look very beautiful tonight."

"Be quiet, Keaton. I'm trying to take your blood pressure."

He stared at her in silence. He couldn't help but admire her radiant skin and luscious lips. The neckline of her halter dress was cut low enough to be sexy, yet classy. Her braids caressed her full breasts and the dress hugged her sensational hips. Her thighs were firm and muscular; the obvious results of years of basketball.

"Well, will I live?"

She took the cuff off his arm. "You're normal, Keaton, but your pulse is up a little."

She handed him a couple of tablets and some water. After swallowing them, he said, "It's your fault that you make my heart beat so wildly."

"Stop it, Keaton," she said, blushing

Standing, he said, "Why don't you believe me?"

She licked her lips. "If I say, you might tell me off."

"Oh, we're back to the weight thing again, huh?"

Keaton walked over to her and wrapped his arms around her. He ran his hands seductively down her back and over her full hips, resting them there. It was Meridan's heart that was racing now.

"See? You fit just perfect. I've never had a woman in my arms that was a per-fect fit before, and I doubt there will be another. Take it for what it's worth, Meridan, because we're not having this weight discussion again. You got it?"

She looked up into his eyes that had taken on a strange appearance. Meridan finally realized he meant business. She swallowed hard and whispered, "Got it."

Twirling her by the arm, he said, "Good! Now let's go because I feel like dancing."

"Me, too, and Keaton?"

"Yes?"

"Thanks!"

Kissing her on the cheek, he said, "Thank me later."

The back door closed behind them and they rejoined the others at the massive tent under the stars.

CHAPTER 21

As soon as they pulled the tent back, Meridan saw a scene nobody should have to witness. Aunt Glo had her dress hiked up on her thighs and she was waving her bottle of unidentifiable alcohol in the air.

Meridan said, "Oh....my...God!"

Keaton laughed. "Your aunt has nice legs."

Meridan playfully elbowed him in the side. "You're no help."

Pointing toward her dad, Keaton said, "Your dad seems to be enjoying the show."

"He's seen these performances on more than one occasion. Aunt Glo needs to sit down. Look! Everyone's laughing at her."

They walked further into the tent, in the direction of her dad's table.

"Daddy, why don't you make Aunt Glo sit down?"

He patted the chair next to him. "Take a load off, baby girl. Your aunt's just having some harmless fun."

Keaton sat next to Meridan and watched along with the rest of the family. Devon and Keyshaun were getting a kick out of playing music that Aunt Glo loved so she'd keep the show going. Meridan's father finally gave them the eye to stop instigating.

He said, "I'll be right back. I'm going to try and talk your aunt into sitting down for a moment before she has a heart attack."

❖❖❖

William was successful in getting Aunt Glo to sit down. About that time, Gwendolyn and Meridan led their father over to the three-tier birthday cake. It was in his favorite colors...crimson and cream. As they made their way over to his table, all one hundred-plus voices sang "Happy Birthday." When the song ended, there was a thunderous applause. Meridan felt a tear slide down her cheek. Her dad was sixty years old and he was in better shape than most forty-year-olds.

A hush fell over the crowd as Meridan's dad tried to find words to express his gratitude to everyone. It was obvious he was overcome with emotion. He smiled at Leona, then looked at his two beautiful daughters and extended family.

He finally cleared his throat. "Tonight has been an extremely special night for me. A lot of people have worked very hard to make this night a success. To my dear friends, I want to thank each one of you for always being around to help me out; no matter how big or small the task. To my wonderful family members, words cannot express how much I love you. To my beautiful daughters, Gwendolyn and Meridan, you are my life. I only wish your mother could've lived to see the gracious young women you both have grown into. I want you to know that I love both of you and I'm so proud of you."

Meridan and Gwendolyn were both crying at this point. William was trying his best to hold back his tears. His voice cracked as he struggled to finish his speech.

"This night isn't about me turning sixty. This night is about love, friendship and happiness. Lastly, I'd like to thank Leona for always being there to support and comfort me. I love you, sweetheart, and if you'll have me, I'd like you to be my wife."

Everyone was shocked, even Ms. Leona, as they watched William pull a ring out of his pocket and place it on her finger.

She hugged and kissed him. "Yes, William! Yes, I'd be honored to be your wife. That is, if it's okay with Gwendolyn and Meridan."

The sisters walked over and hugged and kissed both Ms. Leona and their father with acceptance.

William turned and said, "With all of that said and done, I'd like to invite all of you back out here in the morning for Sunday service. The good reverend said he'd love to conduct the service under this beautiful tent. So, without further ado, I'll blow out these candles so we can continue on with the celebration."

He closed his eyes and made his wish. The room remained hushed. Finally he opened his eyes and, in two breaths, he had all the candles blown out. Everyone screamed, clapped and cheered as he hugged and kissed his daughters. Other family members made their way up to congratulate Mr. St. John and Ms. Leona. Meridan was still wiping her tears away with her hands when a masculine hand appeared in front of her holding a napkin. She looked up into Keaton's smiling face.

"I thought you might need this," he offered.

Dabbing her eyes with the napkin, she said, "Thank you, Keaton."

Gwendolyn noticed Keaton's beautiful exchange with Meridan as she wiped her own eyes.

Keaton said, "Your father's speech was beautiful. I'm so happy for him and Ms. Leona."

Folding her arms, she said, "So am I. He's been alone for too long. So, do you want some cake?"

He gently kissed her and whispered, "You're sweet enough for me. Now, come dance with me."

They walked past the line of people waiting on a piece of cake. Devon had put on one of the most romantic songs ever made, "Reasons" by Earth, Wind and Fire.

Meridan looked up at him and he gave her two thumbs up. She discreetly mouthed the words, "thank you." Keaton was secretly counting his blessings also. Holding Meridan was what he'd been waiting for all night. Jacob watched from the sidelines as Keaton and Meridan danced their way into each other's hearts. Keaton was in the way. He'd come all the way home to propose to her, and now he'd have to wait until Keaton wasn't around.

When the song ended, Keaton escorted Meridan back to their table. Aunt Glo was standing there, winking at Keaton.

"Meridan, you don't mind if I dance with your boyfriend, do you?"

She didn't know what to say. Keaton didn't give her any indication if he wanted her to save him. She looked at her aunt and said, "It's up to Keaton, Aunt Glo, but you'd better behave yourself."

She swayed her hips. "What you say, cutie? You sure are a tall glass of tea. Do you think you can handle this old woman?"

"No, Ma'am, but I'll dance with you."

Keaton winked at Meridan as he entered the dance floor with Aunt Glo.

Meridan gnawed on her nail and yelled, "Aunt Glo, I'm serious!"

"Hush, chile, and go dance with Jacob or something!"

Meridan couldn't stand around and witness what Aunt Glo might do to Keaton. She decided to go back over to her father's table and pray nothing embarrassing happened.

Keaton arrived back at the table, exhausted. Aunt Glo was still on the dance floor, with another victim in her clutches.

"Meridan, your aunt's wild, but I like her. She's one of a kind. Oh, she grabbed my butt."

Shocked, she yelled, "She did what? Daddy!"

CHAPTER 22

Hours later, when the crowd had reduced to only a few helping to clean up, Keaton and Meridan were still slow dancing. It was about one a.m. and William and Ms. Leona were holding hands, saying goodbye to guests. Meridan rested her head again on Keaton's chest and closed her eyes.

"Tired, huh?"

"Very," she admitted.

He stopped dancing and swung her up into his arms. Some of Meridan's family members laughed as they noticed the loving exchange between the two.

Startled and slightly embarrassed, she yelled, "Keaton! What are you doing?"

"I'm walking you home," he answered as he carried her across the yard.

Blushing, she said, "It looks more like you're carrying me home. I can't leave right now. I have to stay and help clean up."

Continuing to walk, he said, "Meridan, you've been going nonstop since early this morning. I'll stay and help. You need to go lie down because you're not going to be any help anyway. There's enough of us here to finish up. Okay?"

William smiled and shook his head as he noticed Keaton carrying his daughter across the yard.

"Maybe you're right. Do you think you could put me down so I can at least tell Daddy and Ms. Leona goodnight first?"

He kissed her hard on the lips before placing her feet on the ground. "I guess I could, but you'd better go straight to bed. Got it?"

Fingering her braids, she said, "Got it."

At the house, some of the aunts and cousins were busy putting food away for the night. The St. John house had always been Grand Central Station for the family and someone was always coming, going, or spending the night.

Meridan's Aunt Cora asked, "Are you headed to bed, baby?"

Aunt Cora was known as "Sugar" by those who knew her since she was the best baker in the county.

"Yes, Ma'am. I'll see you tomorrow. I can barely hold my eyes open. If you didn't already know, Devon and Keyshaun are staying here tonight."

"William told me. Don't let those boys disturb you and your guest," she warned.

"Sugar, I don't believe I'd hear a bomb drop after my head hits my pillow."

Aunt Cora hugged and kissed Meridan goodnight.

"You're so much like your mother, God rest her soul. Go on and get some rest now."

"Goodnight everyone."

In unison, everyone told her goodnight.

Meridan took a quick shower and crawled under her comforter. As she lotioned her legs, she heard a soft tap on her door. Opening the door she found Gwendolyn standing there.

"Hey, Sis."

"Hey, Gwendolyn. I hope you haven't come up here to start anything about Daddy and Ms. Leona. I don't have the strength."

Walking past her, she said, "I'm not here to argue, Meridan. I'm happy for Daddy. I see the way his face lights up when he's with her, or talks about her."

Closing the door, she asked, "Then what do you want? I'm tired."

Sitting on the bed, Gwendolyn fumbled with her words.

"Meridan, look, I'm sorry about earlier tonight. I was out of line about Daddy and Ms. Leona. I realize I haven't been the best big sister I could've been over the years. To tell you the truth, I've been a little jealous of you. You were always Momma and Daddy's favorite. Hearing Daddy's speech tonight touched me. I realized it's not your fault and it's stupid of me to be jealous. You're my sister and I do love you."

Meridan couldn't believe what she was hearing. She couldn't understand what Gwendolyn was talking about. If anything, she was the favorite.

"What do you mean, favorite? You're the one who got to do everything and go everywhere. Momma and Daddy had me on serious lockdown."

Gwendolyn played with designs on the comforter in silence.

"Meridan, you look just like Momma. Daddy loves you more."

Coming to sit next to her, she said, "No, he doesn't. All he talks about is you and how proud he is of you. You're the one with the successful temporary employment agency. You built that company from the ground up. You have a wonderful husband who loves you to no end and two great kids. What do I have?"

"You have more than you give yourself credit for. You've accomplished so much, to be so young. You have your own medical practice and you're the best female basketball player I've every seen in my life."

"Yeah, yeah, yeah, Gwendolyn, but I'll never be able to give a man what they want most…children. I don't even know why I'm wasting Keaton's time."

She touched her sister's cheek, turning her to face her.

"Meridan, you're not wasting Keaton's time. I can see he really cares about you."

"How do you know?"

"I have eyes. I watched his expressions when you were talking to Jacob, or any other man tonight. The love radiates from his eyes. Plus, we talked a little tonight and got to know each other somewhat. Look, all I'm saying is if he's the one and if you care about him, give him the benefit of the doubt. He's a nice guy and he's so hot."

Laughing, Meridan said, "Listen at you, talking about another man! You're married."

Standing, she said, "I know, but I'm not dead. Seriously though, are you in love with him?"

Blushing, Meridan softly said, "Yes."

"Does he know?"

Lowering her head, she said, "No, he doesn't know."

Hugging Meridan, she said, "You'll know when to tell him. You should go for it! But you need to be honest with him about your situation. I know you're still dealing with what happened to you, but if you love Keaton, he has a right to know. Okay?"

"We'll see. Thanks for talking to me tonight and explaining everything. I've missed talking to you, but we'll be talking more since we have a wedding to plan."

"Yes, we do. Thanks for coming by, Gwendolyn."

"You bet. Now, let me get out of your way so you can get some rest."

"I love you, Gwendolyn."

"I love you, too, little sister."

As Gwendolyn opened Meridan's bedroom door to leave, she found Keaton standing there ready to knock.

Smiling, he asked, "Am I interrupting anything?"

Hugging him, Gwendolyn said, "No, not at all. I was just leaving. Goodnight, Keaton."

"Goodnight, Gwendolyn," he said as he hugged her back.

Meridan and Keaton watched Gwendolyn disappear down the hallway. Keaton turned back to Meridan and asked, "Ready to be tucked in?"

A chill traveled over her body, giving her goose bumps. It wasn't what he said; it was how he said it. Trying to hide the effect he had on her, she leaned against the door frame for balance and said, "Just about. Did everything get cleaned up?"

"Everything's done and Devon and Keyshaun are camped out in the den playing video games. William has taken Ms. Leona home. Do you want me to wait up for him?"

"That's so sweet of you, but no. I'm not sure Daddy's coming back home tonight."

Smiling, he said, "He's a lucky man. Well, I'll let you get some rest. Goodnight, Meridan."

As Keaton turned to walk toward his room, Meridan folded her arms and asked, "You mean to tell me I don't get a goodnight kiss, Keaton Lapahie?"

He turned back to her, pulling her into his arms, kissing her hungrily. Meridan returned the favor by pulling him to her, allowing his hands to caress the silk fabric covering her body. She was so full of emotion that she began to sob.

"What's wrong, sweetheart?" he asked with concern.

Wiping her tears, she said, "I'm sorry, Keaton. It's just that I appreciate everything you've done for me and my family this weekend. You're very special to me, Keaton. I've developed some very strong feelings for you, and it's getting harder for me to keep them under control."

He lifted her chin. "Why try to control them?"

Meridan looked up at him, feeling slightly embarrassed. She knew if she allowed herself to lose control with Keaton, there's no telling where it might lead.

"Because you leaving, that's why," she solemnly said.

"Meridan, you're special to me also. My feelings for you should be obvious. It's been torture keeping my hands to myself when I'm around. As far as me leaving, well, the end of that story depends on you."

She looked up at him. "How?"

He nuzzled her neck and ear, and whispered, "Because I don't want it to end."

She kissed his cheek and said, "Keaton, you just don't know how hearing that makes me feel. You're a true gentleman and for those qualities and many others, I crave your hands, lips and anything else you want to give me. I want you, Keaton Lapahie, like I've never wanted anything in my life. I know you're leaving soon but, before you go, I want you to make love to me. You have no idea what I've gone through to get to this point."

Keaton swallowed hard. He'd finally heard the words he thought he'd never hear. He'd decided, after their second near sexual encounter, that he'd wait for Meridan to approach him, but he didn't expect her to do it here...Now.

"Meridan, I wouldn't be comfortable here—"

She hugged him and pressed her face against his warm neck, kissing it, causing him to let out a long sigh.

"I know, Keaton. I can't wait to get back to Philly so I can feel your skin against mine."

Keaton swallowed hard again and felt his body respond. He knew the inevitable would greet them the moment they stepped off the plane, but tonight a cold shower would be his sleeping pill. In Philly, he'd finally get to show Meridan St. John how much he loved her. Yes... Loved her.

CHAPTER 23

S unday after church service, a lot of the family members gathered for dinner at the St. John household. As many as thirty family members came to eat more delicious food. Jacob came back also, to bid Meridan goodbye. He wanted her to take a walk with him so they could talk. She agreed since they hadn't had an opportunity to talk alone. Keaton noticed them walking arm-in-arm out the back door and through the garden.

As they walked, Jacob asked, "Are you and that guy in there getting serious?"

"Where is that coming from?"

Jacob stopped walking. "I'm curious. You know I've always loved you, Meridan."

They stopped walking and sat down on a bench in her mother's prize flower garden.

Meridan held his hand. "Jacob, I'm not going to sit here and lie. When we were younger, I had feelings for you. I even fantasized about being married to you, but that was a long time ago. I went away to college and so did you. People change, you know that. You'll always be my first love, but that's all in the past now. I care about you as a friend, but that's as far as it goes. You understand me, don't you?"

Jacob reached up to touch her hair and asked, "Does he know what happened to you and that you can't have children?'"

Meridan's body tensed. She trembled slightly since she hadn't had the conversation about her condition with anyone in a while.

She bit down on her bottom lip. "No, he doesn't know and it's my decision to inform him, or anyone else, about my condition. I can't believe you'd even bring that up to me. I told you that as a friend, in confidence."

"Meridan, I'm sorry for upsetting you, but don't you think he has a right to know? Just in case—"

Angrily she asked, "Just in case what?"

"Just in case he's falling in love with you. I've noticed the way he looks at you. Honestly speaking, I think he's already in love with you."

Meridan stood. "That's none of your business. We should be getting back to the house. Have a safe trip back to Atlanta."

He put his arms around her waist and hugged her tightly. "I love you, Meridan. I always will. I wish nothing but the best for you. So where you feel I'm meddling, I'm just being concerned. Call me sometime, okay?"

She returned his hug. "I will, and thank you. I'll always love you, Jacob, but I can't offer you the kind of love you want from me."

He kissed her cheek lovingly before walking back toward the house. Jacob's comment had shaken her. She hadn't had any reason to be concerned about discussing her condition. That was, until Keaton Lapahie entered into her life. She didn't plan on falling in love with him. Now that she was, she feared once he found out she couldn't bear children, he wouldn't have anything else to do with her. In the meantime, she'd enjoy the pleasure he could give her before returning to Texas. Yes, when he left, her heart would be broken, but her secret would remain with her.

Back in Tennessee, Sam was released from jail with a revengeful heart. If only Meridan had played along and allowed her mind and body to explore new things. It would've been perfect if that bitch, Nichole, hadn't interfered. If Meridan and Nichole thought what happened in college was bad, they hadn't seen anything yet.

Sam frowned as the recollection of the night Meridan danced and giggled around the room replayed like it was yesterday. Everyone on campus was celebrating a victory that gave the school a high ranking in the NCAA tournament. Most of their circle of friends had gone on to party elsewhere. The liquor they'd been drinking was starting to do exactly what Sam meant for it to do… Relax Meridan. Sam had planned and waited for the moment for weeks, and it was then or never.

An hour later, Meridan finally passed out on the bed and Sam got the opportunity of a lifetime. She was still groggy when she woke up to an unusual sensation. The room was spinning and she felt restrained. Her legs were feeling very heavy, and when she rose up off the bed, she noticed she was nude from the waist down. As her blurred vision cleared, she noticed Sam's head buried deeply between her thighs. Meridan felt like she was dreaming as her body responded naturally to the act being performed on her. She tried to get up and push Sam away, but she was unsuccessful.

Tears welled up in her eyes as she heard Sam whisper, "Chill out, Meridan. I know you like it. Just lay back and enjoy it."

Weak from the alcohol, Meridan tried to scoot away but failed once again. She was drunk, but she was alert enough to know this was wrong, very wrong. Sam had always been only a friend to her. How could their friendship be violated like this?

Meridan could hear Sam humming with pleasure as the assault continued. Her fear was what would come next. Before passing out completely, she watched as Sam stood over her and said, "Damn, Meridan! You're so hot. Are you ready for me? I know you are, so just enjoy the ride."

Back to reality, Sam took the envelope containing all the possessions taken away years back when the doors sealed away the outside world.

Walking away, the guard said, "Don't let me see your ass back in here again, and try to stay out of trouble."

Sam wasn't hearing it. The first thing on the list was looking up Meridan St. John, so they could pick up where they'd left off. Now Nichole, she'd be handled with a special pair of gloves. While in prison, the internet had become a great tool for tracking down old classmates. With addresses in hand, Sam laughed out loud before climbing into a cab that was headed straight to the airport.

CHAPTER 24

Monday afternoon, William took Meridan and Keaton back to the airport. It was bittersweet for Meridan. It would probably be a while before she could come back for a visit.

William extended his hand. "Keaton, you're welcome here anytime. I hope you enjoyed yourself this weekend and that my sister didn't offend you."

Keaton shook his hand. "I appreciate your offer, sir. I did have a wonderful weekend. Don't worry about your sister; her flirting was harmless. She's really a nice woman."

"She has a few issues, but she is a very sweet woman. Well, you guys better get to your plane. I hate that I can't walk to the gate with you. Keaton, take care of my baby."

"I will, sir. Be safe driving home."

William St. John turned to his daughter. Her eyes were filled with tears. Keaton gave them some privacy by stepping away to tend to their luggage.

"I'm going to miss you, Daddy. You should come up for a visit soon."

Hugging her, he said, "I will, Meridan, and I'm going to miss you also." He kissed her forehead. "You like him, don't you?"

"Yes I do, Daddy. Very much."

"Well, for what it's worth, he likes you also."

She leaned back to look at William and asked, "He told you?"

Laughing, he said, "He didn't have to tell me. I like him. He's a good kid. If you want to pursue a relationship with him, you know you have to be honest with him. Have you told him?"

"Daddy, you're beginning to sound like Gwendolyn. She said the same thing. So did Jacob."

"Jacob loves you, Meridan; in spite of the fact that you're not in love with him. He's a good kid also. Just not the one for you, I take it. I've always loved him like a son. He cares about you."

"I know, Daddy, and I promise, I'll tell Keaton when the time is right?"

"Okay. I love you, Meridan. Call me when you get in, and have a safe flight."

"Tell Ms. Leona goodbye for me."

"I will."

Meridan joined Keaton and as they turned the corner in the terminal, they waved goodbye to Mr. St. John. On the plane they quickly found their seats and settled in for the long ride home. Meridan held onto Keaton's arm and rested her head against his chest.

Once the plan leveled off, she dozed off listening to the rhythm of his heart.

Keaton and Meridan stepped off the plane and were met by Philadelphia's chilly temperatures.

"Whew! You can tell we're not in Mississippi anymore, huh?"

"Most definitely. Come on, Meridan, so we can get our bags and get out of here."

Meridan held Keaton's hand and they weeded their way through the crowded airport, after gathering their luggage, Keaton told Meridan to wait at the terminal while he went to get the car. She insisted on going with him; even though it was cold outside. They argued for a few minutes, until an air-port shuttle came along to take them to the area they were parked.

He hugged her and said, "Meridan St. John, you're a stubborn woman."

"Thank you for noticing."

He smiled at her and shook his head. She was sensational and he wanted her more than ever. They took their seats on the shuttle bus.

"Keaton, seriously, I appreciate you trying to protect me from the cold, but the truth is… I didn't want to be separated from you."

"Really?"

"Really."

They finally got to the car after about a ten-minute ride. Keaton started the engine and immediately turned up the heat. Meridan shivered in her seat while Keaton loaded their luggage into the trunk. He jumped in the car and started shivering also. The car had been sitting for a few days, so it was going to take a few minutes for the heat to kick on.

"No wonder Winston got Arnelle that SUV. This piece of junk has seen its last days."

Trembling, she asked, "She doesn't drive it anymore?"

"Not really. Come here," he instructed her. Keaton wrapped his arms around Meridan and tried to warm her up faster with his body heat. "I'm surprised Winston hadn't gotten rid of this piece of junk. I think they keep it around just for me."

Meridan nuzzled his neck and softly said, "Keaton, I'm getting a little warm. Can we go now?"

He looked into her eyes and saw the warmth and sensuality she was feeling. He kissed her on the cheek and said, "You bet. We're out of here."

CHAPTER 25

The drive took about thirty-five minutes. It was around ten-thirty when they pulled into her driveway. Meridan activated the garage door and Keaton drove in out of the cold air. He turned the car off and Meridan lowered the door in silence.

He turned to her and asked, "You okay?"

"Yes, just tired. Come on in. I'll make us some coffee."

They exited the car and Keaton grabbed her luggage and followed her inside the house. Meridan turned on the lights and picked up the telephone to call her dad. While she waited for him to answer, Keaton started making coffee.

"Hello, Daddy?"

"Hello, Meridan. Are you home?"

"Yeah, I'm home."

"Good. It really was good seeing you, sweetheart."

Meridan smiled. "It was good seeing you also, Daddy. Well, I'm getting ready to let you go. It's been a long day."

"That it has. Give Keaton my regards," he insisted.

"I will, Daddy. I love you, and I'll talk to you tomorrow. Goodnight."

"Goodnight, Meridan. I love you, too."

She hung up and leaned against the door frame. Keaton poured her a cup of hot coffee and approached her slowly. "Sugar?"

Playfully, Meridan closed her eyes and puckered her lips. Keaton took her up on her offer. He set the cup down, pulled her into his arms, and kissed her deeply.

A few moments later, she composed herself and said, "Damn!"

"I meant sugar in your coffee, Meridan, but that was much better."

Picking the cup up, she said, "Ditto! Thanks for the coffee."

They stood there sipping their coffee in silence.

"This really hits the spot. I can't believe the differences in climate, but we are in the Northeast."

"Yes, we are."

They finished their coffee and Keaton said, "Well, it's late. I guess I'd better get going, so you can get to bed."

She cleared her throat. "I thought you were going to stay with me tonight?"

His eyes gleamed and danced over her lovingly. "You do know what'll happen if I stay, don't you?"

She wrapped her arms around his waist and cuddled against his chest. Reminding him, she said, "Keaton, I meant what I said in Mississippi."

He ran his hand down the curve of her back and over her hips. "I thought maybe you'd had a change of heart."

She looked up at him. "I'm not going to lie. I am a little nervous, but I've never wanted anything more."

He kissed her forehead. "Me too, babe. Me, too."

She took him by the hand and they headed toward the stairs. He stopped and picked up her luggage, following her upstairs.

Upstairs, Meridan turned on the lamp on her night stand. Keaton sat her luggage down and shoved his hands in his pockets.

She turned and said, "Make yourself at home, Keaton."

"Your home is beautiful," he said as he nervously admired her room.

"Thank you. Come on over and sit down," she said, pointing to a nearby chair.

Meridan went into the bathroom and made sure everything was in order. Nervousness had her stomach turning flips.

"I guess if I'm going to stay, I'll need to get my luggage out of the car."

She smiled.

He walked toward the hallway and said, "I'll be right back, Doc."

Keaton turned slowly and headed to the garage to retrieve his bags. He was unusually nervous and it surprised him. He knew he was in love with

Meridan and had been for quite some time. This was unchartered territory for him and he was still trying to adjust to these unfamiliar emotions. He was so happy that Meridan expressed her feelings for him while they were in Mississippi. Had she not, he didn't know how much longer he would be able to conceal his feelings for her.

By the time he returned to her room, she was already in the shower. He sat his luggage on the bed and opened it. He found himself breathing deeply to calm his nerves. He heard the water turn off and Meridan singing.

"Keaton!"

"Yes?"

"I'll be out in a minute."

"Well, I hope you saved some hot water for me."

Giggling, she said, "I did, so don't worry."

He sat down in the chair and looked around the room. It was elegant and warm. The mauve and cream colors she decorated the room with matched her warm personality. She had a treadmill in the corner and her medical certificates in frames hanging next to the bed.

The door swung open and Meridan appeared in a short, emerald green nightgown. Keaton tried to swallow the lump in his throat, but it was difficult.

"Nice. Very nice," he softly said as he stood slowly.

"I was hoping you'd like it. I got it especially for you." She walked over to him and said, "The bathroom's all yours. Everything you should need is in the linen closet. If not, just holler."

"Meridan, are you sure about this?"

She interlocked her fingers with his. "I've never been clearer about anything in my life. Now, stop it before you make me even more nervous. Okay?"

Smiling, he said, "I'm sorry. I'll be out in a minute."

Keaton entered the bathroom and leaned against the door. Meridan had confirmed everything and there was no turning back now. He'd make love to her and hope he'd be able to return back to his life in Texas in a couple of weeks. The way his heart was beating against his chest, he realized that was unlikely.

After showering, he opened the door to the bedroom. Meridan was sitting on the bed, painting her toenails. She looked up and smiled at him. He stood there with his skin still glistening with water. He walked over with the towel still wrapped around his waist.

Looking down at her, he said, "Let me do that."

"What?"

He sat down on the bed next to her and took the polish out of her hand. "I said, let me do that."

"Are you sure?"

Grabbing her foot, he sat down on the bed and proceeded to paint her toenails.

This man is killing me!

Meridan was being seduced, just by the way he was blowing on her toes. He painted each toe methodically, making sure he didn't make any mistakes.

"You're good at this. You must have done this before?"

He looked up at her mischievously. "Not as much as you might think. MaLeah keeps me busy painting her little fingers and toes."

"I'm talking about big girls, Keaton."

"You're the first big girl I've ever painted. Scout's honor."

Meridan couldn't help but admire his handsome features. The silky hair on his chest had now dried. His skin was a beautiful bronze and his dark eyes were piercing. He wore his hair closely cropped and had a neatly trimmed goatee surrounded by dimples that surfaced with every smile.

"There! You're all done. You have pretty feet."

"Keaton, are you a foot man?"

Keaton put the top on the nail polish and said, "No, I'm just a man. I like everything about you, Meridan St. John, including your feet."

They stared at each other for a moment. He looked down on the bed and noticed the bottle of lotion. She followed his eyes, then looked back up at him.

"May I?"

Handing the bottle to him, she said, "Help yourself."

In her heart, she knew the moment his hands touched her she'd fall apart. Keaton poured some lotion in his hands.

"Ready?"

She swallowed and said, "As ready as I'm going to be."

He rubbed his hands together to make sure they were warm. He started at her feet and worked his way up to her calves, massaging gently. He noticed that Meridan had started to squirm.

"Are you okay?"

Sucking in a breath, she said, "No! You're killing me and you know it."

Laughing, he stopped massaging her legs and leaned over her.

"Meridan… Kiss."

His presence overpowered her, taking her breath. She touched his face lovingly and kissed him tenderly.

"You smell great."

"So do you," she admitted.

He kissed her neck. "Meridan, darling, I… I—"

Meridan ran her hands over his chest and around his neck, pulling him down to her. "Keaton, I want you so much."

He slid his hands up her inner thigh. "Damn, Meridan!" he moaned.

She reached down and removed his towel. She wanted to see him. He watched her reaction of surprise when her eyes scanned him.

"Are you okay, Meridan?"

She sat there, blinking her eyes in amazement. He was unbelievable.

"Are you ready to run out of the room yet?"

"Not on your life," she answered as she swallowed hard.

Keaton walked over to his bag and pulled out a foil packet. He rejoined her on the bed and saw her anxiety. She watched him open the packet and apply the condom.

He kissed her. "Last chance to back out."

"Not on your life," she assured him.

Keaton slid the lingerie over her head and what he saw was stunning. She immediately tried to cover herself, but he stopped her.

"Why are you doing that? You're gorgeous," he stressed.

"Because I'm—"

Pulling her toward him, he said, "I don't want to hear it. Now kiss me."

She reluctantly kissed him and moisture pooled between her thighs.

Releasing her, his eyes danced lovingly over every inch of her body. Chills ran down her spine as he ran his hand over sections of her body, as if he was studying it. He towered over her and kissed her greedily. Meridan felt the evidence of his desire and felt her body become inflamed. He gently ran his tongue over her cocoa skin with precision. She moaned as he kissed even lower to her navel.

"Keaton?"

She was worried he would question the scar on her lower abdomen.

He made eye contact with her and whispered, "Hold on, baby."

He pushed his rigid body into hers and felt unexpected resistance. Meridan held onto him tightly and gritted her teeth.

Meridan moaned, "Damn!"

He pushed a little harder, then realized what was happening. He looked deep into her eyes and stopped.

"Meridan, baby, why didn't you—"

Grabbing his hips, she pleaded, "Keaton, please don't stop."

Keaton tried his best not to hurt her. He couldn't believe it. *She was a virgin.* But why, after all this time, did she choose him? With all these thoughts running through his head, it was becoming even more difficult for him to hold back. Nothing would make him happier than taking her on the ride of her life, but he couldn't. Not yet. He had to settle for a slow, deep rhythm, which was still causing him to slowly lose control. She was glowing and her eyes were full of tears.

In a whisper, he asked, "Are you okay?"

Unable to speak, she nodded her head to acknowledge that she was fine.

She grabbed his hips tighter and finally began moving against him. She had no idea he would feel this heavenly. Yes, she lied. It did hurt at first, but what he was doing now was giving her sensational pleasure. It was obvious he was holding back from her, and she tried her best to get him to relax and let go.

Moments later, Meridan felt her body tremble and an overwhelming sensation rocked her body.

It was over and silence filled the room. The Meridan she had been all her life was no more. She had finally passed a milestone she never expected to. Sam had taken her dignity away and she was determined to get it back with Keaton.

Keaton rose up on his elbows and studied her expression. The tears that filled her eyes earlier had spilled out and were running down the side of her face. She met his gaze, which was filled with concern.

"Sweetheart, why didn't—"

"Just hold me, Keaton. Please, I don't want to talk about it right now."

He kissed her and pulled her into his arms. She clung to his warm body as he pulled the linens over them. Meridan had never felt the love and peace she felt at that moment and it made her a little sad. Sad, because somewhere on the road to making Keaton her first sexual experience, she realized it could never be anything more than just that.

CHAPTER 26

A few hours later, Meridan awoke to find Keaton sound asleep. She slowly eased out of his embrace. He was sleeping so peacefully. She kissed him gently and eased out of the bed and into the shower. She closed the door and turned on the hot water, then climbed in. It was here, the reality of what she had experienced overtook her. She couldn't remember exactly when she had fallen in love with Keaton, but she knew it was long before she had taken him home to meet her family. Tonight basically put everything into perspective for her. She stood in the shower in a daze, slowly rubbing the suds on her skin. The glass door suddenly opened and Keaton appeared in the door.

"Keaton!" She turned her back to him as he climbed in. "Keaton! What are you doing?"

He moved over and embraced her. He kissed her moist shoulder gently and asked, "Why do you keep hiding your body from me? You don't have much that I haven't seen, touched, or tasted tonight."

She shook her head. "It's just this scar."

He turned her around to face him. He tilted her chin so he could make eye contact with her.

"I love every inch of your body, Meridan, and that scar won't make a difference."

He reached down to caress the scar, causing her to flinch. He looked down into her eyes and saw sadness. With concern, he asked, "How did you get it?"

She looked away. "I'm not ready to talk about that; especially not tonight."

He saw fear and more sadness in her eyes. He removed his hand. "It must've been terrible."

"It was, and that's all I'm going to say about it tonight," she said with persistence.

"That scar's not important, Meridan." He pointed to her heart and said, "What's important is what you have in there. This is the last time I ever want you to try and hide your body from me. From where I'm standing, you're flawless. You're built like an athlete and I've had some very erotic dreams about your body. Now, do I make myself clear, Miss St. John?"

"I hear you, Keaton, but something tells me you like your women a lot slimmer."

"What I like is everything I see in you."

Meridan couldn't believe what she was hearing. An eligible, handsome bachelor like Keaton Lapahie wanted to be with a country tomboy like her. She still didn't see herself as desirable and the ugly scar didn't help matters. Being friends with Jacob all her life was safe. She never had to care about what another man thought about her. She had never been in a serious relationship with anyone since Jacob. In college, most men saw her as a conquest they would never get the opportunity to conquer. Since she had met Keaton, she had started wondering why he wanted to date her.

"What exactly do you see in me, Keaton?"

Kissing her tenderly, he said, "I see an attractive woman with a beautiful soul who is full of love and desire. I see a woman who is sexy, independent, as well as loving and caring. I see a woman who has done something I vowed would never happen."

Shyly, she asked, "And what is that?"

He came closer and whispered, "Cause me to fall in love."

"Really?"

"Really. Now, why didn't you tell me you'd never done this before?"

"Would you have gone through with it?"

"Probably not," he answered, fingering her braids.

Looking away, she said, "Now you know why I didn't tell you."

He scanned her lovely face. "I have to admit, I'm a little shocked."

She frowned. "Why?"

He let the water run over his face, then said, "It's just that I don't meet many virgins these days."

She looked away in embarrassment. "It never was that important to me."

Keaton picked up the sponge and put some soap on it. "Weren't you a little curious?"

She looked up at him. "A little bit, but not to the point of actually doing it. I guess you've had your share, huh?"

Keaton smiled as he made a soapy trail on her shoulders. He softly responded, "I've spent time with a few ladies."

"I must've seemed so clumsy to you?"

He continued to sud up her body. Pulling her against his body, he said, "No. You were fine. What I want to know is if you really meant what you said to me, or was it just the heat of the moment?"

Embarrassed, she lowered her chin and bit down on her lower lip. "I meant it. I've been in love with you for some time now, Keaton. I never planned on telling you because I knew you were only in Philly for a short time."

"Well, it's too late now. It's been confirmed by both of us. Now, what do we do about it?"

"I don't know."

He continued to make slow, circular movements with the sponge that caused her skin to tingle. She poured some gel into her hands and rubbed it onto his chest in silence. He stopped bathing her and hugged her. The hot water pounded their bodies as he lowered his head, claiming her lips. The bathroom was full of steam and her knees became weak as his tongue darted inside her mouth, then he went even lower. Meridan did her best to remain standing as Keaton tasted the very essence of her. There was a moment she thought about Sam, but the love she had for Keaton erased that awful memory as quickly as it came. Her body began to spasm as Keaton's tongue took her to the ultimate level of pleasure. She nearly collapsed in the shower when the sensations overtook her. Keaton was able to maneuver her, just where he needed to get the best reaction. He stood and they both moaned as their hands and lips caressed each other's body. Keaton's body was now in full effect.

"Meridan?"

She was delirious and hot.

"Yes?"

"Out… Now!"

Keaton turned off the water and grabbed a towel. He dried their bodies off the best he could, before they fell back onto the tangled sheets on the bed. He hurriedly applied another condom before entering her body once more. She screamed and moaned as he tried to get his fill of her.

"Keaton. What are you doing to me?"

When he saw she was near completion, he moved vigorously inside her moist body. This time, he wouldn't hold back. This time, he had to show her he loved her just as much as she loved him.

"Meridan?"

Breathlessly, she answered, "Yes?"

"Just how limber are you?"

"Oh… My… God!"

He covered her breasts with his hands. The rest was a blur after he placed her legs over his shoulders.

Moments later, he switched positions so they were lying on their sides, facing each other. He ran his hand through her braids and down her back. She snuggled closer to him, kissing his chest. His breathing was rapid and his heart was beating wildly. Keaton held her close to him and whispered, "I love you, Meridan."

Closing her eyes, she answered, "I love you, too, Keaton."

Moments later, they both slipped into a deep, satisfied slumber.

CHAPTER 27

The next morning, Keaton and Meridan made breakfast together. Dressed in his T-shirt, she put the bacon on a paper towel to drain. She blushed as she reminisced about the things they had done the night before. She looked over at Keaton, who was dressed in shorts and a tank top. He was gorgeous. He noticed her staring.

"What you thinking about, Meridan?"

Blushing, she answered, "Nothing."

"I don't believe you. The look on your face tells me you're thinking about something very specific."

Laughing, she said, "Okay, okay! I'm busted."

He stalked over to her and put a buttery croissant up to her lips. She took a bite. "Hmm, yummy!"

"The croissant, or what you were thinking about?"

"Both," she admitted.

"So you're not going to tell me?"

She smiled. "You have to know everything, don't you?"

"Only when it involves us and some heavy breathing."

Meridan laughed out loud and threw a dishtowel at him. He grabbed it and chased her around the kitchen table. He wanted her to think he was going to pop her with the towel.

"Don't you dare, Keaton Lapahie!"

"You're not the boss of me, Meridan St. John!"

He grabbed the back of the T-shirt just as she tried to run out of the kitchen.

Laughing and screaming, she said, "Okay, I give up!"

He held her close, cupping her hips.

"I wouldn't dare pop you back there, Meridan. My baby definitely has junk in her trunk, and I love the way it feels in my hands."

Blushing, she said, "Keaton, you know I'm self-conscious about my hips."

"I don't know why. Any man who's ever been around you, myself included, goes into a trance when you enter the room. I wanted to bust Malik in the mouth at basketball practice because he was looking at you just a little too hard."

"What did he say?"

"Never mind. Now let's eat. Oh, don't forget we have practice this evening, so you need to save your strength."

"Okay. You can turn my hips loose now."

"Do I have to?"

Kissing him, she said, "You're so bad."

The telephone rang so he reluctantly released his grip on her. Meridan smiled as she picked up the telephone. "Hello?"

Silence met her on the other end of the line. She frowned and said hello again. Still, there was silence on the line. Keaton looked over at her curiously as he poured another cup of coffee.

"Hello? Is anybody there?" she asked again.

A baritone voice asked, "Have you missed me?"

She immediately dropped the telephone in shock. It had been years since she had heard that voice, and it was at that moment that reality set in. Sam was out of jail.

Keaton ran over and grabbed the telephone. "What is it?"

Meridan stood there, trembling in fear.

Keaton put the phone up to his ear and frantically asked, "Hello?"

All he got was a dial tone.

Meridan's tears started flowing from her eyes and she ran from the room. Keaton quickly ran after her and found her in the bathroom throwing up her breakfast.

Minutes later, Meridan assured Keaton she was much better and found the strength to get dressed for work. Keaton returned to the kitchen to clean up.

When she came back downstairs he was putting the last cup in the cabinet.

Turning to her, he said, "You look nice, Doc. Are you sure you're feeling better?"

"Not really." She sighed as she sat down to put on her athletic shoes.

"Maybe you should stay home," he suggested as he hung the dishtowel on the rack.

Meridan put her hands over her eyes and said, "I can't miss work today. I'll be okay in a little while."

Keaton sat down in a chair across from her and pulled her foot into his lap so he could lace her shoes for her. As he laced them, he asked, "Who was that on the telephone?"

Without making eye contact, she answered, "Someone from my past."

He looked at her, noticed the tears, and frowned. "Do you mind telling me who it was and what was said?"

She wiped the trail of tears off her cheek and shook her head. "It was awful, Keaton. I've never had anyone make me feel the way—"

She stopped mid-sentence and stood.

He took her hands into his and made her look at him. "What happened to you? Does it have anything to do with that scar?" She nodded. "Is the person who hurt you the one who called?" Meridan nodded again in silence. "Tell me who it is and I'll make sure they never hurt you again. It's obvious this thing is messing with you physically and emotionally. Let me help you, Meridan," he pleaded.

Meridan kissed him on the cheek. "Look, Keaton, I know you want to help me and I appreciate your concern. It was something that happened a long time ago, and I just want to forget about it. There's no need for you to get involved. I can handle it."

He caressed her hand, then said, "It didn't seem like you were handling it a few minutes ago. You were scared."

"I know," she said solemnly. "I'm okay now and I just want to forget about it."

He ran his hand over his head in frustration. "Whoever this is hasn't forgotten about it. Maybe you should call the police," he urged her.

"I don't know, Keaton," she said reluctantly.

"That was true fear on your face, Meridan. I'll go with you if you want me to."

She forced a smile. "There's nothing they can do. It was only a telephone call."

"You're not hiding anything else from me, are you?" he asked with a raised brow.

She kissed him on the cheek again. "No. Now it's time for me to get to work. I'll be okay, so don't worry."

He looked at his watch. "Are you sure you're going to be okay? I'm going to be worrying about you all day. I don't like seeing you like this."

"Don't do this to yourself, Keaton. If it'll make you feel better, I'll call you every hour on the hour."

"If you say so. Hold on a sec while I run upstairs and get my things."

He hurried past her, kissing her on the lips. In her bedroom, he jumped in his sweats and grabbed his bag. They had taken a shower together earlier in the morning so that was taken care of. He looked around the room and smiled before meeting back up with her in the kitchen.

"Ready, babe?"

Meridan slowly walked over to him and put her arms around his neck. He hugged her waist and looked into her eyes. It was at that moment that she kissed him deeply. She wanted him to know the depth of her affection. No words were spoken, because everything that needed to be said was spoken with their eyes. They finally released each other, picked up their bags and headed out the door. He put Meridan's gym bag in her trunk, then came around to her window.

"I guess I'll see you this evening?"

"Save your strength, Keaton, because I plan on working you very hard," she said suggestively.

With a devilish grin, he asked, "Are you talking about on the basketball court or in the bedroom?"

Raising the garage door, she blushed. "At the gym, silly. Goodbye and drive carefully."

"Meridan… Kiss."

He stuck his head in her window and gave her one last kiss. They both backed out of the garage and headed in two different directions. Inside the house, Meridan's telephone rang. When the answering machine picked up, a familiar voice sounded.

"Hey, Meridan, it's Jacob. I was just making sure you made it back safely. Give me a call when you get a chance. I wanted to see if you could fly down next weekend and go to this dinner with me. We don't get to hang out anymore and I thought next weekend would be a good time for us to get together. It was good seeing you this past weekend. I've really missed you and I want us to have a chance to talk some more. You have all my numbers. I'll wait to hear back from you. I love you. Later."

CHAPTER 28

Keaton made it back to his sister's house in little to no time. He walked through the door and was met by Winston and MaLeah in the hallway.

Winston shoved his hand into his pockets and said, "Weeeell! Look who decided to finally come home!"

MaLeah, dressed in her lavender Bratz outfit, saw her uncle and danced and yelled, "Uncie Key!"

Keaton dropped his bag and picked her up into his arms. He kissed her and asked, "Have you been a good girl, Shorty?"

Winston interrupted by asking, "My question is, was Uncle Keaton a good boy while he was away?"

Frowning, Keaton said, "Don't start, Winston. Where's Arnelle?"

"She just left. So, did you have a good time with the good doctor in Mississippi?"

Keaton sat MaLeah down. "Yeah, I had a good time. She has a very nice family."

Winston stared at Keaton, but he wouldn't make eye contact with him. Instead, he continued to play with MaLeah's ponytails.

Leaning against the wall, Winston asked, "So, when did you guys get back?"

Before he realized what Winston was doing, he answered, "Last night."

As soon as he said it, it dawned on him that Winston had tricked him. The last thing he wanted to do was open the door for Winston Carter III, attorney-at-law, to put him on the witness stand.

He folded his arms. "Last night, huh?"

Finally making eye contact, Keaton frowned. "Yeah, last night."

Keaton took MaLeah by the hand and led her into the family room. He sat down and clicked on the TV. MaLeah crawled up into his lap and started watching TV with him. Winston followed them into the room and sat down in the chair. He continued to study Keaton's mood as he watched his daughter feed him her animal crackers.

Without looking away from the TV, Keaton asked, "Are you going into the office today?"

Still studying him, Winston answered, "Nah, I'm going to work from home since I don't have any court cases today."

Looking around, Keaton asked, "Where's Fredrick?"

"He's upstairs asleep," Winston answered, still staring at him. Without warning, he leaned forward and whispered, "You hit it, didn't you, Keaton?"

Keaton laughed out loud and nervously replied, "What did you just ask me?"

MaLeah turned to her daddy. "Who did Uncie Key hit, Daddy?"

Waving her off, he said, "MaLeah, go play. I'm talking to your uncle."

She turned to Keaton and asked, "Did you hit somebody, Uncie Key?"

He laughed, kissed her, and said, "No, Shorty, I didn't hit anyone. Your daddy's being silly." He looked over at Winston. "I can't believe you sometimes, Winston."

Ignoring Keaton's obvious disgust, he smiled and asked, "Well, did you?"

Perturbed with Winston's continued prying, Keaton answered, "That's none of your business, Bro. You take things too far sometimes."

Winston leaned back in his chair and crossed his legs. With a sarcastic grin he said, "Sorry, Bro, but when did you start getting so sensitive about me asking you about your sexual conquests? It's never been a problem with any of the others," Winston reminded him.

Keaton stood up. "It doesn't matter. I'm tired and I'm not up for your games today."

Winston smiled, knowing he had struck a nerve with his dear brother-in-law. "Look, Keaton, I'm not trying to get under your skin. I'm not asking you anything I don't normally ask you after your dates."

Keaton walked toward the hallway. "Whatever, Winston. Look, I'll holler at you later. I'm going upstairs to unpack. Are we still practicing this evening?"

Winston took a sip of his coffee and said, "Five o'clock straight up."

"Okay. I'll see you in a little bit. I'm going to lie down for a minute."

MaLeah stood up, looking from her daddy over to her uncle. She didn't know which one she wanted to hang with. She hadn't seen Keaton in a few days and sort of wanted to hang with him. But it was her daddy who had just bought her the new Barbie Doll townhouse with accessories and was going to be home all day.

Keaton looked down at her. "You wanna take a nap with me, Shorty?"

"No, Uncie Key! I wanna play with Daddy and my new dollhouse."

"Go on and play with your little doll, you little traitor. Give me a hug, and you better not come up to my room waking me up either."

"K!"

Keaton left the room and Winston sat back, analyzing their brief conversation. He knew the answer to his question the moment Keaton snapped at him. In his heart, he knew he had won the bet and with time, he'd verify it just to be sure. He and Arnelle would be enjoying their new summer home in Florida sooner than expected.

Upstairs, Keaton sat on the bed in disbelief. He couldn't believe what had happened to him since arriving in Philly. His vow of eternal bachelorhood was beginning to crumble right before his eyes. He sighed and picked up his cell phone and dialed his best friend, Gerald. As he waited for him to answer, he smiled and reminisced about the previous night's activities.

"Well, it's about damn time you called. I was beginning to think you had moved to Philly permanently!" Gerald yelled at him.

"Damn! I hate that caller ID. You can't even surprise people anymore and, to answer your other question, no, I haven't moved here permanently. Forget about that right now. I need to talk to you about something."

"What's up, Dogg?"

Keaton stood and paced the floor. He took a breath and said, "You're not going to believe this but I've fallen in love with someone up here."

There was brief silence on the telephone before Gerald asked, "Excuse me?"

"I know! I can't believe it either. Her name is Meridan and she's...She's perfect."

"Get the hell out of here! Are you for real, man?"

Keaton sat down in the chair and put his head in his hand.

"Yeah, and she's everything I could ever want in a woman. Guess what?"

"What?"

"She was a former All-American point guard in college and played in the WNBA briefly. She turned down an extended contract, so she could go to medical school. You have to see her, Gerald. She's stunning."

Gerald was silent again on the other end of the telephone. He couldn't believe his ears. His best friend and former teammate sounded like he was on his way to the altar. He cleared his throat and asked, "Have you already told her how you feel about her?"

"Yeah, and I mean it. I'm serious, Gerald. She's perfect. You should see how she handles the rock on the court. Talk about poetry in motion."

"You're sprung, aren't you?"

"Like a mutha! The thing is… I don't mind because I'm not letting her get away."

Laughing, Gerald said, "Damn! I never thought I'd hear you say anything like this."

Keaton said, "Laugh all you want to. This is the real thing. Unfortunately, this is going to cause me to lose a bet with my brother-in-law, but she's worth every penny."

"In that case, I can't wait to meet her."

Keaton grinned. "I can't wait to introduce you to her. You'll see."

"I'm happy for you, Keaton. When are you coming home?"

"Soon, but I have to get my relationship set with Meridan first. Have you been by my restaurant lately?"

"I was there last night. They're doing a good job running the place without you. All your employees need raises," he joked.

Laughing, Keaton said, "Whatever! I'll holler at you later. Thanks for keeping an eye out on my place."

"No problem. Take care of yourself and hurry back. I haven't played a decent game of ball since you left. Oh! Someone asked about you."

Knowing exactly who he was talking about, he warned, "I don't want to hear it. She's history and that's the way I'm going to keep it."

CHAPTER 29

It was only lunchtime and Meridan had seen three children with strep throat and two more with ear infections. After checking with her receptionist, she found out she had several more children to examine after lunch. She entered her office and took off her stethoscope. She smiled and thought she would call Nichole. She didn't call Keaton every hour like she promised, but she did call to assure him she was fine.

As she dialed Nichole, she thumbed through a magazine and came across some wedding gowns. She sighed, knowing she probably would never get to wear one.

"Contract Department, this is Nichole."

"Hey, girl!"

"Heeeeey!! When did you get back?"

Closing the magazine, she answered, "Last night."

Nichole twirled around in her chair. "So, how did your dad like Mr. Tall, Dark and So Fine?"

Laughing, Meridan said, "Can you believe he already knew him? So did the rest of the males in my family. Nikki, Keaton used to play pro ball with the San Antonio Spurs."

"How did you miss that one, Dee?"

"He said he was going to tell me, but he wanted to surprise me since I shocked him about UT."

"That's great. So, how are you two getting along? You guys have been hanging pretty tight lately. I feel sort of left out."

Solemnly, Meridan said, "Now you know you're my girl. Please don't say that."

Nichole smiled. "I really am happy for you, Dee."

"Thanks, Nikki."

Laughing mischievously, Nichole asked, "So have you guys done the nasty yet?"

"Nikki!"

"Don't Nikki me. Well, have you? You sound a little different, Dee. All it'll take is one look in your eyes and I'll know for sure."

"Girl, you're stupid, but check this out. Guess who called me?"

Nichole curiously asked, "Who?"

"Sam," Meridan said with her voice cracking.

Nichole stood. "Are you serious? That fool has a lot of nerve, calling you. Dee, you didn't get spooked, did you?"

"I've been spooked ever since that mess happened, Nikki. Sam told us payback was going to be hell and I believe it."

Nichole sat back down and said, "I know, but I showed that idiot that I don't play. Sam had better not start any shit!"

"Don't forget you're on the hit list, too."

They were both quiet for a minute, then Meridan admitted, "Keaton was at my house when Sam called. I freaked out so bad, Nikki. He knows something's wrong. You know I've never been a good liar."

"Wait, he was at your house? Hold up! There's something you're not telling me, Dee!"

Meridan sighed. "Can't we talk seriously for one second?"

"We are talking seriously, but you're leaving out all the good parts," Nichole came back at Meridan. "Look, Dee, I'm not afraid of Sam, and you shouldn't be either. Mind games; that's all it is. You should go ahead and tell Keaton what happened, so if that idiot does come at you, he can be prepared to handle it."

A soft voice followed. "I love him, Nikki. I don't want to run him away."

"What did he say?"

Meridan rubbed her forehead. "He saw the scar and asked how it happened. I told him I didn't want to talk about it."

Trying to comfort her, Nikki said, "I'm sure he loves you, too."

"He said he did," Meridan added.

Smiling, Nichole asked, "Then I assume there are no more cobwebs?"

"No more cobwebs, Nikki."

In a serious tone, Nichole firmly said, "Good. Tell him the truth as soon as possible. Don't mess this up with Keaton. I like him, Dee. That should tell you something."

Meridan laughed. "It tells me you are the best friend a woman could have. I love you, Nikki."

"I love you, too," she responded. "Now get back to work and forget about Sam."

"I'll try. I'll call you later."

"Bye."

They hung up and went back to their daily work.

Across town, Sam tucked the .9mm inside the waistband of the prison-issued jeans before stepping out of the dark alley. It was so easy to purchase a gun on the street. Jail had hardened any ounce of goodness left. Revenge was the only thing that consumed the attacker's heart and it would be revenge that would free this soul.

Before eating lunch, Meridan decided to check her answering machine at home.

She listened as she heard Jacob's message inviting her to Atlanta. She looked at her calendar and realized that was the same day of the basketball tournament. She might be able to swing it, since the games started on Saturday morning. She could catch an evening flight out, but it was going to be tight. Meridan hung up and her pager vibrated. She looked at it and saw a text message appear.

Just sitting here thinking about the way suds look on your brown skin. I can't wait to see you. Love, Keaton

She smiled, then joined her staff in the lounge for soup and sandwiches and decided to wait and return Jacob's call when she got home. It was going to be a long day.

The day ended and Meridan had been thrown up on once and coughed on countless times by her little patients, but she loved her job. In her office, she changed into her practice clothes. She looked at the clock and realized she had only twenty minutes to get to the gym.

CHAPTER 30

Keaton and the guys were shooting around on the court when she got there. Winston made it a point to watch Keaton's expression when Meridan walked in. As expected, his face lit up with the biggest smile he'd ever seen. She hurried in and put her bag down.

"Sorry I'm late. Traffic."

Keaton walked over and kissed her hard on the lips. Comforting her, he said, "You're not that late."

She took off her sweat pants and revealed a sporty outfit.

He yelled, "Dayum!"

Meridan smiled and asked, "Does it look okay?"

He bounced the ball and said, "You're killing me, Meridan."

"I don't mean to," she said innocently.

"I know, but if Malik says one thing out of line today, I *will* bust him in his damn mouth," Keaton promised.

Lacing up her tennis shoes, she said, "Don't worry. I only have eyes for you. Now come on, so I can give you a workout."

"I love it when you talk dirty to me," he answered with a mischievous grin.

Only Craig and Winston paid attention to their little exchange.

Craig walked over and asked, "Did I just see Keaton kiss Meridan?"

Winston responded, "You sure did. I think they're an item but they're trying to keep it on the down low."

"Well, she's a fine woman and she can play ball better than some men I know. If Keaton doesn't want her, Malik would be happy to step up. He won't shut up about her."

"Is that so?"

Craig laughed. "Don't get any mess started between them, Skeeter. Malik mentioned that Keaton told him she was spoken for a few weeks ago when he inquired about her."

"I'll be cool. Let's get to work."

Winston called the group together. As he talked to them, Meridan went through a series of stretches. Keaton saw Malik watching her again. He frowned, then threw the basketball at him to make him stop looking at her. Malik looked at him in confusion. When Winston finished going over the fundamentals, they broke up and started practicing.

Meridan still held the spot of point guard and she pushed them up and down the court with some precise passes. Byron showed up for practice. He was happy to get out of the house for a while after becoming a new dad. Since Meridan had been filling in so well for him, the guys voted for her to start at point guard. Byron was amazed at Meridan's skills and felt the guys had made the right decision.

Practice lasted until around seven-thirty and before everyone left, Winston reminded the group about the time of their first game.

Malik yelled, "Nine o'clock!"

Winston said, "Yes, and make sure you go to bed early, Malik, so you'll be well-rested."

Meridan asked Winston, "If we go all the way, what time should the last game end?"

"Probably around three o'clock."

Putting on her sweats, she replied, "Thank you."

Winston clapped his hands together and said, "I know you're all hungry, so dinner's on me at Mae Pearls; if you guys are up for it."

Meridan said, "I'll take a rain check, Winston, but you guys go right ahead. It's been a long day and I'm tired."

Malik chimed in, "Ah, come on, Meridan. You can hang out with us a little while longer."

Keaton looked at Malik and shook his head. The man wasn't going to stop.

"No, really guys, thanks, but I need to get home." She turned and asked, "Winston, is our last practice Thursday?"

"Yes, five o'clock."

Picking up her bag, she said, "Thanks. I'll see you guys Thursday. Goodnight."

In unison, they said, "Goodnight, Meridan."

Keaton grabbed his bag and yelled, "Wait! I'll walk out with you."

Winston asked, "Keaton, you coming to dinner?"

"Yeah, go ahead. I'll meet you guys there."

Keaton took Meridan's gym bag from her hand and escorted her out the door. Once outside he got in the car with her as she started the engine. "You okay?"

"I'm fine. Just a little tired."

He covered her hand with his lovingly. "Would you like me to bring you something from the restaurant?"

Smiling, she asked, "You'd do that for me?"

"Of course. I know you're tired, but you still have to eat. You were great, as usual, out on the court today."

Interlocking her fingers with his, she said, "So were you and now that I think about it, I would like something from the restaurant. If they have a shrimp or chicken alfredo dish, I'd be so ever grateful to you."

"I don't mind at all," he answered as he caressed her hand.

Meridan leaned over and kissed him. He'd been waiting to kiss her properly all day.

"Whew, Keaton! That was sweet!"

"Ditto that."

Rubbing her neck, she said, "Well, I'd better get going. My bubbles are calling my name."

Smiling naughtily, he said, "That's a nice visual. I might just get my dinner to go."

"You're so bad. Go on and hang with your boys. I'll see you later."

He looked at her seriously for a moment. "I won't be long. Meridan, have you had any more phone calls?"

She looked away. "Nah."

He opened the car door and climbed out. He walked around to her side of the car and said, "That's good. Drive safely, and don't fall asleep before I get there."

"I won't, and Keaton?"

"Yes?"

"Kiss," she proclaimed as she closed her eyes in anticipation.

CHAPTER 31

Meridan turned on the water in her tub. She stripped out of her sweats and decided to return Jacob's call.

"Hello?"

"Hey, Jacob, it's Meridan. I got your message."

Clearing his throat, he said, "I'm glad you called back. I really need you to do this favor for me. I really don't want to go to this dinner with anyone else."

"Why? What kind of dinner is it?"

"It's a benefit banquet that I'm chairing."

"Congratulations, Jacob, but couldn't you have told me about this when we were in Mississippi?"

"Yes, but it slipped my mind. Look, I realize this is short notice, but I really could use your company. Can you make it?"

She sighed. "I have something I can't miss Saturday morning. What time does it start?"

"Eight o'clock."

"If you can get me a flight out of here by five o'clock, I just might make it. I'm gonna beat you up when I see you. You'd better be glad you're my boy."

Laughing, he said, "I'll take care of everything. Do you have a dress? It's formal. If not, I can pick something up for you."

"Thanks, but I think I have something that will be appropriate. Make sure you get me back to Philly on Sunday; no later than six o'clock. Okay?"

"Okay, and thanks, homegirl."

"Goodnight, Jacob."

"Goodnight, Meridan."

She hung up the telephone and sighed. She didn't have any definite plans with Keaton Saturday night, but she'd hoped for some. She would break the news to him when he came over later. Returning to the bathroom, she turned on the jets and climbed in the hot swirling water.

At the restaurant, Keaton enjoyed his time with the guys. He constantly checked his watch to keep up with the time.

Winston noticed and decided to tease him.

"Hey, Keaton. Why do you keep checking the time? You got somewhere you need to be?"

Keaton gave Winston the eye. "As a matter of fact, I do."

He motioned for the waitress and put in the order for Meridan's dish.

Everyone was silent and listened to him place the order. Malik, in particular, was interested in the order.

He asked, "Who are you ordering for?"

"If you all must know, I'm ordering it for Meridan," he answered with a frown.

Winston said, "I think it's nice of you to do that for her. I'm sure she's hungry."

Craig smiled. "So you going to drop it off by her house, or are you going to stay and feed it to her?"

The group laughed.

"If Meridan wants me to feed her, I'll feed her. Is that okay with you guys?"

Keaton didn't see the humor in their comments, but he should've expected it. Preaching about being a bachelor for life was coming back to haunt him.

Malik asked, "So, Keaton, are you and Meridan seeing each other seriously?"

Getting angry, he asked, "Why do you want to know?"

"I just wanted to know because after you go back to Texas, I thought I'd ask her out."

Keaton's blood pressure shot up instantly. He wasn't about to let Malik or any man get within ten feet of Meridan St. John... Ever! Winston stared at Keaton. What he saw in Keaton's body language was a man whose temper was about to blow. Now was better than any time to intervene.

Winston stood and said, "Malik, stop getting Keaton all worked up. Meridan's too busy to fool around with either one of you clowns."

Malik took a sip of his water. "Well, I'll just have to see for myself."

Malik knew he was getting under Keaton's skin and he took pleasure in pissing him off.

Keaton calmly looked at Malik and said, "Knock yourself out, man."

The waitress brought the order to the table and he stood to pay her.

Winston stared at him, knowing Keaton could take a swing at Malik at any moment for taunting him. He also knew Malik had Keaton close to his boiling point.

To make sure he was okay, he asked, "You cool, Keaton?"

Shaking his hand, he said, "Yeah, I'm cool, Bro."

"Should I wait up for you?"

They all laughed again.

"Funny, Winston. I'll holler at you punks later. Peace!"

He grabbed his jacket and headed out the door.

Meridan met Keaton at the door, wrapped in a towel.

She smiled and said, "Hurry, hurry! It's freezing out there!"

He looked her up and down and asked, "You're still soaking?"

Opening the Styrofoam plate, she said, "Yes, Sir. Oooo! Thank you, Keaton. This smells so good!" She turned and ran back up the stairs. Yelling back to him, she said, "Come on up and bring the plate with you!"

He laughed and followed her up the stairs. By the time he made it to her bedroom, she was back in the tub. He sat her plate on a table and entered the bathroom.

Looking down at her, he asked, "Do you want it now?"

She smiled up at him. "What exactly are you offering me, Keaton?"

He knelt down and put his hand over in the hot water, touching her thigh. "Whatever you want," he said, with love in his voice.

Keaton could feel her eyes on him. His heart rate accelerated.

Meridan took a deep breath and asked, "Do you want to come in? I don't mind sharing. I know your muscles are just as tired as mine."

He swallowed and watched the bubbles dance around her brown skin. He stood, pulling his sweatshirt over his head. He discarded his pants as well. She didn't have to invite him but once. Meridan watched him as he shed his clothes.

As he eased into the waters, he grunted, "Damn, Meridan! This water is scalding hot!"

"That's how I like it," she boasted. "I'm sorry, sweetheart. Do you want me to cool it down a little?"

He gritted his teeth and eased further into the water. "Nah, just give me a minute. I'll adjust."

Keaton finally settled in and let out a loud sigh.

Meridan smiled and asked, "Are you okay?"

"Finally. I don't see how you take it."

"I'm a country girl, remember? I have thick skin."

Closing his eyes, he said, "You're funny, and you're spoiling me."

Leaning forward, she asked, "Didn't I tell you? That's one of my specialties."

He laughed.

She closed her eyes and lay back. "Keaton?"

"Yes?"

"Remember that telephone call this morning?"

He opened his eyes and stared at her before answering, "Yes, what about it?"

"There's something I need to tell you and it's not going to be easy for me. I need to tell you how I got this scar."

She stared back at him, waiting for his answer.

"Okay," he answered.

Pleased, she said, "Thanks again for bringing me dinner."

He closed his eyes again and said, "No, thank you."

They closed their eyes and enjoyed the hot, steamy bath in silence. Keaton had no idea what he was going to hear. Whatever it was, he knew it was going to have some heavy weight to it.

CHAPTER 32

Winston walked into his bedroom and found Arnelle, MaLeah, and Fredrick all cuddled up in their bed. The kids were asleep and Arnelle was watching a movie. He walked over and planted a wet kiss on her lips.

Smiling, he said, "It looks a little crowded in here.

She turned off the movie. "They tried to wait up for you. How was practice?"

Unlacing his shoes, he said, "It was good, and your brother is out there."

Pulling back the linens, she asked, "What do you mean, out there?"

Winston laughed. "Hold up. Let me take the kids to their room."

Arnelle sat there frowning as she thought about Keaton playing with Meridan's heart. Winston returned, closing the door behind him. Arnelle reached over and turned on the baby monitors. He sat down so he could take off his socks.

"You should've seen him kissing on Meridan before practice. She didn't stay for dinner, so your brother took her a carryout."

"I think that's sweet but I'm afraid she's going to get her heart broken by him."

Discarding his clothes, he said, "You worry about Keaton too much. I thought he was going to jump on Malik at dinner. He was going on and on about asking Meridan out when Keaton goes back to Texas. I didn't like the direction the conversation was heading in so I had to cool things down."

Worried, she asked, "They didn't get into it, did they?"

"Almost, but they're cool. I wouldn't wait up for him, though. He'll probably spend the night with her again."

Arnelle sat up and asked, "What do you mean, again?"

Winston laughed and disappeared into the bathroom. He returned to the bedroom and said, "He told me they got back from Mississippi last night, but he didn't come home until around eight-thirty this morning. I think he slept with her."

Arnelle got out of the bed.

"This is exactly what I was afraid of. Poor Meridan's probably already fallen in love with him."

"Calm down, Arnelle. Like I told you before, Meridan's a grown woman."

"I know she is, Baby, but I know my brother can be reckless with women's hearts."

He stood before her, naked. "They'll work it out. Stop worrying about them. Okay?"

She smiled. "You want me to wash your back for you?"

"You bet."

"Go ahead. I'll be right in," she coaxed.

Arnelle slid out of her nightgown and joined Winston in the bubbles. She produced two glasses of wine.

"Thank you."

"You're welcome."

They sipped their wine as Arnelle laid back against his chest. "Winston, I know you told me to leave it alone, but I'm worried about my brother."

Winston kissed her shoulders. "Don't because Keaton is fine. His blood pressure is normal and he'll be going back home in a couple of weeks. The kids have really enjoyed him since he's been here. It's going to tear MaLeah up when he leaves."

"I know. He has really spoiled her and she loves him so much."

Winston caressed her body and kissed her neck.

She kissed him lovingly and said, "He reminds me so much of you."

Laughing, he said, "I agree and I believe there will be a wedding in the near future."

Straddling his lap, she said, "That would be nice. I love my brother but I guess it's time I quit trying to be his big sister, huh?"

"Nah, you're going to always be his big sister and you're going to always worry about him. You're just going to have let him live his life and hopefully he won't make any bad choices. If so, he'll learn from them. Okay?"

She hugged him and said, "You're right. Now, how about some hot, sweaty loving? Do you think you can serve that up for me?"

He palmed her rear, pulling her closer. She wrapped her arms around his neck and kissed him. As a married couple with two small children, they tried their best to have as much quality time as possible. He ran his tongue over her breasts, taking her into his mouth.

"You do know what I like, Counselor," she moaned as she threw back her head.

She guided him inside her body and they took each other on a wild ride to ecstasy.

Winston worked to get even deeper. Arnelle was already gasping as his hips met hers.

"Arnelle, you know I love you, don't you?"

Breathlessly, she moaned, "Oh yes, Baby. Yes! I love you, too."

Winston was always weak to her making love on top. That was usually when she talked dirtiest to him and it turned him on even more. Moments later Arnelle and Winston yelled out in satisfaction. She kissed his chest, neck, and lips while trying to catch her breath.

"Now that's what I'm talking about."

"Damn it, Arnelle, you're going to make me wake up the kids."

She ran her tongue in his ear and whispered, "And to think... I'm not even through with you yet. Just wait until I get you into bed."

"You know you're playing with fire, don't you?"

She giggled. "The hotter, the better. Come on, Winston."

He kissed her hard.

"As soon as we're done here, I'm all yours."

Arnelle smiled and took a sip of her wine. Winston caressed her body and asked, "How are things at the clinic?"

"Great. Venice is amazing. She really knows how to bring in clients. We just picked up a couple more high schools. I don't know where she gets the energy; especially since she has the twins."

Winston smiled. "She is an amazing woman. She's strong-willed, and she's been through a lot. I didn't care for her when we first met because of what she put Craig through. But, I had to step aside and let Craig handle his business because he loved her; regardless of my opinion. Somehow through all of that, we've become the best of friends. With her help, I was able to wake up and put my foolish pride aside so I wouldn't lose you. I'm so glad I did because I don't know what I would've done if I had lost you."

Cupping his face, she said, "Winston, you were never threatened by any other man. I would've waited a lifetime for you."

"What about Damon Kilpatrick? You ran off to Florida with him."

She kissed him tenderly and said, "You broke up with me, remember? Besides, you came and got me."

"How could I forget? We did have a beautiful wedding that night, didn't we?"

"Yes, we did, even though the one my family arranged for us in Texas was just as beautiful."

Winston ran his finger down her chest. "I need to call Venice and Craig and see about getting Brandon over here for the weekend. MaLeah would love that. It's been a while since they tore up the house."

Standing up, she looked down at him. "Sounds like a plan to me. Now come to bed."

He caressed her legs. "Don't move."

Staring down at him in confusion, she asked, "What?"

He sat up and repeated, "I said, don't move."

Arnelle sucked in a sharp breath as his lips came in contact with her body. She braced herself against the wall and closed her eyes.

"Winston Carter III, you are *sooo* bad."

CHAPTER 33

Meridan crawled into bed after finishing the delicious dinner Keaton brought her. He was down the hallway putting his clothes in the washer. Since he didn't get a chance to pick up a change of clothes, he'd ask Meridan if he could use her washer. He walked back into the room with a towel around his waist.

"Did you find everything okay?"

Crawling into bed, he said, "Just where you said it would be. How was your dinner?"

"Delicious. I really appreciate you bringing it to me. That was so sweet."

Fluffing his pillow, he said, "I didn't mind at all. What time do you have to be at work in the morning?"

"I'm the early bird. I have to be there at eight."

"Wake me up when you get up, so I can get out of your way."

She leaned down and kissed his cheek. "You can sleep in, if you like. I don't mind. Just call me when you get up so I can tell you how to set the alarm. There's no reason for you to get up if you don't have to."

Keaton's heart fluttered. He could see the love in her eyes. "Are you sure?"

She turned toward him. "Yes. Now kiss me so I can tell you about that phone call."

He kissed her tenderly. He tried his best not to get too greedy. She faced him and he pulled her closer.

She stared at him. "Keaton, I need to tell you this because it's now or never."

He took a breath. "I'm all ears."

Meridan swallowed hard. "One of my classmates cut me with a broken bottle because I didn't want to be any more than a friend. If Nikki hadn't come along and hit 'em over the head with a brick, it could've been a lot worse. I lost a lot of blood and for a while, they didn't think I was going to make it. It's hard for some people to accept no for an answer."

Keaton was horrified. He stroked her cheek and asked, "Why would anyone want to hurt you?"

"Keaton, you know yourself there are people in this world who have some serious issues. I'm just glad Nikki was there."

Angry, he yelled, "You could've been killed!"

Meridan wiped away a tear because she knew she was still leaving a lot of the story out.

"I know. I think about that night every time I look in the mirror."

He sighed. "What happened to him?"

Meridan stared at him and said, "Served time for attempted manslaughter."

"Wow! I'm so sorry, Baby," he said as he closed his eyes and pulled her into his arms. "No wonder you didn't want me to see the scar. Just remember what I told you before… That scar doesn't make the woman."

"Thank you."

They lay there, holding each other in silence.

"Meridan?"

"Yes?"

He caressed her face and asked, "Would you please tell me who this person is so I can protect you?"

She looked into his eyes and answered, "I don't want you to get in the middle of this, Keaton."

"Were you threatened?"

Sighing, she said, "Thankfully, no."

"You will at least mention it to the police? They need to know you're being stalked and harassed."

"If I get any more phone calls, I will."

"Good."

She snuggled closer. "Keaton?"

"Yes, Dear."

"There's one more thing I want to talk to you about."

He looked at her curiously and asked, "What is it?"

"Jacob wants me to fly to Atlanta Saturday evening to go to a banquet with him. I told him I would go this time, but he'd better not call me on short notice like this again. I'll be spending the night at his house and flying back on Sunday. You don't mind, do you?"

Hiding his true feelings, he said, "I was kind of hoping we would spent the evening together after the game, but I guess I'll just have to miss you."

"I'm sorry, Keaton. I couldn't say no. I'll definitely miss you."

Jealousy leaped into his heart.

"You make sure Jacob knows it's hands off," he said with anger in his voice.

Rubbing his cheek, she said, "Keaton, you have nothing to worry about. Jacob and I are just friends."

Keaton stared at her. He felt like he had just been punched in the stomach. He saw the way Jacob looked at Meridan when they were in Mississippi. He didn't want to think about her on the arm of another man. What made it worse was that she was going to be spending the night at his house. Yes, he understood they were childhood friends, but the eyes never lie. Jacob was a man who still carried a lot of love for Meridan St. John.

Snapping him out of his trance, Meridan said, "Keaton, you do know you don't have to sleep in that towel, don't you?"

"If you wanted me to stay over to cuddle, it's best I do."

She laughed. "We'll see what the morning brings. Goodnight, sweetheart."

"Goodnight, babe."

Keaton woke up and for a moment, he forgot where he was. Then he picked up Meridan's heavenly scent and smiled. He remembered Meridan planting feather kisses all over his body earlier that morning before getting out of bed. In doing that, he had no choice but to give her a dose of his loving before sending her off to work. He pulled back the covers and noticed that she had laid his clothes out on the chair. Stretching, he headed toward the shower.

After showering, he returned to the bedroom and sat down to apply lotion to his body. The telephone rang and he froze. He didn't feel comfortable being there to hear Meridan's private phone calls, but it was her idea for him to sleep in. The telephone rang a couple more times before her answering machine picked up. Jacob's voice abruptly came over the answering machine.

"Hey, Meridan. I made your flight reservations. You leave on American Flight 280 at five-thirty. Your ticket will be at the gate when you get there. It'll put you here in plenty of time to get ready. I was also able to get you back to Philly Sunday evening like you wanted."

He sighed and held the telephone in silence for a moment. Jacob's voice was cracking and it sounded like he was crying.

"Meridan, sweetheart, I love you so much and I can't wait to see you. You mean everything to me and I mean, everything. We're going to have a great time. You'll see. See you Saturday. Love You."

Jacob hung up the telephone and Keaton stood there, not believing what he'd just heard. Meridan may not think he had anything to worry about, but he knew better. He'd been a determined man all his life and Jacob seemed to possess those same qualities. It was obvious he was madly in love with Meridan. Now he had something else to worry about. Keaton had now become even more uneasy about this trip. He stood in the middle of the bedroom, totally confused on what to do. He'd never had to deal with anything like this before. He always got the girl. Composing himself, he picked up the telephone and called Meridan.

"Dr. St. John's office, how may I help you?"

"Keaton Lapahie for Dr. St. John," he answered.

The operator replied, "One moment, please."

Keaton waited and his mind was traveling at 100 miles per hour.

"Keaton?'"

"Good morning, Meridan."

He could hear the smile in her voice.

"Did you sleep well?"

"Thanks to what we did this morning, I slept very well."

"I'm glad. Are you getting ready to leave?"

He looked at his watch and said, "Well, it's around ten o'clock. I think I've had enough sleep for the day.

"I enjoyed your company and everything else."

"So did I. Now, what do I need to do before I lock up?"

Meridan gave him the code to her alarm system, as well as where to find the other garage door remote. He noted her instructions and told her he would talk to her later. He slowly placed the telephone back into the cradle and put his head in his hands. It was at that moment the telephone rang again. Keaton looked over at the answering machine and listened as the caller held the telephone. In the background the chilling music from the horror flick *Halloween* was playing. He could hear the caller breathing heavily on the extension.

Angry, Keaton picked up the telephone and yelled, "Who the hell is this?"

The caller's laugh was hoarse and eerie, then he hung up within seconds. There was no name on the caller ID. His heart was beating wildly in his chest. He feared for Meridan's safety. Someone was playing games with her and she needed to take these calls more seriously. Concerned, he decided to drop by her office and let her know about the telephone call. Little did Keaton know, he was finding out more about Meridan's past than she was prepared for him to know.

CHAPTER 34

Keaton surprised Meridan at her office for lunch just so he could keep an eye on her. All the women in her office were whispering and lusting over his tall, dark, and handsome frame. Meridan introduced them, then told them she would see them later, before closing the door to her office.

"What a nice surprise! You see what you've started?"

Smiling innocently, he asked, "What did I do?"

She hugged him. "You have disrupted my office by coming in here looking so sexy."

Meridan was right. Keaton showed up in some faded jeans and a black leather jacket. The jeans molded to his round derriere. Any woman with warm blood in her veins would be drooling over him. In Meridan's office, it was unanimous. They shared some hot chili, prepared especially by him. He made sure he brought enough for her staff.

"Keaton, this is delicious. What did you put in it?"

He wiped the corner of her mouth with a napkin and said, "It's a secret."

"That's not fair!"

"All is fair in love and war."

She blushed and continued to savor the hot, spicy chili.

"Keaton?"

He looked up at her.

"Do you mind staying over with me Friday night? I really would like to spend some time with you before I fly out to Atlanta. We could get up and go to the game together. I would like you to drive me to the airport, if you don't mind."

He stared at her. He couldn't help but think about her kicking it with Jacob. He was starting to get angrier about the whole set-up. He frowned.

"What's wrong, Keaton?"

"I don't want you to go to Atlanta, and I'm worried about your attacker. I believe he called your house this morning."

Shocked, she asked, "How do you know?"

"It's on your answering machine. When I heard spooky music, I picked up the phone. All he did was laugh."

Meridan sat there shocked. She didn't know what to say to him. Sam was pulling Keaton into the drama and she was trying to keep him out of it.

He put down his spoon and ran his hand over his head.

Meridan said, "Keaton, I don't know what to say. I don't know why all of this is happening."

"You need to call the cops, Meridan. I'm not going to tell you again. It doesn't seem like this fool is playing."

She looked up at him, seeing he was having a hard time with the whole situation and it was understandable.

She hugged his neck. "Keaton? The last thing I want to do is pull you into some drama."

He looked at her and said, "I love you and that makes me responsible for you. I will not allow anyone to hurt you. That goes for Jacob, too. Understood?"

She looked at him curiously and asked, "Why Jacob?"

"I don't want you down there with him. He has feelings for you."

She sat in his lap and snuggled. "I have feelings for him, too, but it's nothing like the feelings I have for you. Nothing is going to happen between me and Jacob. I'm just going to escort him to this banquet. Besides, I've known Jacob all my life. He knows where I stand."

"You trust him to behave?"

Smiling, she asked, "Oh course I do. Do you think different?"

"I'd be a fool not to think that."

She looked down at her hands. "Look, Keaton. I appreciate your concern. It's very sweet, but I can handle Jacob. I can take care of myself in both matters. Okay?"

She hugged his neck.

"Nothing is going to happen. Okay?"

He returned the hug, then looked her in the eyes.

"Meridan, I'll break Jacob's damn neck if he steps one inch out of line. Do you understand me?"

She saw the seriousness in his eyes. She buried her face in his warm neck and said, "I understand and thank you for caring about me so much."

"Always... Always."

Meridan and Keaton spent Friday night making love and playing video games. She modeled the dress she was going to be wearing to the dinner with Jacob. Seeing the way the fabric clung to her body made Keaton tense even more.

Frowning, he asked, "Don't you have something less revealing to wear?"

Laughing, she said, "Keaton, don't start."

"I'm just asking," he yelled as he threw his hands in the air.

Meridan changed out of the dress so she could finish packing. Moments later, she climbed into bed with Keaton.

She kissed him and asked, "Do you think we'll win tomorrow?"

"I hope so. I'm glad we're playing for charity. That prize money will do the children at the youth center a lot of good."

She sat up and asked, "How's your knee?"

"It's great. That's why I work out so hard. Arnelle makes sure I don't do anything to damage it. It doesn't hurt to have a sports doctor in the family."

"I agree. Well, I guess we'd better turn in, huh?"

He rolled over on top of her and kissed her neck. "Hmm. I'm going to have a hard time putting you on that plane tomorrow."

She cupped his face and said, "I'm coming back to you, my love. Now kiss me."

"Don't mind if I do."

He dove under the comforter, causing Meridan to scream out loud.

CHAPTER 35

The buzzer sounded to notify the team it was time to take the court. Meridan was cool as a cucumber. She was used to this, even though it had been a while since she had competed. Winston had purchased them some nice uniforms and all of them seemed anxious to get started. Meridan pulled her braids up into a ponytail and kept moving so her muscles would stay loose. Winston gave them their pep talk and they took to the court. Keaton walked over to Meridan and whispered, "Good luck, sweetheart."

Smiling, she responded, "Good luck to you, too."

They won the toss and the game began. The gym was standing room only. Most of the spectators were there to see the female they had heard about. Meridan meticulously drove the team down the floor. She had quick hands and handled the ball beautifully. She had most of the spectators rooting for their team.

Minutes later, they were ahead, but it was close. The competitor Meridan was guarding tried to intimidate her. When he saw she was playing him tight, man to man, it angered him. On one drive to the basket, he purposely ran her over. Meridan went down hard. Malik helped her up while Keaton walked over to the guy on the other team and discreetly said, "Do that again and your ass is mine."

"Hey! If she can't handle it, she shouldn't be on the court."

The competitor ran back down the floor, after having been charged with a foul. Keaton walked over to Meridan and asked, "Are you okay?"

"I'm fine, Keaton. I can handle him, but thanks."

Meridan went to the foul line and shot her free throws. She hit nothing but net.

On the last play of the game, Meridan drove down the court. The competitor who had been guarding her all day was talking a lot of trash. She smiled at him. "Take this, punk!"

She discreetly elbowed him sharply in the ribs and charged in for the lay-up. The buzzer sounded and they won. The competitor was holding his stomach, screaming to the referee about a foul. The referee told him if he couldn't handle it, he shouldn't be on the court. The game was over.

The time passed slowly as each game came to a close. There were games in between theirs, which gave them time to rest. Venice, Arnelle, and their kids were in attendance to cheer the team on. Nichole was there as well.

Venice said, "Meridan, gurl! You are showing out!"

In agreement, Arnelle said, "You sure are."

Meridan said, "Thank you. How are my favorite twins and company?"

Brandon and MaLeah both hugged Meridan's leg as she kissed the twins on the cheek. She sat down, taking Fredrick into her lap.

Arnelle leaned down and whispered, "You okay? You took a hard fall out there."

"I'm okay. I got him back."

Arnelle laughed and thought just how perfect Meridan was for her brother. She wasn't a pushover at all. Nichole tapped Meridan on the leg and whispered, "What's that guy's name that helped you up?"

Surprised at Nichole's question, she asked, "Why do you want to know?"

"He's cute. Is he spoken for?"

"Not that I know of, but aren't you spoken for?"

Crossing her legs, she smiled. "That's okay, Dee. I'll find out for myself, but thanks anyway. Damn! He sure is fine!"

Meridan laughed. "You better not let that cop you're dating hear you talking this trash. You guys are still dating, aren't you?"

"Yes, but I still like to keep my options open. What does that guy do for a living?"

Frowning, Meridan said, "I don't know. The subject has never come up."

"It really doesn't matter anyway. He's a cutie."

"Knock yourself out, Nikki, but I must warn you. Malik's very outspoken."

"That's how I like my men. Thanks for the heads up."

"Good luck, Nikki."

Hugging Meridan's neck, she said, "Thanks, Dee! Now you guys better kick butt in this next game."

"Oh, we will."

Hours and several games later, Winston's team played in the finals. It was a long, hard-fought game, but sadly they lost. They still were able to make a donation to the charity that had been chosen as the runner-up recipient. The team members received their trophies and awards. After saying good-bye to everyone, Meridan looked over at Keaton and said, "We need to get going. I want to take a quick shower before we leave for the airport."

"Go ahead. I'll wait right here for you."

Meridan hurried to the locker room and took a quick shower.

On the way to the airport, Keaton's heart kept fluttering. He occasionally looked over at her. It was still killing him that she was getting ready to jet off to spend time with another man. He had a good mind to make her miss her flight. That way, they could be together.

"Keaton, what time is it?"

"It's about four-fifteen. We're almost there, baby. Relax."

"I hope I have everything. If not, too bad. His butt shouldn't have called me on such short notice."

Keaton parked in short-term parking and hurried in with Meridan. She checked her bag and they ran down the concourse. When they got to her gate, the passengers were already boarding the plane.

She turned and said, "Come on, give me some sugar before I go."

Keaton didn't want to say goodbye to her. He wanted to throw her over his shoulder and run out of the airport.

Instead, he put his arms around her waist. "I'm going to miss you. Have a safe flight, and you'd better call me as soon as you get in. Promise?"

"Promise."

He kissed her passionately, lifting her completely off the floor.

Meridan wrapped her legs around his waist and breathlessly said, "You sure are making it hard for me to get on this plane."

"Just remember what I said. I will hurt your homeboy if he disrespects you in any way. Do you hear me?"

"I hear you. I love you. Be safe driving home."

He set her back on the floor. "I love you, too. See ya!"

She waved and hurried down the ramp to the plane.

When Meridan stepped off the plane, she immediately saw Jacob standing there. He smiled and waved to her. She walked over, handing him her bag. He sat it down and pulled her into his arms, planting a big kiss on her lips.

Meridan pulled back and yelled, "Jacob!"

Surprised, he asked, "What's wrong?"

She pulled her purse up on her shoulder. "What's wrong is you kissing me like that. You know better."

He sighed. "You used to like my kisses. Look, I'm just glad to see you, okay?"

She stared at him and looked her watch.

"Whatever. Don't you think we should be going?"

He picked up her bag and wrapped his arm around her waist.

"You're right. Our chariot awaits us. We're going to have so much fun tonight. Thanks again for coming."

"I'm still going to beat your ass for calling me on short notice."

He laughed as they walked through the airport. When they got outside he took her hand and led her over to a stretch limo.

"What's this, Jacob?"

"Our chariot."

"You're not doing this for me, are you?"

The chauffeur opened the car door for them.

"No, I'm doing it for us. Besides, the champagne will be flowing and I wouldn't dare put you at risk."

"Well, that was thoughtful of you."

They sat down and waited for the driver to pull away from the curb.

CHAPTER 36

Keaton arrived back at his sister's house, feeling a little down. He had hoped to be spending the night with Meridan. When he walked in, MaLeah immediately ran over, requesting that he pick her up. He set his bag down, picked her up, and sat down on the sofa.

Arnelle saw the solemn look on his face and asked, "Are you okay?"

"Yeah."

Arnelle didn't know what was wrong with her brother, but she figured it had something to do with Meridan. She watched him as he played with MaLeah. Little Fredrick squealed from the playpen. He went over and picked Fredrick up so he could join them.

As he sat down, Arnelle asked, "You going out with Meridan tonight?"

Tickling MaLeah and Fredrick, he said, "She had to go out of town."

"When is she coming back?"

"Tomorrow. Where's Winston?"

"He's upstairs taking a shower."

Keaton stood and said, "Hey, I'm going to run over to the mall for a while. Can I borrow your truck?"

"Of course. Are you sure you're okay?"

Putting Fredrick back into his playpen, he said, "Yeah, can I take MaLeah with me?"

"Sure. What do you want for dinner?"

He walked over and got MaLeah's coat out of the closet.

"It doesn't matter. I'm not really hungry anyway."

"Okay. Drive carefully and, MaLeah, behave."

"K!"

When they left the room, Fredrick cried large crocodile tears. Arnelle picked him up and said, "I know, Sweetie. I think your uncle feels the same way. Come help Momma cook dinner."

Keaton and MaLeah had spent a couple of hours walking through the mall. There were plenty of colorful displays, and entertaining music was in the air. MaLeah wanted everything in sight.

"Uncie Key! I want that!"

Keaton looked over and saw the Barbie Corvette that MaLeah had pointed out. He laughed. "What are you going to do with that?"

"I wanna drive, Uncie Key!" MaLeah sat in the Corvette and tried to make the car go. "It's broke, Uncie Key!"

Keaton laughed at her and started playing a PlayStation 2 game. His cell phone rang.

"Hello?"

"Hey, sexy," Meridan said seductively in his ear.

Smiling, he said, "I take it you've arrived safe and sound?"

"Yes, I did. Right now, I'm trying to get into this dress."

Keaton frowned. "I'll be damned if you get *him* to help you."

"Calm down, Keaton. It was just a figure of speech. Actually, I'm ready. So, what are you doing?"

Taking a breath, he answered, "I'm at the toy store with MaLeah."

"Well, have fun and give her a kiss for me. Don't forget to pick me up tomorrow."

"I won't. Has everything been cool?"

"Everything has been normal. Stop worrying, Keaton. I'll call you when I get in tonight. Okay?"

Pouting, he said, "I guess."

"I love you."

Pausing, he said, "Love you, too."

"Talk to you later."

"Aight. Goodbye."

"Bye."

Keaton hung up the telephone and watched MaLeah play with a baby doll. They walked further down the mall, looking in the windows of other stores.

MaLeah had conned Keaton out of a huge lollipop. What MaLeah didn't know was that her uncle had secretly bought her that Barbie Corvette and doll she had been playing with. Holding her hand, he stopped when he came upon a jewelry store. Looking in the window, he saw something that caught his eye. He couldn't take his eyes off it.

"Come on, MaLeah. Your uncle sees something he wants to look at a little closer."

With a sticky face, she said, "K!"

Keaton and MaLeah had been in the mall for some time. He'd made several purchases; mostly presents for his family members since he knew this was his last week in Philadelphia. By the time they got back to the truck, MaLeah was asleep. He pulled around to the dock so the Barbie Corvette could be loaded inside. He also picked up a scooter for Fredrick. For Winston and Arnelle, he got them a weekend getaway at a local hotel. It was going to be bittersweet for him when he went home; mostly because of Meridan. Long distance relationships were hard to sustain, but he was willing to do whatever he could to keep her in his life. He just prayed she would go for it.

When Meridan stepped out of the bedroom, Jacob was waiting for her. His eyes widened. Her black gown was strapless and hugged her curves.

"Meridan, you look fabulous. Are you ready to go?"

"As ready as I'm going to be. You look nice, too, Jacob. I guess you'd never know we're a couple of country kids from Mississippi, huh?"

Laughing, he kissed her on the cheek. "You can take us out of the country, but you can't take the country out of us."

Meridan giggled and nudged him playfully with her elbow. "I'm glad I came. I miss hanging with you."

"I'm also glad you came. Let's roll."

Meridan and Jacob got in the limo and headed to the hotel. He poured two glasses of champagne and asked, "So, how's your friend? What's his name? Keaton?"

Taking a sip of champagne, she replied, "Keaton's doing fine."

"You're glowing. What's up?"

Blushing, she answered, "Nothing's up."

He smiled while studying her.

"Why are you looking at me like that? Stop it."

"Meridan St. John, I will get to the bottom of this before the night is over. I guarantee it."

She sipped her champagne. "You're silly, Jacob. There's nothing to get to the bottom of."

The limo pulled up to the front of the hotel. There were dozens of people going inside, dressed in their formal attire. The driver opened the door so they could join the many people attending the banquet. As they stepped out, Jacob held his arm out for Meridan to take it.

She looked at him, dressed in his tuxedo. "Good luck tonight."

"I wish my parents could've come, but Momma's not feeling well. Daddy didn't want to leave her."

"I understand. I guess we'd better get inside."

Taking her hand into his, he said, "Let's go."

CHAPTER 37

K eaton pulled into the garage with a sleeping MaLeah in tow. It had been a long day and he was exhausted. He pulled MaLeah out of her car seat and entered the house. Winston was in the kitchen fixing his plate.

"What's up, Bro?"

Closing the door, he said, "Nothing much." He handed Winston the envelope with the certificate for the weekend getaway.

Winston frowned and asked, "What's this?"

"Just a little thank you for letting me hang out with you guys these past few weeks."

Winston opened the envelope and smiled. "You didn't have to do this, Keaton. You're family."

Keaton repositioned MaLeah. "I wanted to."

"Thank you, Bro. I'm sure we'll enjoy this," he said with gratitude.

Grinning, Keaton said, "I'm sure you guys will."

Sitting the envelope down, Winston asked, "Do you want me to take MaLeah?"

"Nah, I got her. Oh, you can take the items out of the truck that I got for the kids."

Winston looked worried. "What did you get them?"

Laughing, Keaton walked out of the kitchen without responding. Winston knew very well how much Keaton spoiled the kids on their birthdays and holidays. He was afraid to see what awaited him in the garage.

Meridan and Jacob were enjoying their meal. The ballroom was full of people and the banquet would be beginning soon. Jacob leaned over and occasionally pointed out dignitaries in the crowd. There were a lot of politicians and entertainers in the mix; some that Meridan would otherwise not get this close to.

"Jacob, I'm so proud of you. You've really done well for yourself here."

"It would be so much better if you would share it with me."

Taking a bite of her dessert, she asked, "What are you talking about?"

He whispered in her ear, "We'll talk about it back at the house. Okay?"

Confused, she shrugged her shoulders. "Okay."

Jacob was recognized for chairing the banquet and after that portion of the program was over, the guests were ushered over to another room where a band was set up for dancing. Jacob introduced Meridan to several colleagues and friends. Meridan loved the South and being in Atlanta was no different. The climate, food, and hospitality were like nowhere else. It was an enjoyable night after all.

On the ride back to Jacob's house, Meridan fell asleep on his shoulder. Once the limo pulled up in front of the house, he gently woke her up. The chauffeur came around and opened the door. Jacob handed him an envelope and thanked him for his services.

"Meridan. Wake up, baby. We're home."

Yawning, she took his hand and followed him up the stairs. Inside, Meridan yawned again. "I had a good time, Jacob. I'm glad I came."

"I told you it would be fun," he said as he locked the door.

They walked into his den and Meridan slipped out of her shoes. She lay on the sofa and smiled at Jacob. His eyes were red and glazy. He took off his jacket and sat down next to her. He pulled her feet into his lap and began to massage her feet.

"Coffee?"

"No, I'm okay. You look tired though. How are you holding up? You had a lot to drink tonight. That's not a problem for you, is it?"

Looking over at her, he said, "Nah, I'm cool." He continued to massage her feet in silence, then said, "Meridan?"

With her eyes closed, she said, "Uh-huh?"

"Sit up for a second. I want to talk to you."

He pulled her up, so that she was sitting close to him. She ran her hand over his closely cropped hair and asked, "What do you want to talk about?"

He held her hands. "I know you got my message on your answering machine. I couldn't help but pour my heart out to you. It's just that I love you so much. I've been trying to figure it out, what was so different about you all night, and I think I know."

"I know you love me, Jacob. I love you, too, but there's nothing different about me. We've already had this conversation. Remember?"

Lowering his head, he said, "No, no, Meridan. I don't think you realize where I'm coming from. I've wanted to be with you all my life. As we grew up and you told me you couldn't have children, I still wanted you. Meridan, marry me. There aren't many men out there who would want a woman who couldn't give them children, but I'm the exception. I'm the only one who truly loves you for you. That punk up in Philly could never make you happy."

Punk? Where is this coming from?

Meridan was first shocked, then furious. So furious that tears formed in her eyes in disbelief.

She jumped up and yelled, "What the hell is wrong with you, Jacob? What makes you think I want to marry anyone? Like I told you when we were home, my issue is *my* issue. I'm so sorry I ever told you anything about my condition."

Jacob stood and paced the floor angrily. "You're screwing him, aren't you? That's why you're acting so different. That's also why you won't marry me. You can't deny it because I can see the change in you."

"You must be drunk! Furthermore it's none of your damn business!! You make me sorry I ever came down here! I've told you, I don't love you like that! What is it about that don't you understand?"

He stalked over to her. "So, I guess what you're saying is you're in love with him? He'll never marry you, if that's what you're hoping. I saw the way he looked at the kids playing when we were home. I'm the only one who could accept you with all your flaws. You'll be back."

She folded her arms and stared at him. Before turning to walk out of the room, he walked over and said, "I'm sorry, Meridan. I shouldn't have said that to you."

She yelled. "You should be!"

"Give me a hug, so I'll know you're not mad," he calmly begged.

Meridan hesitated for a moment, then decided to bury the hatchet. Jacob pulled her to him and tried to kiss her. She was able to prevent him but, as she tried to push him off, he was able to hold onto her so he could place a large passion mark on her neck.

"Take that back to Philly with you and try to explain that to your boy."

Meridan slapped him hard across the cheek. "You make me sick!"

She backed away from him when he started toward her. He stopped halfway and rubbed his cheek, then laughed.

Meridan didn't like the look in Jacob's eyes. It was almost like he was someone else. She backed out of the room. "Stay away from me, Jacob. I mean it!"

"You know I speak the truth. Just think about what I said, okay? My offer is still on the table."

"Go to hell, Jacob!"

He watched her as she ran out of the room and up the stairs. From the foyer, he yelled, "Sweet dreams, my love!"

Meridan continued up the stairs and locked the bedroom door. She sat down on the edge of the bed and burst into tears. Looking at the clock, she noticed it was around one. She looked in her bag, pulled out her cell phone, and placed a call.

CHAPTER 38

Back in Philly, Meridan stepped off the plane and walked down the ramp to the concourse. She'd had an emotionally draining evening and knew she had to get away from Jacob as soon as possible because he really scared her.

It was around five a.m. when her plane landed. She was able to pack, call a cab, and slip out of Jacob's house undetected. With all the liquor he drank, he was in a deep, coma-like slumber when she left. Nichole was the only person she could call and when she saw her, she hugged her and started crying.

Nichole hugged her back. "What's wrong, Dee? Are you okay? Did that fool hurt you?"

Shaking her head, she answered, "I'm just glad to be home. Thanks for meeting me. I couldn't call Keaton."

"Why not? I'm sure he'd rather pick you up."

Meridan wiped her tears. "If I had called him, he would've showed up in Atlanta ready to draw blood. He told me before I left that he would hurt Jacob if he got out of line. Nikki, Keaton was dead serious."

Nichole put her arm around Meridan's shoulder. "Well, you're home now so come on. You don't have to worry about Jacob anymore. I'm taking you to my house so you can get some rest. You can call Keaton when you wake up."

"Nikki, that's not the worst of it."

Nichole frowned. "What do you mean?"

Meridan lowered her turtleneck and showed her the passion mark on her neck. She gasped. "Yikes! He didn't—"

Shaking her head, Meridan said, "No! He did it to make Keaton think something happened between us. How am I going to make him believe nothing happened? You know how men are."

"Keaton's going to be pissed, but he trusts you. Don't worry about it. Just tell him what happened. If you try to hide it, that's what will make him suspicious."

"I hope you're right. Thanks, Nikki. I owe you big time."

"No, you don't. Let's ride."

Moments later, they pulled into the driveway. Nichole said, "Now I know I left the lights on when I left." She looked over at her neighbors' houses and their lights were on. "Humph. That's odd."

Meridan looked around and asked, "What's wrong?"

Opening the door of the car, Nikki said, "It must be a blown fuse."

Grabbing her arm, Meridan said, "What if it's not? What if Sam's in there waiting?"

Nikki looked at Meridan. "Are you serious? You think Sam would be stupid enough to do something like this?"

"Sam's capable of anything; you know that," she said nervously.

Nichole sat there, contemplating what to do next. She looked over at Meridan and asked, "What do you want to do?"

"It might be a good idea to call Deacon so he can check things out."

Picking up her cell phone, Nikki said, "That might not be a bad idea, Dee."

Minutes later, Deacon was there and sure enough, someone had broken in through the back door and shut off the power in the house. Nothing was stolen, but spray painted on the living room wall were words which shook both of them to their core. Deacon took pictures and filed an official report. Worried, he advised Nikki to stay with him for a while. He also told them he would check in with Sam's probation officer to get more information. Nikki refused to leave her house and decided to keep her handgun closer to her. Before Deacon left, he helped them paint over the words which read, *Get ready to meet your maker.*

CHAPTER 39

Keaton woke up early for some strange reason. He was a little concerned that he hadn't heard from Meridan. She'd told him she would call when the banquet was over, but she hadn't. He looked over at the clock and noticed it was around five a.m. He turned over and found MaLeah asleep on the pillow next to him. He smiled and kissed her on the cheek. He decided he would try and call Meridan in a couple of hours.

Jacob woke up with a serious hangover. Some of last night was a blur, but he remembered his confrontation with Meridan. He crawled out of bed and walked over to bedroom Meridan slept in. He knocked on the door. "Meridan? You up?" There was no response. He knocked again, but there was still no answer. He turned the knob and said, "I'm coming in."

He looked at the bed and noticed that it hadn't been slept in. On the pillow was a note:

Jacob,

I don't know who you were last night. You've really hurt me. I can't believe you said the things you said. I can't believe you would intentionally try to ruin our friendship. No one and I mean no one can make me do anything I don't want to do. I'll always care about you, but I'll never look at you the same way ever again.

Goodbye,

Meridan

Jacob sat on the bed and stared at the note. Had he lost Meridan forever?

MaLeah woke Keaton up, singing her favorite nursery rhymes. He turned over and asked, "What are you doing in here?" She had been there for a while and he knew it, but decided to tease her.

She giggled. "Monsters were in my room."

"Why didn't you go wake up your daddy?"

Frowning, she answered, "He was making a funny noise."

"What kind of noise?"

MaLeah started snorting her nose like a pig.

Keaton tickled her. "He was snoring, Shorty. Are you hungry?"

"I want ice cream, Uncie Key!"

"Shhh! Come on so I can fix you some breakfast."

"K!"

Downstairs, Keaton pulled out a skillet and the eggs. MaLeah turned on the TV and started watching the *Rugrats*. He pulled bacon from the refrigerator and placed it in the pan. Staring at the clock, he'd waited as long as he could. He reached for the telephone and dialed Meridan's cell phone. It rang several times before her sleepy voice picked up.

"Hello?"

Just hearing her voice made him melt. He smiled. "Good morning. I'm sorry I woke you up, but you said you were going to call me last night."

She took a breath and said, "I'm sorry, Keaton. It was so late."

"It's okay. I can't wait to see you this afternoon." A brief silence followed. "Meridan?"

Solemnly, she answered, "I'm here. Keaton, I'm already back in Philly."

"What do you mean, you're back in Philly? What happened? Why didn't you call me?"

Fear swept over his body, then he got angry.

Sitting up in bed, she said, "I'm fine, Keaton."

Cutting her off, he asked, "Are you at home?"

"No, I'm at Nikki's house."

That confirmed to him that something was very wrong.

He gritted his teeth. "I'm on my way over."

"Keaton!"

The telephone went dead.

Keaton turned off the stove and picked MaLeah up and hurried toward the stairs. He gave her a Pop Tart and said, "MaLeah, Uncie Key has to go somewhere. Come on so you can get in bed with your parents. Okay?"

"I wanna go, too!"

Running up the stairs, he said, "Not this time, Shorty."

Keaton hurriedly dressed and ran out the door in record time. He knew in his heart something had happened to Meridan. He was trying not to let his imagination get the best of him, but if Jacob had harmed her in any way, he was a dead man.

Keaton came to a screeching halt in Nichole's driveway. She met him at the door and could see the stress on his face as he stalked toward her.

Gritting his teeth, he asked, "Where is she, Nichole?"

Trying to block his path, she said, "Keaton, calm down. She's fine. You can't go barging upstairs upsetting her."

He grabbed Nichole's shoulders, shaking her. "What did he do to her?"

Meridan walked into the room and softly said, "I'm okay, Keaton. You can stop shaking Nikki."

He stared at her for a moment. He didn't know what he was expecting to see, but he felt instant relief.

He hugged Nichole and said, "I'm sorry. Did I hurt you?"

Rubbing her shoulder, she answered, "It's okay and, believe me, I understand how you feel. But, damn, you have a grip!"

Keaton had already tuned Nichole out. Meridan walked over to him and laid her head against his chest. His voice cracked when he spoke to Nichole. Trying to hold his composure, he asked, "Nikki, could you give us a minute?"

She gnawed on her nail. "Sure, holler if you need me. I'll be in my room."

There was silence in the room for what seemed like hours. Keaton picked her up into his arms and sat down on the sofa, placing her in his lap. Meridan was unable to look at him at the moment.

"Are you ready to tell me what happened and why you didn't call me when you got in?"

She cleared her throat. "Jacob and I got into a big argument. He yelled, I yelled, and I just thought it would be best if I didn't spend the night there."

He swallowed hard and calmly asked, "Did he put his hands on you?"

Meridan looked into his eyes and saw fire. She could tell he was trying to be calm. She knew he was a ticking time bomb, but she couldn't lie to him.

He cleared his throat and asked again, "Meridan? Did he put his hands on you?"

She opened her robe and showed him the mark on her neck.

He jumped up from the sofa, nearly knocking her to the floor. He paced back and forth across the floor. "Son of a bitch! What did he do to you?"

Closing her robe, she said, "That's all he did, Keaton. He did it just to piss you off."

"Well, he succeeded. I'm going to break his damn neck! Do you hear me!"

Meridan stood up and tried to calm him down. He continued to pace the floor and started mumbling in his Navajo dialect.

Grabbing his hands, she yelled, "Keaton! Keaton! Listen to me! Forget about him. Please don't get yourself all worked up over Jacob. You have to think about your blood pressure and he's not worth it. You're all I care about so please don't! I would never forgive myself if you made yourself sick over Jacob. I should've listened to you. I should've never gone down there."

Meridan hugged his waist and cried. She cried because Keaton loved her enough to defend her honor.

He hugged her tightly and softly said, "Get your things. I'm taking you home."

Shaking her head, she said, "I don't feel like going home right now."

"No, you're going home with me to Texas...Today!"

Keaton wanted to get Meridan out of the environment so they could regroup. For all he knew, Jacob could come to Philadelphia, looking for her. If he did that, he would have to kill him for sure. What he didn't know was Jacob was the last person he should be worried about.

"Texas! I can't leave my job and run off to Texas!"

Nikki rushed into the room after hearing all of the yelling. "Why are you two yelling? Meridan, did you tell Keaton about Sam?"

Keaton stopped yelling and looked over at Nichole curiously. "Who the hell is Sam?"

Nikki and Meridan looked at each other in disbelief.

Meridan sat down and said, "Damn, Nikki!"

Stuttering, Nikki said, "What? You didn't tell him?"

With her head still hanging, she answered, "No, not yet."

"My bad, Dee," she apologized.

Keaton folded his arms and angrily yelled, "When is somebody going to tell me what the hell is going on?"

"This is such a mess, Keaton." Meridan sighed. "Besides what went down with Jacob, that classmate of mine is…is—"

Confused, he folded his arms and asked, "What?"

Meridan sat down. "Keaton, remember when I told you about how I got this scar?"

"Yes," he responded with a frustrated look on his face.

Hesitating, she said, "Well, it happened because I pressed charges against the person who sexually assaulted me in college. Me, Nichole, my friends Chris, Freddie, Valerie, Steve, and Sam were hanging out in the dorm. I had too much to drink and it just happened. Sam was the person who assaulted me and stabbed me with the bottle."

Keaton's eyes widened as he listened. He swallowed hard, then asked, "I thought you were a virgin?"

"I was, Keaton," she whispered. "You don't have to have intercourse to be sexually assaulted."

A lump formed in Keaton's throat but he was able to say, "Is this the same person who's been calling on your phone?"

"Yes," she said, hesitating.

He embraced her. "I'm sorry, Meridan."

Meridan continued, saying, "Sam's out of jail and threatening both me and Nikki. Someone broke in here last night and spray painted a threat on the wall. We both believe Sam is behind it."

"What kind of threat?"

She sighed. "One that intends to do harm to both of us."

Keaton really didn't know what to think or what to say. He had always felt Meridan had been holding back information about her scar all along, but he never dreamed it was something this serious.

He turned to Nikki and asked, "Did you call the police?"

She gnawed on her nail again. "My boyfriend, Deacon, is a policeman. He came by and took pictures and filed a report."

"It's not safe for you guys to be here. Nikki, do you have somewhere else to stay?"

She frowned. "I'm not leaving my house because of Sam!"

He walked over to Nikki. "Look, it's obvious this Sam person is unstable. What do you think would've happened if you two had been here? I don't want to see you guys hurt. Now, if you don't have anywhere to stay, you're welcome to come to Texas with us, but you're not staying here until the police close the case. Now go pack, Nichole!"

Defeated, she said, "You don't have to yell, Keaton. I guess I can stay with Deacon."

"Good, now get moving." He turned to Meridan and said, "Get dressed. I'm going to take you by your house to get some clothes, then you're going with me so I can pick up my luggage. We're going to Texas and that's final!"

"But, Keaton—"

He cut her off. "Don't you understand what could've happened to you guys tonight?"

She lowered her head. "We're okay, Keaton. Nothing happened."

"I'll take you by force if I have to, Meridan. I know you don't want me to get your dad involved because he would be acting worse than I am. I'm trying to protect you. Let me... Please!"

"What about my job?"

He tilted her chin. "Take a personal leave. I don't care, but you're not staying here!"

They were all silent for a moment.

Keaton walked over to the window. "Look, this situation isn't good and you know it, so stop trying to play it down. Please act like you have the good sense God gave you. This maniac is trying to kill you! What is it that you don't understand?"

Meridan walked over to the window and stood next to him. She touched his arm and said, "Keaton, I hear you. I know I've laid a lot of drama on you tonight. We're all emotional right now and, under the circumstances, I'm trying to be reasonable and think this thing through."

He turned to her. "Dad's last fund-raiser for his campaign is coming up soon. A change of environment will do us both some good; plus it'll give you a chance to meet my parents."

"I don't know, Keaton. I have a lot of patients who depend on me."

"What good are you to them if you're dead?"

He wrapped his arms around her.

She sighed. "I guess you're right."

Tightening his hold, he said, "Good!"

Meridan was torn. She wanted to be with Keaton so much; especially after her ordeal with Jacob and now that it seemed Sam was back to finish her off. Keaton was right about one thing. She didn't want her father to find out what happened with Jacob. He wouldn't think twice about taking a shot at him. Neither would any of the other men in her family. Most dangerous were her teenage cousins, Devon and Keyshaun, who were attending Morehouse College in Atlanta. They never liked Jacob and would take him out in a heartbeat.

Back at her house, Meridan reluctantly packed as Keaton made sure her house was secured. She was still upset about the altercation with Jacob. Never in her wildest dreams did she think her life could get to this point.

Keaton walked in and compassionately asked, "Are you ready?"

"Keaton, I have no idea what to take or how much."

"Don't worry about it. Just take what you think you need. If you need anything else, we can get it once we get there."

She looked at him. She could see the hurt and helplessness in his eyes. "Are you sure about this, Keaton?"

He zipped up her suitcase. "Yes, I'm sure. Now, let's go."

Her telephone rang and they looked at each other. She picked it up. "Hello?"

"Why the hell did you run out like that?"

She closed her eyes. It was Jacob. "I don't have anything to say to you right now, Jacob."

Keaton frowned and angrily said, "Give me the telephone." He snatched the telephone from her hand and said, "Jacob, this is Keaton. You come near her again and your ass is mine. You touch her again, I'll kill you. Do I make myself clear?"

Laughing, Jacob said, "This is between me and Meridan."

"Not anymore! Stay away from her!"

Laughing again, he said, "We'll see how you feel when you find out the truth about her. She's not what you think she is. I'm the only one who can give her what she needs and she is what I need."

Keaton hung up the telephone. He was pissed! Meridan noticed the change in the color of his skin.

"What did he say?"

Keaton grabbed her luggage. "Don't worry about it. Let's go."

CHAPTER 40

O ver at his sister's house there was total chaos. MaLeah and Fredrick were crying; Arnelle and Winston were in shock. The sudden news of Keaton telling them that he was leaving and taking Meridan with him left them in awe. Winston grinned and tried to comfort MaLeah. The moment he said he was leaving, she started screaming. They knew this day was coming, but they didn't expect it so suddenly.

Arnelle looked at her brother and Meridan and asked, "What's wrong?"

Keaton hugged her and said, "I'll explain later, but we have to get going."

He ran upstairs to get his clothes. Winston followed him so they could talk. Arnelle escorted Meridan into the family room. She could see the worry on Meridan's face.

Arnelle held Fredrick in her lap and asked, "Do you want to talk about it, Meridan?"

"Oh, Arnelle, it's a mess. My childhood friend and I had an altercation while I was in Atlanta. He wants me to marry him, but I don't love him like that. He purposely put a passion mark on my neck just to piss Keaton off and, of course it worked. Then I have this former classmate that recently got out of jail for assaulting me and it seems the idiot has come back to try and finish the job."

Shocked, Arnelle asked, "Assaulted you?"

"Yes," she admitted. "Because I pressed charges, that criminal got angry and tried to kill me."

Shocked, she said, "Oh my God! Why?"

"It's a long story, Arnelle. It all started because I wouldn't have a relationship with the thug. Now, Keaton wants me to go home with him to get away. Arnelle, I saw Keaton's temper and it's scary. I don't want him to get hurt or make himself sick because of me."

Arnelle patted her hand to comfort her. "Don't worry about Keaton. It's so obvious he's in love with you." She sighed. "Look, Meridan, none of what Keaton's doing probably makes any sense to you. The reason is... He's never had anyone to care about like this before. He'll probably fumble his way through it, so just bear with him and let him go through the motions. He cared about someone once before, but it was nothing like what he's feeling for you. Things didn't work out with that other person, thank goodness."

Meridan wasn't surprised to hear that Keaton had once been seriously involved with someone else. As a matter of fact, she was surprised he wasn't already involved with someone before she met him.

She sighed and said, "I'll do my best, Arnelle. I just hate that he's caught up in the middle of all my drama."

"Do you love him, Meridan?"

"Yes, I do, very much."

"Have you told him?"

Blushing, she said, "Yeah, I guess you can say I reluctantly told him."

Curious, Arnelle asked, "How did he react?"

Meridan blushed again. "He handled it rather well."

"I'm not surprised," Arnelle added. "It's past time for my dear brother to settle down with the *right* woman. What did he say when you told him?"

Softly, she answered, "He told me he loved me, too."

Arnelle hugged her. "Good, so you have nothing to worry about! Then the only thing he's caught up in is being in love with you. I'm so happy for both of you."

"Thank you, Arnelle," Meridan told Arnelle as she stood.

Upstairs, Winston and MaLeah watched Keaton pack. MaLeah was still pouting.

As he packed his clothes, he said, "Hey, Shorty, I'll see you real soon. Aight?"

She crawled out of her daddy's lap and over to Keaton so she could hug his neck. "Don't go Uncie Key," she said with tears streaming down her face.

This broke his heart. "I'll see you soon, sweetheart. Please don't cry."

Winston leaned back on the bed and motioned for MaLeah to come to him. "What's going on, Keaton? Why are you jetting out of town and taking Meridan with you?"

Continuing to pack, he said, "Long story, Bro. It's too much to tell you about tonight. I will say that punk ass fool she grew up with got a little physical with her when she was in Atlanta yesterday. But that's not the most serious thing going on."

Winston sat up and asked, "What do you mean?"

Keaton sighed. "Meridan told me she was stabbed by some dude in college because she wouldn't kick it with him. He served time and now it seems he's out and coming back to finish the job."

"Damn! I had no idea," Winston whispered. "Did her homeboy in Atlanta hurt her?"

"Nah, just scared her a little bit. I had a little talk with him when he called her house a little while ago. Had the nerve to say Meridan isn't what she seems, or some shit like that."

MaLeah had stopped crying and was not lying across Winston's chest. He kissed his daughter. "Well, don't get yourself mixed up in anything you can't get out of but you know I got your back."

"Yeah, I know. Thanks."

"You must really love her, huh?"

Keaton sat down and covered his face. He knew this was the question Winston had been waiting for him to answer for some time. There was no use denying it anymore.

"Yeah, man. I love her."

He got up and walked over to his dresser. He pulled out a box and tossed it to Winston. Catching it, he slowly opened it.

"Dayum!"

Keaton softly said, "Tell me about it. I saw it last night in the jewelry store."

Winston sat up, looking at the huge platinum diamond ring. He had to admit that he really didn't expect Keaton to do something like this so quickly. "Are you serious?"

Laughing, Keaton said, "Yeah. I'm tripping about it myself, but when I saw it, I knew it was the one just for her because she's the only one for me."

"She doesn't have a clue, does she?"

"Not about the ring, but she knows how I feel about her."

Smiling, Winston said, "You didn't even see this coming did you, Bro?"

"Hell! No!"

"Do you have any regrets?"

"Not a one," he said with pride.

"I tried to tell you, but you didn't believe me. So it looks like we'll be getting that summer home after all, huh?"

"Only if she says yes."

Winston stood up, hugged Keaton, and said, "Congratulations."

"Thanks, but don't say anything to anybody; especially Arnelle."

Picking MaLeah up, he said, "I'll be cool. We're going to miss you around here."

Zipping his luggage, Keaton said, "I'm going to miss you guys also. But I'll see you soon at Daddy's campaign dinner."

"That's right. Well, call us when you get in."

"I will."

Winston stood. "I guess I'll let you finish packing. I'll see you downstairs."

"Aight."

"Come on, MaLeah."

She jumped up and down on the bed and said, "I wanna stay with Uncie Key!"

"No, come on, sweetheart."

Keaton smiled. "She's okay. Let her stay."

"See, that's the problem. It's bad enough that you bought her that Barbie car. We'll have drama every night when it's time for her to go to bed."

Laughing, Keaton said, "She's my niece. It's my job to spoil her. Just wait until Fredrick gets a little older. I'm going to repeat the same things with him."

"Whatever. See you downstairs."

Winston left the room, leaving MaLeah and Keaton to say their goodbyes.

Picking her up, he said, "MaLeah, let me talk to you a second." She sat in his lap and he hugged her. "You know you're my girl, don't you?"

"Uh, huh."

He kissed her and said, "I want you to be a big girl and take care of Fredrick while I'm gone. Okay?"

"K!"

"Kiss!"

Keaton kissed MaLeah, then picked up the telephone and dialed. A female voice picked up the extension.

"Hello?"

"Hey, Momma."

"Hey, Baby! How are you doing?"

"I'm fine, Momma. Look, I'm coming home later today and my plane lands at noon. I need you and Daddy to bring my car to the airport if you don't mind."

"Why can't we just pick you up?"

He paused. "Because I'm bringing a young lady home with me. MaLeah's right here. Do you want to speak to her?"

"Of course I do," his mother beamed happlily.

Keaton handed the telephone to MaLeah, who lay back on the bed. MaLeah giggled and talked to her grandmother, who she hadn't seen in a while. After a few minutes, she handed the phone back to Keaton.

"Momma, thanks for bringing my car to the airport."

"No problem! We'll see you two later. Have a safe flight."

"Okay, Momma. I love you."

"I love you."

Keaton's mom hung up the telephone and said, "Herbert! Keaton's bringing MaLeah home with him today. Their plane lands at noon. He wants us to get his car and drive it to the airport for him."

Herbert Lapahie smiled. "It's going to be so nice to see my grandbaby."

Keaton was confused on why his mom didn't quiz him. He figured she'd wait until they got there.

Arnelle didn't have the heart to ride to the airport to see her brother off. Besides, she knew that MaLeah would go into another crying fit. Instead, Winston drove them and sent Keaton off with his blessings.

CHAPTER 41

Meridan was nervous the whole ride to San Antonio. Keaton held her hand. "Relax, Meridan. Everything will be okay," he assured her.

"I can't relax, Keaton. I'm worried about meeting your parents."

He kissed her cheek. "They're going to love you; now relax. Besides, you've already met them."

"Not like this," she reminded him. "They probably don't even remember me."

He looked at her and said, "They might not recognize you in the braids, but they'll remember you."

"If you say so."

The plane landed on time and Keaton and Meridan walked down the ramp into the airport. He could see his parents waving at him.

He smiled and said, "There they are."

Meridan remembered Keaton's parents being an attractive couple. His mother was a striking woman for her age. They walked over and he hugged both of them.

Laughing, his mom asked, "Where's MaLeah?"

Confused, he asked, "What do you mean?"

Meridan was standing there feeling awkward.

He laughed. "You said you were bringing her home with you."

He pulled Meridan around in front of him and said, "No, Momma, I said

I was bringing a young lady home with me. This is Meridan St. John, the kids' pediatrician. Remember? You met her when Fredrick was born. Meridan, you remember my parents, don't you?"

Keaton's parents stood there in shock. Keaton had never brought a girl home before. Like robots, they extended their hands to Meridan.

Keaton's mother finally snapped out of her trance and spoke up. She then pulled Meridan into her embrace.

"Oh, Honey, I'm so sorry. Of course we remember you. When Keaton said he was bringing a young lady home, we just assumed—" Waving her off, she said, "Well, never mind about all that. It's so nice to see you again."

Meridan shyly stepped out of her embrace and said, "Nice to see you again, too. I know it's been a while since we first met."

Keaton's father said, "That it has, but it's nice to see you. I hope you'll excuse us for being surprised."

"Momma, I'm sorry I didn't make myself clear. We can talk about it later. Right now, I want to get home and rest a bit. Is my car outside?"

Herbert replied, "Yes, it's right out front. Meridan, it's a pleasure and we hope to see you two at dinner tonight."

She looked at Herbert and said, "Likewise."

Keaton took her hand and said, "We'll be there. Let's go get our luggage so we can get out of here."

The four of them walked out together.

When Keaton's parents got inside their vehicle, they looked at each other and burst out laughing.

"Zenora, can you believe it? He actually brought a woman home."

"Did you see how he was holding onto her? Herbert, I thought I was going to pass out right there in the airport. She's so tall and beautiful. They really look good together."

"I know, I know. You have got to call Arnelle when we get back to the house. I want to know how this happened. That boy swore up and down he would *never* fall in love and you could see it all over his face."

Pulling onto the expressway, she said, "She seems to be a nice girl. I can't wait to get to know the woman that finally stole my son's heart."

Herbert grinned. "I'm glad he didn't end up with that other woman. What was her name?"

Zenora frowned. "Sierra. Keaton never said what happened between them, but whatever it was must've been big. I could tell she wasn't genuine."

"She was beautiful also, but Keaton didn't seem happy when he was with her. He looks happy with this one."

Zenora sat there clapping her hands with happiness. Herbert looked over at her and said, "Slow your roll, honey. Let's not get our hopes up too high too soon."

Meridan was quiet as she rode through the streets of San Antonio. Keaton looked over and noticed her staring out her window. "Are you okay over there?"

She looked at him and smiled. "I'm okay," she said with a whisper.

"I'm sorry about the way my parents reacted. I had no idea my mother would assume that I was bringing MaLeah home. All I told her was I was bringing a young lady home."

Looking back out the window, she said, "Don't worry about it, Keaton."

Taking his eyes off the road briefly, he looked over at her and said, "But I am. I don't want you feeling awkward while you're here."

She turned to him. "Your parents are very nice. I'm fine, really."

Keaton thought he would leave the subject alone. He continued to drive, taking them out of the city.

She asked, "How much farther?"

"Just a few more miles. Did you tell your father where you were going to be?"

"I'll call him later. I don't want him getting suspicious."

Traveling down a country road, Meridan noticed the uniquely styled homes, most of which sat on what looked like several acres of land. Some even had horses running around in adjoining pastures. "It's beautiful out here."

"That's why I like it. I'm still close to the city, while having country living. I like seclusion."

Several miles later, he pulled in his driveway. He stopped to check his mailbox, just in case his parents had forgotten. He got back inside, handing a stack of mail to Meridan.

"Where's your house?"

"It's just over the hill."

Keaton continued down his driveway. The entrance was lined with a grove of trees, flowers and shrubbery. He topped a small hill and as he descended it, Meridan gasped.

"Oh, Keaton. It's gorgeous!"

"Thank you," he said proudly.

The house looked like something you would see in Arizona or New Mexico. It was made of stone with detailed western architecture. He pulled up to the house and parked.

"Come on in. I know you're tired."

He jumped out and walked around to open her door. Extending his hand, he said, "Welcome to mi casa."

She looked up at the two-story home and asked, "How many rooms do you have in there?"

"A few. I'm a man who loves his space," he said with a smile.

"No kidding."

Opening the trunk, he pulled out their luggage.

"Wait, let me help you with those," she offered.

Meridan took a couple of the bags and walked up on the porch with him.

She couldn't help but notice the Indian-style blankets folded neatly over the wicker chairs. There was a porch swing and several potted plants that added beauty to the porch. Keaton fumbled with his keys like he was nervous.

"Here it is," he said happily as he found the right key.

Meridan looked out over the yard. While the house seemed massive, it was quaint and serene. Keaton finally got the door open and it was obvious his parents had been there. The house smelled fresh and fragrant. He sat their bags inside the foyer and placed the keys on a hallway table. Meridan took one step inside the door and was frozen where she stood. She was totally taken back by the interior of Keaton's house.

He looked at her and asked, "You like?"

"Keaton, I love it. Did you decorate it yourself?"

Laughing, he said, "Most of it, but you know Arnelle and my mother had a lot to do with it. But, they know what I like. Let's get these bags upstairs."

She followed him up the stairs, taking in every detail. The hues of red, orange, and beige blended perfectly to his personality. Orange represented his sense of humor; the color beige for his patience and understanding nature and, lastly, red for his fiery passion and hot temper.

Upstairs, she stopped again. There was a small rocking chair sitting in the hallway. Resting in the chair was a doll, which resembled a small Indian girl.

"Oh, Keaton, how cute!"

"I had that made when MaLeah was born. This way she's always with me."

She smiled at him. "You amaze me, Keaton Lapahie."

He laughed. "Get in here, woman."

They walked inside his bedroom and Meridan said, "I can't take anymore."

Grinning mischievously, he said, "We'll see about that."

Setting their luggage down, Meridan's eyes were drawn to the king-sized bed. It was a large cherry poster bed. As her eyes scanned the room she saw nothing that she expected. The house was neat and organized. While Keaton went through his mail, he looked up and said, "Go ahead, make yourself at home."

She slowly walked around his bedroom admiring the artwork and a large bookshelf full of books. Keaton had the novel *The Pact: Three Young Men Make a Promise and Fulfill a Dream* turned face down on the desk. It was obvious he was still in the process of reading it.

Next she noticed the French doors that led out onto a balcony overlooking a pool and huge yard. Peeping around the corner, she found the bathroom. Walking inside, she found a massive tub with shiny gold fixtures as well as a large shower. Ivory and gold decor accented the bathroom, which was also spacious and had a large skylight overhead.

Keaton walked in and asked, "You find everything okay?"

Turning, she said, "Yes, everything is very nice."

He stood there admiring her beauty. He walked over to her and pulled her into his arms lovingly. He touched the area on her neck that Jacob had violated and asked, "Are you hungry?"

"Not really, but I am a little sleepy."

"Do you want to take a nap?"

She put her arms around his neck and whispered something seductively into his ear.

Frowning, he yelled, "Jesus, Meridan!"

What she had whispered to him instantly aroused him. He playfully threw her over his shoulder and headed toward his large bed. Meridan giggled as he gently placed her on his bed.

He sprinkled her body with kisses and said, "I'm glad you're here."

"I'm glad I'm here also," she said as she softly caressed his face. They stared at each other passionately. "Keaton?"

"Yes?"

"Kiss!"

He kissed her neck, cheek, and lips. "Guess what?"

She moaned and asked, "What?"

"I have something even better for you."

"Really?"

"Oh yeah!"

He unbuttoned her blouse and unzipped her jeans. Moving lower, he pulled off her shoes and jeans. She sat up on her knees and pulled his shirt over his head. As she kissed his neck and chest, he removed her clothing, leaving her in only her white lace undergarments. Meridan reached down and unsnapped his jeans, unzipping them slowly. He discarded them and they sat there smiling at each other. He ran his hand up her thigh and lowered her panties. Their eyes met and in silence, he unsnapped her bra, tossing it on the floor. He shook his head in disbelief of the woman lying before him. Never in his wildest dreams did he ever think he would ever find a woman like Meridan.

Snapping him out of his trance, she whispered, "Keaton?"

"Yes?"

"Drop 'em."

CHAPTER 42

D inner at the Lapahies was calm and relaxing. Zenora Lapahie had whipped up one of her specialties for the occasion. Their home was just as beautiful as Keaton's.

"Mrs. Lapahie, these chicken enchiladas are delicious."

"Thank you, Meridan, and I insist you call me Zenora."

Keaton and his dad made eye contact as they listened to the ladies talk.

He wiped his mouth and asked, "So, Meridan, how long are you planning on visiting?"

"Not long because I have to get back to my patients."

Zenora said, "Well, I'm sure they miss you, but feel free to stay as long as you like. Keaton, did you get enough to eat?"

"Yes, Momma, I'm fine," Keaton answered as he leaned back and rubbed his stomach.

Zenora stood and asked, "Anybody up for dessert? All I need to say is chocolate and whipped cream."

Smiling, Meridan said, "No thank you. I'm stuffed."

"Herbert? Keaton?"

"I might try some tomorrow, Momma."

Herbert smiled. "I'll take a piece, Zenora."

She put the dessert on a saucer and handed it to him. Smiling at Meridan, she asked, "Are you going to come back for Herbert's final fund-raiser? It'll be here before we know it and everyone will be there."

"Yes, Ma'am. Keaton told me all about it. It sounds so exciting."

Herbert said, "It is, but it's exhausting also. I've been all over this city campaigning. I've met a lot of people in all levels of income and I must say there's a lot of work to be done to make this city even better. I believe, with help, I can do the job."

"Well, good luck to you, Mr. Lapahie. I'm sure you'll win."

He took a bite of his dessert and said, "My dear, I must agree with Zenora now. Please call me Herbert."

"Thank you, but it's so hard. My daddy brought me up to be respectful."

Zenora sipped her water and asked, "Where are you from, Meridan?"

"I grew up in a little town not far from Jackson, Mississippi."

Herbert laughed. "Jackson, Mississippi! Now, those are some good people. What does your father do there?"

"He's a farmer," she said with pride.

Zenora said, "Good for him! You know there are not many black farmers still around. I know you're proud."

"Very."

Zenora said, "You know, I come from a family of farmers also and it was a great place to grow up. I remember having so much fun. My granddaddy farmed in Alabama. It was rough back then, but my parents made sure I got my education. I moved out here to work and met this handsome young lawyer. I haven't been myself since because he swept me off my feet."

Meridan saw Herbert and Zenora smiling at each other. So did Keaton.

Meridan blushed. "How romantic."

"Yeah, Momma. I didn't know Daddy had you sprung like that."

She threw her napkin at him and said, "Hush your fuss, Keaton!"

Herbert cleared his throat. "Keaton, speaking of sprung—"

Keaton stood up quickly. "Well, it's time for us to go."

Meridan laughed. "No, Keaton. We're not leaving until we do the dishes."

Zenora giggled. "You don't have to do that, Honey."

"Zenora, *we* insist. Let's get busy, Keaton. I'll wash, you dry."

He mumbled as he helped Meridan clear the dishes.

In the kitchen they carried on a discreet conversation about their afternoon delight.

Keaton said, "You think this afternoon was something, you're going to pay for this when I get you home."

"What are you gonna do? Spank me?"

He laughed. "Worse. I just might have to tie you up and get out my special feather."

"Keaton, you are so bad."

He kissed her ear and stuck his tongue inside it, causing her to let out a loud scream.

Whispering, she said, "Behave, Keaton."

"Who are you going to tell...my parents? They're freaky, too."

"Keaton, you are so wrong."

"Sweetheart, I've only just begun. You just wait. You are so mine when we get home."

Meridan started to get a little worried. Keaton was back on his home territory and there was no telling what he had up his sleeve.

CHAPTER 43

It had been two days since Meridan arrived in Texas. Keaton had given her a tour of his land and today he was taking her by his restaurant. He wasn't scheduled to return until next week, but he wanted to treat Meridan to lunch. They walked through the front door and his hostess immediately screamed. She ran over and hugged him.

He smiled. "Tracy, if I didn't know any better, I would think you've missed me. How have things been around here without me?"

"Keaton, you know you've been missed, but Trenton has done an excellent job running things. You know how he is."

"Yes, I do. That's why I left him in charge."

"So, how are you feeling?"

He shoved his hands in his pockets. "I'm one hundred percent." Taking Meridan's hand, he said, "Tracy, I want you to meet Meridan St. John. Meridan, this is Tracy Davenport, the best hostess in San Antonio."

Shaking hands, Tracy said, "It's so nice to meet you."

"Same here," Meridan responded.

Tracy winked at Keaton. She elbowed him and asked, "Are you guys here for lunch?"

"Yes, we are."

Tracy grabbed two menus. "On that note, welcome to Lorraine's. Right this way, boss."

"Cut it out, Tracy."

She giggled. "Welcome back, Keaton."

"Thanks."

They sat down and Meridan started scanning the menu. She looked up and asked, "Who's Lorraine?"

He smiled and proudly said, "My grandmother."

Looking away to scan the menu once more, she responded, "I see."

He studied her expression with curiosity. "Who did you think Lorraine was?"

"I figured it was one of your lady friends," she answered with a jealous tone.

He took her menu out of her hand. "Well, you were wrong and, just for the record, I only have you, so you have nothing to worry about."

Smiling with contentment, she asked, "May I have my menu back?"

He handed the menu to her and smiled.

Jacob had just finished examining the last patient for the day. He retired to his office and opened his desk drawer. He sat there staring at the glass vial. He studied it for a moment, then pulled out a small mirror. Emptying the contents of the vial on the mirror, he worked the powdery substance until he got it just like he wanted it. He leaned forward and inhaled the substance until it was gone. Leaning back in his chair, he punched the intercom and told his staff they could go home for the evening. Sitting there with the lights low, he reminisced about the good times he and Meridan had growing up together.

He picked up the telephone and dialed her number. The telephone rang until her answering machine picked up. He listened to her greeting, then hung up. Feeling the effects of the white powder, he dialed her cell phone. He figured there was no way she was still mad at him.

"Hello?"

"Meridan. It's Jacob."

Sighing, she asked, "What do you want, Jacob? You need to leave me alone right now because I have nothing to say to you. I don't know what has happened to you lately."

"Where are you, Meridan? We need to talk."

Standing in the mirror in the restaurant's ladies room, she answered, "That's none of your business, goodbye."

"Wait! I'm serious! I really need to talk to you."

"Forget it, Jacob. You and I have nothing to discuss. Not anymore."

"Meridan, please!"

He heard a click and couldn't believe Meridan hung up on him. He leaned back in his chair and put his hands over his face.

"Meridan, you will talk to me, sweetheart, whether you like it or not."

Returning to the table, Keaton stood as she approached. He could see stress on Meridan's face. "What's wrong?"

Sitting down, she said, "Nothing. Lunch was delicious. Can we leave now? I really would like to give Daddy a call."

Standing, he said, "Okay. Are you sure you're all right?"

Sliding her arm around his waist, she hugged him and said, "I'm sure. How about you let me drive back to the house?"

Dropping the keys in her hands, he asked, "Can you handle a stick?"

"Buckle up and watch my smoke, chief."

He jokingly said, "I'm so afraid."

Back at Keaton's house, he gave Meridan some privacy to call her dad. He went out to the patio as Meridan used the cordless telephone. She walked around the kitchen and into the family room.

"Daddy?"

"Hey, Meridan. How are you?"

She closed her eyes briefly, sat down in the oversized chair, and sighed.

"I could be better, Daddy. I don't know what's going on with Jacob. He's acting weird."

Sounding worried, he asked, "What do you mean? Did something happen when you went to visit him that I should know about?"

"Daddy, I don't want to upset you, but I don't trust Jacob anymore because of his erratic behavior."

"What happened between you two?"

Sighing, Meridan said, "Daddy, don't get yourself all worked up over him. I just know our friendship will never be the same. I have nothing to say to him right now."

"Meridan, I think Jacob is having a hard time seeing you with another man. I guess he believed you two would end up together when it was all said and done."

"Well, he needs to get over it, Daddy. He was acting like he was on something."

"What do you mean? Do you think he's on the bottle?"

"He did drink a lot at that banquet. I don't know, Daddy, and I don't want to speculate. What I do know is he scared me a little."

Mr. St. John firmly said, "Meridan, if that boy did something to hurt you, you'd better tell me. You know I'll kill him before he takes another breath if he did. I don't care who he is."

"Calm down, Daddy. All Jacob did was try and put some demands on me. He even forced a passion mark on my neck to make Keaton angry."

Raising his voice, he asked, "He did what?"

"Daddy!"

"Meridan, that boy has gone too far. Where's Keaton?"

"Daddy, Keaton overreacted just like you are right now. Jacob may be a little out of sorts, but I don't think he's crazy."

"If he's on something, you don't know what he's capable of. I appreciate Keaton getting you out of town for a few days. If you don't take Jacob's behavior seriously, I'm glad Keaton is."

"Jacob is the least of my worries right now."

William anxiously asked, "What is it, Baby?"

"Remember Sam?"

"How the hell could I forget?"

Meridan braced herself and said, "Well, it looks like Sam is out of jail and is coming after me and Nikki."

William was quiet on the other end of the telephone.

"Daddy?"

"I was afraid something like this would happen," he solemnly whispered. "Have you called the police?"

Meridan wiped away a tear. "Nikki's boyfriend is a policeman so he's checking things out and hopefully can find that monster. Daddy, we think Sam broke into Nikki's house."

"Have you told Keaton?"

"I told him some of it and it was the worst thing I ever had to do. He was in total shock."

William smiled. "Keaton loves you, Meridan. Did you tell him about how Sam's attack affected you?" There was silence on the phone. "Meridan?"

"I can't, Daddy," she whispered.

"Meridan, I'd advise you to tell him immediately. He has a right to know; especially since he's emotionally involved with you."

"I know, Daddy," she admitted.

Assuring her, he said, "It'll be okay. Call me tomorrow, and tell Keaton hello."

She stood and said, "Daddy?"

"Yes, darling?"

"I'll try."

"Do your best," he encouraged her.

"Oh, Daddy, be looking for an invitation from Keaton's family. His dad has invited you and Ms. Leona to come to his last mayoral fund-raiser next week. Do you think you can make it?"

"I will and I love you, Meridan. Give my best to Keaton and his family."

"I will. Tell everyone hello. Goodbye."

"Goodbye."

Meridan hung up the telephone and walked outside. She found Keaton examining the landscape surrounding his house. He looked up and asked, "How's your dad?"

"He's pissed off about the mess I'm in, of course."

Rearranging some flowers, he said, "I can't say I blame him."

Looking down at her manicured toes, she asked, "I know. I just wish all of this would go away."

He towered over her. "So do I. How would you feel about me having a few friends over for a barbecue? I want them to meet you."

She interlocked her fingers with his. "It sounds very nice, Keaton. I'd love to meet your friends."

He hugged her. "Good."

She smiled. "So, what's on the agenda for the rest of the evening?"

"Whatever you want to do is fine with me," he said as he knocked dirt from his hands.

She walked up toe to toe with him. He looked at her curiously. "Are you up for a little one on one?"

Smiling, he wiped his hands on his pants. "On the basketball court or upstairs?"

Turning on her heels, she said laughed. "I'll meet you on the court in five minutes, chief."

Following her, he asked, "You're serious, aren't you?"

"What's wrong Keaton? You're not scared of a little competition, are you?"

His baritone laugh filled their serene surroundings. He pulled her against his hard frame. "Meridan St. John, the only thing I'm afraid of is... Well, I'll keep that to myself for now."

"So, does this mean you're game?"

Gently kissing her on the lips, he said, "Most definitely. Do you care to place a little wager on this?"

"I don't know. What do you have in mind?"

He leaned forward and whispered, "I'll think of something."

She closed her eyes as chills ran over her body. Looking up into his eyes she said, "Mr. Lapahie, you have yourself a deal. Are you ready for some basketball?"

Several games later, the count was tied and they were exhausted. Keaton had started out taking it easy on Meridan, but when she scored four straight three-pointers over him, he started playing her tighter. When it was all over, Keaton won and Meridan lost the bet.

She turned to him. "Are you really going to hold me to that bet?"

"Of course. You said we had a deal, so yes, you have to pay up." Tucking the basketball under his arm, he took her by the hand. "You might as well get it over with. Let's go."

"Keaton!"

Laughing, he said, "Don't be scared. I can't wait to get into those bubbles. Besides, you're going to look so sexy in what I picked out for you. By the way, I love strawberries and whipped cream with my champagne and I would love some before my full body massage."

She giggled and followed him upstairs, realizing she was in for a long night.

CHAPTER 44

A couple of nights later, Meridan's cousins Devon, Keyshaun, and several friends found a way to get inside of one of Atlanta's most popular gentleman's clubs, called the Chocolate Cat. The club was packed and the ladies were wall to wall.

Devon looked at Keyshaun. "You do know if we get caught up in here, our asses are grass."

Watching a half-naked woman walk past him, he answered, "It'll be worth it, Bro. Damn!"

The guys found an empty table and proceeded to get their drink orders. Only two in the group were old enough to drink. The rest of them lied, telling the waitress they were either on medication or on duty so they couldn't consume any alcohol. Instead, they ordered sodas.

Woman after woman graced the stage doing acrobatics never seen before. Devon enjoyed placing his money in their g-strings. He was amazed when one dancer in particular made his five-dollar bill disappear without using her hands. Looking around the club, he noticed a familiar face.

"I'll be damn. Keyshaun, look over there."

Across the room, they saw Jacob getting a lap dance. Meridan's Aunt Sugar had called and told them what happened between Jacob and Meridan. She told them to be on the lookout for him. To Devon and Keyshaun, that meant kick his ass if they saw him. Both men were now distracted from the entertainment in front of them. They had some business to take care of... Family business. You don't mess with family and with both of them standing about six-three, two hundred thirty pounds, they didn't play. They watched and waited until Jacob got up to go to the restroom. Devon and Keyshaun discreetly followed.

Inside the men's room, they waited for Jacob to come out of the stall. There were other men inside the bathroom, but when they saw the expressions on the boys' faces, they hurriedly left. There was a flush and Jacob exited the stall, snorting and wiping his nose.

"Hey, guys! What are you two doing here?"

Devon walked over and punched Jacob as hard as he could in the stomach. Jacob fell to his knees and gasped for air. Keyshaun walked over and punched him hard in the face.

Jacob yelled, "What the hell is wrong with you two?"

Devon said, "You touch Meridan again and we'll kill you. You come near my uncle's house again, we'll kill you. Do you understand?"

Jacob couldn't answer. All he could do was lie in a tight ball on the floor in his designer suit. He was bleeding from his mouth and nose. Keyshaun grabbed a stack of paper towels and tossed them to him.

"Wipe that shit off your face and get the hell out of here."

Unfortunately, they didn't notice the cocaine residue on his nose. Otherwise they might have been prepared for what would come later.

Keyshaun and Devon's night at the Chocolate Cat turned out great. Their friends were all hanging outside, waiting for the valet to bring their car around. While Devon was trying to imitate one of the dancers, a car sped by and gunshots rang out. Screams could be heard as patrons rushed back inside the club to avoid the bullets. When things had calmed down, one person lay bleeding on the sidewalk from broken glass. It was total chaos. Devon got up off the ground and looked around for Keyshaun. His other friends also got up and looked around to try and make sense of what happened. The bodyguards were frantically talking on their radios as police arrived. Devon finally found Keyshaun helping a patron who was injured in the stampede. When they made eye contact, relief swept over both of them. Keyshaun came over and hugged Devon.

"Man, that was too close for comfort, huh?"

"Hell yeah. Let's get out of here."

Several blocks down the street, Jacob smiled as his black Mercedes slowed its pace. He placed the .9mm back in his glove compartment and headed home.

Zenora Lapahie picked up Meridan to go shopping. Keaton was at home making sure everything for the barbecue was in order. He was excited about Meridan meeting his friends and other family members.

When Zenora and Meridan returned to his house hours later, they could smell the aroma of barbecue in the air.

"Zenora, that smells heavenly."

Laughing, she answered, "That's my son. He's an excellent cook and he really cares for you, Meridan. I see the way he looks at you."

Taking her bags out of the trunk, she blushed. "I really care for him also, Mrs. Lapahie."

Grabbing more bags, Mrs. Lapahie said, "For the last time, child, it's Zenora."

Laughing, Meridan said, "I'm sorry. I'll try not to forget."

"Well, Meridan, let's go in and see what's cooking."

"I'm right behind you."

Keaton was busy in the backyard giving instructions on where to place the tables.

There were approximately five people from the caterers decorating and setting up the area.

Zenora and Meridan stepped out onto the patio.

Zenora said, "Keaton, sweetheart, everything looks beautiful. Do you need any help?" He was so busy staring at Meridan, he didn't hear a word his mother said. "Keaton!"

Snapping him out of his trance, he said, "I'm sorry, Momma. What did you say?"

Laughing, she said, "Never mind. You're something else, son."

Meridan folded her arms. "I'm impressed and the food smells heavenly."

He kissed her cheek. "Thank you, and so do you."

Looking at his watch, he realized time was flying by. "You guys had better get changed. Guests will be arriving in about an hour. Don't forget it's casual, Momma."

Waving him off, she said, "You don't have to remind me, boy."

"Yes, I do."

Headed upstairs, she yelled back, "Your father will be over later."

"Okay! Meridan, don't believe any stories she tells you about my childhood."

He could hear her giggling. He already knew his mother had filled her head with all sorts of stories during their shopping spree together. He shuddered to think of what she had told her.

CHAPTER 45

Across town, Gerald stood in the store, trying his best to pick out a wine to take to the cookout. He had narrowed his search down to two choices. As he pondered over them, he heard a sultry female voice say, "Well, well, well, long time, no see."

He looked up. "Hey, Girl!"

Keaton's ex-girlfriend, Sierra, walked over and gave Gerald a warm hug. He hugged her back and looked her up and down.

"Damn, Girl, you look better and better every time I see you."

"It's good to see you, too, Gerald."

"Nah, you really look good," he announced openly.

Sierra twirled around in her short dress. "Well, I do what I can."

They laughed together, then experienced a moment of awkward silence. Sierra broke the silence by saying, "So, what are you up to tonight?"

He smiled. "Look at you, all up in my business. But if you must know, I'm trying to make a decision on a wine. Can you help?"

Sierra leaned over. "What kind of food are you having?"

"Pork and maybe beef."

"In that case, get the red."

"You always were good at stuff like this."

"Thanks, Gerald. So, tell me, how's Keaton?"

Sitting the white wine back on the shelf, he looked away. "He's cool."

She folded her arms. "You know I still love him, don't you?"

"You had a sick way of showing it, Sierra," he said with a frown.

"I know you and Keaton hate me for what I did. I had too much to drink that night and Neil offered to give me a ride home. One thing led to another."

"Look, Sierra, I'm not trying to get up in the middle of your and Keaton's business and I don't hate you."

She sniffed and said, "I never wanted to hurt Keaton. I can't even get him to look at me."

"Damn, Sierra! Do you blame him?"

"I made a mistake, Gerald. Men do shit like that all the time."

Gerald laughed. "Sierra, you committed the ultimate betrayal. First, you're caught screwing another man. Second, you did it in your man's house."

"I wasn't screwing him."

"If Keaton hadn't caught you, I'm sure that was next on your list."

Sierra teared up. "I miss him so much."

"Put yourself in his position, Sierra. What if it was you who walked in on Keaton getting busy with some chick?"

Sierra was silent. She knew everything Gerald was saying was true. The fact remained that she did still love Keaton and something told her Gerald was getting ready to hook up with his boy. This might be the perfect opportunity for her to try, once again, to talk some sense into him.

Walking toward the checkout line, Gerald said, "I'm sorry things didn't work out between you two."

"Me, too. Well, it was good seeing you. Tell Keaton I said hello."

Hugging her once again, he said, "I will. Take care of yourself."

"You do the same. Goodbye."

Gerald shook his head as he watched her walk out the door.

Keaton's yard was filled with almost fifty close friends and family members. There was great music and good food, Texas style. Meridan wore a long, straight, gold skirt with a matching blouse. She put her braids up into an upswept hairdo, leaving some hanging loose. Keaton introduced her to all his family members and friends. She was very impressed with Keaton's family.

Their backgrounds were similar to hers: country. They worked in various levels, whether it was blue or white collar but they never made her feel inferior.

As Keaton refilled his drink, he turned and spotted the last person he thought he would ever see at his house again: Sierra. She was tall, slender, and very beautiful. Meridan noticed her immediately and picked up on the fact that Keaton was shaken by her appearance. Keaton immediately walked over to Sierra and started a conversation with her. Meridan couldn't hear what was being said, but after a few words, she saw him hustle Gerald into the house.

"Damn, Gerald! What is Sierra doing here?"

Playfully punching at Keaton, he said, "I ran into her on the way over here. I guess she followed me."

Keaton grabbed him by the collar and pulled him further into the house.

"I don't need this shit tonight. Meridan is here and I don't want any trouble. You need to get rid of her."

Rubbing his chin, he said, "I'm sorry, Keaton. But you have to admit, she looks great. Doesn't she?"

Sighing, he said, "Yeah, she looks great. Sierra always looks great, but she's in my past now."

Gerald put his hand on Keaton's shoulder. "Do you really want me to get rid of her? I mean, I don't want her to cause a scene."

Walking toward the backyard, Keaton said, "Don't worry about it. I'll handle Sierra."

"What are you going to do?"

"I'm going to try and get her to leave without causing a scene. Follow me. I want you to meet Meridan."

Keaton introduced Gerald to Meridan. From across the yard, Sierra noticed the gleam in Keaton's eyes when he looked at one particular woman. As she stared at the woman, she noticed she was plain and nowhere close to being any serious competition. Her main motive tonight was to get Keaton back. As she stood there, she thought back on the reason for their breakup.

Months ago, Keaton had caught her in a compromising position with another man in of all places…his house. He had been out of town for a couple of days on business and trusted her alone in his home. Unfortunately for her, he came back a day early. He hadn't looked her way or returned her calls since. Even though he was a man who had dated many women, Sierra had basically become his main woman. What sickened him most wasn't the fact that she was with another man. It was the fact that she disrespected him by bringing the man into his house.

The party was in full swing and Sierra had been trying her best to get Keaton alone all evening. Finally she saw him retire upstairs so she followed.

Up in his bedroom, Keaton went to the medicine cabinet and pulled out some pain medicine. He had decided that it was best that he ignore Sierra, instead of chancing an ugly scene. When he came back through the bedroom, he found Sierra standing there. The short dress she had on accented her long, slender, cocoa brown legs.

Keaton frowned. "What are you doing up here?"

Walking toward him, she said, "This used to be our favorite spot."

Popping the medication, he solemnly said, "You said the key words, used to be. What do you want, Sierra?"

"I've been trying to get you alone all evening. We need to talk."

Laughing, he said, "Why don't you just leave, Sierra? You weren't invited and we have nothing to talk about. You're lucky I haven't thrown you out of here."

He walked past her and she grabbed his arm. "Keaton, don't you miss me at all? I'm sure you remember how good we were together."

He looked her in the eyes. "Not at all. What I do remember is walking into my house and finding you with your head in some guy's lap. Now, I would appreciate it if you would get the hell out of my room and out of my house, because you're not welcome here."

Sierra folded her arms. "What's wrong? You afraid your little transvestite girlfriend will get the wrong idea with me up here with you? She's a little muscular for a woman, don't you think? You might need to check the Adam's apple, Keaton."

Keaton had taken all he could take. He looked at her in anger and stalked toward her. Sierra realized she had gone too far. She knew he would never hit her, but he wouldn't think twice about throwing her out of his house in front of all his guests. He'd done it the night he caught her with the man and never looked back.

Meridan stepped through the door at that precise moment. "Is everything okay in here?"

He turned and firmly said, "Everything's about to be just fine because Sierra was just leaving. Weren't you?"

Sliding past Keaton cautiously, Sierra said, "Yes, I was. Goodnight."

With Sierra gone, Keaton sat down on the bed and let out a loud sigh.

"What was that all about?"

"We used to date a while back. She was trying to provoke me and she almost succeeded. I'm glad you came in."

Meridan walked over to him. He pulled her close, resting his head against her stomach. She caressed his neck to soothe him. They were silent for a minute.

"I caught her giving oral sex to another man in my house," he announced.

Stilling caressing him, she said, "I'm sorry, Keaton. That must've hurt."

He said, "I'm glad I found out her true colors before it was too late."

Meridan didn't respond. It was obvious he'd had feelings for this woman at one time. He raised her blouse and kissed the soft skin of her abdomen. "Enough about her, because she's history. I'm ready for everyone to get out of my house because I want to be alone with you. You're all I care about."

Meridan smiled and asked, "Really?"

"Most definitely. I'm ready to have you all to myself."

She kissed him lovingly. "I'm ready whenever you are."

Taking her hand, he said, "Good! Come with me so I can throw everyone out."

Giggling, she asked, "You're not serious, are you?"

"I don't care where they go, but they have to get the hell out of here."

He winked and led her out of the room.

CHAPTER 46

Keaton didn't put everyone out like he threatened. In fact, they enjoyed another hour or two of fun and games. Later, when all the guests and food were finally gone, the caterers started cleaning up. Keaton asked his parents if they could hang around until the caterers finished because he had a special surprise for Meridan. He noticed that she seemed to really enjoy herself playing cards and Taboo with his friends, which made him love her even more. He had shared her with his friends and family; now he was ready for some private time with her.

Keaton's parents were unaware of the plans Keaton had made. They thought it was humorous when he blindfolded Meridan and walked her out to the car.

"Goodnight, Meridan!"

"Goodnight!"

Before turning to walk back into the house, Judge Lapahie yelled, "Keaton, you drive carefully with that young lady. You hear me?"

"Yes, Sir. Goodnight, Momma! If you need me, call my cell."

"We'll be fine. Goodnight."

Keaton started the car and started down the driveway.

"Where are you taking me, Keaton?"

"Just sit back and relax, sweetheart."

He kept driving and finally came to a stop. Meridan could hear all sorts of unfamiliar sounds; especially the sound of water. He came around to her side of the car and opened her door. Taking his hand, she cautiously let him lead her. His hands were warm and strong as he pulled her forward. After a series of steps he pulled the blindfold from her eyes. Before her was a room filled with candles. She looked around the room and asked, "Where are we?"

"We're on a yacht. It's called the Ecstasy," he said as he lit the candles.

"Keaton Lapahie, you are something else. It's beautiful."

There were two empty glasses on a small table. He walked over and poured the champagne that was chilling in a silver bucket into the glasses. Walking over to her, he handed her a glass and touched it to hers. "To a long life full of love and happiness, Meridan St. John."

"Ditto that, Keaton Lapahie." They sipped the champagne together in silence. Sipping more champagne, she walked around the room admiring it. "Your barbecue was a hit, Keaton. Your family and friends were so nice to me."

"They fell in love with you," he announced proudly.

"Really?"

"Really."

Blushing, she asked, "So what's the occasion? I thought we were going to relax at your house."

"Can't a brotha pamper his woman without it being an occasion? Besides, there's no telling what time those people finished cleaning up. I didn't want them to hear you moaning from upstairs."

Laughing, she said, "Keaton, you can pamper me anytime and as far as the moaning, we'll just have to see, won't we?"

Taking her hand, he said, "I guess we will. Follow me."

They retired to the deck. It was so peaceful. Meridan hugged him affectionately.

"This is a very nice surprise and this yacht is unbelievable."

Playing in her hair, he said, "We're staying overnight, if it's okay with you."

"Oh, Keaton! Wait! I don't have a change of clothes."

He sipped his champagne. "Yes, you do. I packed some things for us. They're in the trunk."

She hugged his waist again. "You thought of everything, didn't you?"

He kissed her neck. "I try. I'll be right back. Let me get the bags out of the car."

Releasing him, she said, "Hurry back."

Keaton returned to find Meridan refilling her glass. She said, "It's getting a little cool out here. We should go inside."

"It sure is. Come on so I can show you around."

They went below deck and Keaton walked down the long hallway. The yacht had four bedrooms and three bathrooms, along with a kitchen and a family room. He opened the door to a huge bedroom. Once again Meridan was in awe.

"Just whose yacht is this, Keaton? It's like a house on water."

Grinning, he said, "A couple of teammates bought it together. Now come on so I can give you the complete tour."

After the tour, Meridan kicked off her shoes and lay lazily across the bed. The champagne relaxed her.

Keaton smiled and asked, "Tired?"

"Not really. I think this champagne is making me sleepy."

Keaton climbed onto the bed next to her, pulling her closer. She buried her face against his warm neck and closed her eyes.

He softly said, "Meridan, we need to talk."

Kissing his neck, she asked, "About what?"

"About us," he answered as he played with her braids.

Keaton had finally found the courage to propose to her.

"What about us?"

"Meridan, I never thought I would find a woman that would fit me so well. I love you so much and I want to be with you...forever."

Oh my God! He can't mean what I think he means.

He kissed her lips tenderly. "How much do you love me, Meridan?"

She nervously kissed him back. "I love you a lot, Keaton."

"How much is a lot?"

Meridan's heart was full and she was speechless. She did love Keaton and wanted to be with him more than anything in the world, but she couldn't. She would never be able to give him the family she knew his heart desired. She now realized she had let things go too far. She should've told him about her condition a long time ago. She never expected Keaton to invest himself emotionally into their relationship, even though she already had. At this point, she didn't know what to do. Trying not to panic, she said, "Keaton, you know I love you, but—"

Damn it, Keaton! Why are you complicating things?

Cutting her off, he ran his hand up her arm and asked, "But what?" He'd always loved the feel of her skin. "Meridan, I don't think you understand what I'm trying to say."

He took her hands into his and caressed them. Tears streamed out of her eyes as she tried to form words but, once again, she was unsuccessful. She leaned forward and kissed him. Keaton welcomed Meridan's aggressiveness. Their kisses spoke for both of them as they became even more passionate. She unbuttoned his shirt as he slid her skirt over her hips. Kissing his chest she closed her eyes and inhaled his scent. She knew in her heart that he was on the verge of proposing to her, but she just couldn't let him. Making love to him was the only way she could distract him from saying anything else. The truth was she was afraid. In the morning, she would tell him their relationship could never be more than it was right now.

Keaton picked up on the fact that Meridan didn't want him to finish what he was trying to say, but why?

He thought to himself, *Meridan St. John, I will make you mine. It was obvious you didn't want to talk about us tonight, but you'll have to eventually. This ring in my pocket is for you and only you.*

CHAPTER 47

T he next morning, Keaton found Meridan sitting out on deck sipping coffee. She seemed to be in deep thought. They didn't get much sleep the previous night from being entangled in each other's arms. They had run out of condoms near midnight, but that didn't stop them from continuing to show their affection for each other. That simple act tested all the faith Meridan had in him. She knew he would never put her at risk and she also knew there was no reason to worry about him getting her pregnant.

Kissing her cheek, he said, "Good morning, sweetheart."

Looking up, she blushed. "Good morning."

Joining her at the table, he asked, "Why are you up so early? I missed you."

"I just couldn't sleep. I have a lot on my mind."

Pouring a cup of coffee, he said, "I figured you did. Look, Meridan, I know I acted irresponsibly last night. I want you to know that I would never take a chance with your life because you mean too much to me. I don't have any diseases and I've never made love to *any* woman without protection until now."

She looked at him. "I know you wouldn't put me at risk, Keaton, and I could've stopped you if I wanted to. I didn't want any barriers between us anymore."

Reaching across the table, he held her hand. "Meridan, if I've gotten you pregnant, I'm here for you and my child because it was conceived out of love and that's what is important."

She smiled. "Thank you, Keaton, and I appreciate you saying that."

"You know, that's a nice thought. I wouldn't mind having a couple of kids with you. I never really gave it much thought until now. Then again, it took me a while to find you, didn't it? I'm in love with you, Meridan."

The sadness crept into their conversation the moment he mentioned having children. She stood and he came around to her side of the table and embraced her lovingly. He kissed her slowly.

She smiled and said, "That was nice."

"I'm glad you like. Can I ask you something?"

She swallowed hard. "Sure."

He continued to hold her in his arms. He sighed and said, "Did you understand anything that I was saying to you last night?"

She looked away and answered, "I think so."

"What are you so afraid of?"

She looked up into his eyes. "You don't understand, Keaton. It's complicated."

"It can't be that bad," he added as he played in her hair.

Meridan was trying to find the courage to tell Keaton the truth about her inability to have children.

"Keaton, there are things out of my past that haunt me, even now. Things have happened to me that have left me incomplete and I've been trying to find the courage to explain everything to you but it's so hard," she said as she visibly struggled with her words.

He caressed her back. "I'm sure whatever it is, I'll understand."

At that point she started trembling uncontrollably in his arms. She was so afraid of losing him.

"Calm down, Meridan, it's okay. We don't have to talk about it any more today. I'm not letting you go and if you're trying to run me away, you're wasting your time because I'm not going anywhere. Do you understand me?"

She nodded in agreement because she knew she would eventually have to stop hiding the truth.

He leaned down and kissed her tenderly on the lips and asked, "Are you hungry?"

"After last night, I'm starving," she answered as she tried to compose herself.

Teasing her, he said, "You were sort of wild, Miss St. John."

She smiled at his effort to cheer her up.

At that moment they heard the phone ring.

He smiled. "Don't move."

She looked around at the blue water surrounding the boat. "I won't."

He laughed and disappeared downstairs. Seconds later he came back out. "That was your telephone ringing."

He handed it to her and she answered, "Hello?"

"Yo cuz, this is Keyshaun. You don't have to worry about that punk ass Jacob anymore."

Standing up, Meridan asked with worry in her voice, "Why? What did you do?"

"Let's just say me and Devon let him know that he doesn't mess with anyone in our family."

"Keyshaun, did Daddy tell you what happened?"

"It doesn't matter. We just let Jacob know where we stand. Aight?"

"Keyshaun! Stay away from Jacob and you two keep your heads in your books. Do you hear me? You and Devon stay out of this."

"I hear you, Meridan. I'll holler at you later. Love ya."

Sighing, she said, "I love you, too. Just stay out of trouble. Okay?"

"Aight. Bye."

Meridan hung up and rubbed her temples.

Keaton took the phone out of her hand and said, "I'm sorry, Meridan. Keyshaun told me what happened. I told them to stay away from him. I think they'll listen."

"Those knuckleheads have an uncontrollable temper. They're too young to mess up their future over Jacob. Daddy was wrong for telling them my business."

"They're family and they're trying to look out for you. No more than what I'm trying to do, Meridan."

"This is getting out of hand. I don't want anyone getting hurt over this. I wish everyone would just forget about everything!"

He folded his arms and calmly said, "It's not that simple, Meridan. It's a man thing."

"Well, it's ridiculous," she said angrily. "Look, I'm going inside to take a shower."

She stood and went back inside the yacht, clearly upset. Keaton smiled as he watched Meridan's hips sway as she disappeared into the yacht. Her fiery temper was another thing he loved about her.

He turned and looked out over the blue water, then mumbled, "Looks like hell has frozen over."

CHAPTER 48

A couple of days later in Philly, Nichole made her daily stop at Meridan's house to check on things. She gathered the mail, then pulled into the garage. When she entered the house and sat her purse on the counter, she quickly filled a pitcher with water so she could water the plants. Making her way upstairs, she decided she would start at the top and work her way back down.

After watering the plants upstairs, she decided to check Meridan's messages for her. There were about twenty hang-up calls and a few calls from Meridan's coworkers.

After listening to the last message, she went into the family room to water the last of the plants and check the doors to the deck. When she returned to the kitchen, what she saw made her drop the pitcher and scream out in fear.

Keaton needed to conduct some interviews at his restaurant. He was reluctant to leave Meridan alone, but she assured him she would be fine. After a small verbal battle, Meridan won. Still dressed in her robe, she dropped his car keys in his hands and pushed him out the front door.

He smiled. "I can't believe I'm letting you kick me out of my own house."

"Keaton, contrary to what you might believe, I don't need a babysitter. All I'm going to do is read, make a few calls, and snack out in front of the TV. Don't worry about me. Go handle your business."

"Are you sure? I could get Momma to come over and keep you company."

"I'm sure, but thanks."

He pulled her into his arms and kissed her. He unconsciously started untying her robe.

Smacking his hand, she laughed and yelled, "Keaton Lapahie! You are so bad."

Backing away, he put his hands in his pockets. "You can't hurt a man for trying."

She folded her arms. "I guess not."

Walking closer to her, he tilted her chin upward and said, "I won't be long and, remember, I do want to finish the conversation we had on the yacht. I know you're struggling with something serious and all we need to do is talk it through. Okay?"

She leaned in and kissed him lovingly on the lips. "I know, now go!"

He laughed and walked down the steps to his car. Before climbing inside, he said, "Lock the door and set the alarm."

"Yes, dear."

Meridan did as she was told before retiring into the kitchen to make herself a sandwich. As she prepared her sandwich, she thought this was a good opportunity to check in with her office. She was relieved to find out that everything was going smoothly in her absence and she was grateful. When she hung up, her cell phone immediately rang.

"Hello? Hello?" Meridan could hear the person breathing, but they wouldn't say anything. The caller ID was blank so she had no idea who was calling. "Hello!"

Still no answer, so she hung up. The telephone rang again and she yanked it up answering, "Hello!"

"Why are you yelling, Meridan?"

Solemnly, she said, "I'm sorry, Daddy. Someone just called here holding the phone. How are you?"

"Do you think it was Jacob or Sam?"

"Who knows, Daddy. How are you?"

"Oh, I'm doing well," he answered. "I guess you know that Jacob had the nerve to call here last night."

"What? What did he want?"

William angrily said, "We never got around to much talking. He asked where you were. I told him to stay away from you; then I hung up on him."

"Daddy, you shouldn't have told Devon and Keyshaun what happened. I don't want them to get into any trouble. Keyshaun called and said they got into some type of altercation with Jacob. Please talk to them and I would appreciate it if you wouldn't tell them anything else. You know what kind of tempers they have."

Mr. St. John sighed. "I didn't directly tell them. I told your Aunt Sugar so she must have relayed the info back to them. I'll be more careful in the future. I'll call the boys and calm them down."

"Thanks, Daddy."

"No problem. How are Keaton and his family?"

"Everyone is fine but, Daddy, I think I need to get back to my office."

"It's too soon, but you do what you feel you need to do. I'm going to worry about you, but God has a special angel looking over you. Has there been any news on Sam?"

"No."

"That's a damn shame. You watch your back, Meridan."

"Thanks, Daddy, and I will. I'll call you later. I haven't talked to Nikki today and that's not like her."

"I hope everything's okay. When you talk to her, give her my love."

"I will. Goodbye."

Nichole's head was still throbbing when she regained consciousness. As she leaned again the cabinet door, she realized the water had soaked her pants. She slowly reached over to pick up the water pitcher. Still feeling dazed, she pulled herself up off the floor and tried her best to remember what happened. As she placed the pitcher in the sink, she heard a low voice say, "It's about time you woke up."

Startled, she turned to see Sam sitting at the table holding a gun on her. Unable to scream, she could feel her heart beating wildly inside her chest.

"What are you doing here? How did you get in here?"

"Don't worry about how I got in here. You just tell me where Meridan is."

She couldn't show the fear ripping through her body at that very moment. "Why don't you leave Meridan alone? It was nobody's fault but your own that put you in prison."

"No, it was Meridan's fault. If she had just gone along with the program, everything would've been fine."

Nikki said, "Meridan didn't like you like that and you know it. You took advantage of her."

Sam laughed. "That what they all say. After we party a few times, they come begging for more. It's happened too many times for me to count." Shoving the gun closer to Nikki, he said, "I will have Meridan, one way or the other, or no one will. Now tell me where she is, or you won't see the light of another day."

Trembling, Nikki answered, "I don't know where she is. She just told me she was going out of town to clear her head."

"Wrong answer, bitch!"

The loud sound of the gun discharging radiated throughout the house and Nichole fell bleeding onto the floor.

CHAPTER 49

Hours passed and Meridan still had not been able to reach Nikki. Her cell phone and work phone went directly into voice mail. The messages she'd left on her home phone hadn't been returned. She hadn't been able to get into the book she was reading because she was trying her best not to worry about her. As she sat out on the deck, she continued to wait for Nikki to return her calls. Keaton had called a couple of times to check in on her, but she decided not to tell him she was worried. Just as she was about to close her book, the telephone rang. She anxiously answered it.

"Hello?"

"Is this Meridan St. John?"

With concern, Meridan answered, "Yes, it is."

"This is St. Moriah Hospital calling in regards to a Nichole Adams. She was transported here with a gunshot wound and your phone number shows up on her cell phone."

Meridan jumped up. "Is she okay?"

"She's lost a lot of blood and she's in a coma. Other than that, we don't know."

Frantically, Meridan said, "How did this happen?"

"I'm not sure, Miss St. John. I just know she was transported here in the last twenty-four hours."

"What is your name?"

"This is Sharon Baxter of Patient Services."

Meridan scribbled the caller's name on a piece of paper, then said, "Ms. Baxter, I'm out of town at the moment, but I'll be there as soon as I can get a flight. If Nikki wakes up, please tell her I'm on my way."

"I will, Miss St. John. Have a safe flight."

Meridan hung up the telephone and started trembling. The tears immediately streamed down her face as she ran up the stairs to pack. Rushing upstairs to the bedroom she pulled out her suitcase. She dialed the airlines to get the next flight information out of San Antonio. Coming up with the lie for breaking up with Keaton would have to come later. Right now, all she would tell him is that she was needed back at the hospital to take care of Nikki. She hurriedly dressed in a warmup suit and packed her clothes as fast as she could. Tears continued to stream down her face and she knew becoming hysterical was not an option right then, which was difficult. At that moment, she heard the doorbell.

"Who could that be?" Cautiously, she walked downstairs and peeped out the window. It was Keaton's mother. Before opening the door, she tried her best to compose herself. Opening the door, she said, "Hi, Zenora."

Zenora knew immediately something was wrong. She could see it in her eyes. She pulled her purse upon her shoulder and asked, "What's wrong, Meridan? Did you and Keaton have a fight?"

"No, Ma'am. Please come in. Did Keaton tell you to come over?"

She closed the door. "No, I thought I'd come by to see if you wanted to go shopping."

Zenora had on beautiful red pantsuit with matching shoes and purse. She walked further into the house and held the concerned look on her face.

She turned to face Meridan and said, "Meridan, I know something is wrong and it's obvious you've been crying. Please tell me what's wrong."

Meridan looked at her watch and quietly walked up the stairs with Zenora following closely behind. Zenora knew when trouble was brewing. She just hoped it was nothing her son had done because Meridan was Keaton's match. Normally she stayed out of Keaton's business, but since Meridan had come into his life, she didn't want him to lose her.

Quietly they entered Keaton's bedroom and Zenora immediately noticed Meridan's luggage. They made eye contact and she asked, "Are you leaving?"

"Yes, Ma'am. I received a call from Philadelphia and I need to get back. A friend of mine has been shot."

Zenora walked over to her and worriedly asked, "Does Keaton know?"

"No, I just got the call and I have to hurry to the airport. I'm planning on calling him on the way."

Zenora held Meridan's hands and said, "Honey, is there anything I can do to help?"

"Thank you, Zenora, but I really have to get going."

"Well, can I at least drive you to the airport?"

"Yes, Ma'am," she said thankfully.

"Only if you call Keaton, because he needs to know what's going on. My son is more sensitive than he seems. He loves you, Meridan."

Stifling her tears, she said, "I love him, too, Zenora."

"Okay, now let's get you to the airport."

Keaton held the telephone up to his ears, but he couldn't believe what he was hearing. Before he knew it, he had raised his voice. "What do you mean, you're on your way to the airport?"

"Nikki's been shot and she's in a coma, but that's all I know right now."

"Why don't you wait and let me go with you? I'm sure Sam was involved and I don't want anything to happen to you."

Frantic, she stuttered, "All I care about right now is getting to Nikki."

Worried, he said, "I could've taken you to the airport."

"Your mom stopped by, so she's driving me. I'll call you when I get in and let you know what's going on."

Keaton was quiet again on the extension. He sighed and softly whispered, "I have a bad feeling about this, Meridan."

Meridan choked back her tears. "I know. I'll keep you informed. I promise."

"I'm not cool with this," he admitted while tapping his ink pen on the desk.

"I'm going to call Deacon and see what I can find out. Don't worry."

"I love you, Meridan, and please, please be careful. I'm a little uneasy about you going back there all by yourself. Why don't you wait and let me go with you?"

Trying to be cheerful, she said, "I need to get back and take care of Nikki."

"You'd better be careful, call me the minute you get in, and keep me posted on everything until I can get there. Have a safe flight, sweetheart, and please watch your back. I'll try to get out there as soon as I can."

"Okay. Goodbye."

He leaned back in his chair and rubbed his temple. "Goodbye, sweetheart."

Zenora watched Meridan's facial expression as she talked to Keaton. She had a funny feeling there was more to Meridan's story than she was revealing, just by their conversation she overheard.

When Meridan hung up the telephone, she leaned back against her seat and closed her eyes. She couldn't break down. Not here in front of Keaton's mom.

"Meridan, how did Keaton take the news?"

She opened her eyes and stared down at her hands. "I guess as well as to be expected under the circumstances."

"I see."

Silence surrounded them for a few minutes, then Meridan asked, "Zenora, would you like to have more grandchildren?"

Smiling, she answered, "Meridan, I'll take as many grandchildren as my children give me. You know I'm not trying to look like a grandmother, but I love being one."

Solemnly, Meridan said, "I wish my mother could've lived longer to see my nieces. I know she would've spoiled them rotten."

"I know you miss her. It had to have been hard on you and your sister to lose her at such a young age."

"It was," Meridan said solemnly.

"So when are you and Keaton going to quit playing around and get married? I stopped by the house the other evening and saw you two playing basketball in the backyard. It was the sweetest sight I've seen in a long time."

Surprised, she asked, "Why didn't you let us know you were there?"

Laughing, Zenora said, "Oh no! I wasn't about to interfere on your evening. I called before I came out, but I didn't get an answer. I didn't think you two were at home until I heard you guys laughing."

"We wouldn't have minded at all. You should've stayed for a visit."

"I know, but you two were having so much fun, so I got what I came for out of the garage and left."

Meridan couldn't hold back her tears any longer. She was worried about Nikki, she hated leaving Keaton, and she desperately wanted *his* children. In that instance, Meridan burst out crying.

Pulling into the airport parking lot, Zenora said, "Meridan, don't cry. I know you're probably feeling overwhelmed right now and you're worried about your friend."

"Zenora, it's not that. It's just Keaton… Zenora, I—"

She pulled into a parking space and turned the motor off. Hugging her, she said, "There, there, Meridan. Please stop crying. Whatever is heavy on your heart will work itself out. You'll see."

Blowing her nose, she said, "No, it won't Zenora! I wish it could, but it won't!"

Worried, Zenora asked, "What is it? What has you so torn up that involves my son?"

Meridan sighed, then said, "I shouldn't burden you with any of my problems."

"Why not? I care about you and so does my son."

"Zenora, I'm sorry I let things with Keaton get to this point. I should've told him a long time ago."

Concerned, Zenora asked, "You should've told him what, Meridan?"

"I can't have children. That's why Keaton and I could never get married. I know he wants children of his own and I could never give them to him."

"I'm so sorry, Meridan. Is that why you asked if I wanted more grandchildren?"

"Yes," she answered as she wiped her nose with a tissue.

Zenora sighed. "Meridan, children are truly a blessing. Just because you can't have your own doesn't mean you can't be a mother. As far as me wanting more grandchildren, that's not up to me. It's up to what God has planned in my children's lives."

More tears fell from Meridan's eyes as she said, "Keaton wants his own children."

"Honey, have you talked to him about this?"

"The other night on the yacht, I think Keaton was about to propose to me.

I panicked and did whatever I could to stop him. He could tell something was wrong so the next morning he questioned me about it. Zenora, I tried to tell him the truth but I started feeling scared and I couldn't do it. I love him so much, but I'm so afraid of losing him because of my lies!"

Zenora patted Meridan's hands and said, "Darling, it's okay. All you need to do is pray, then sit down and talk to Keaton about this. He deserves to know the truth and he needs to hear it from you. You need to know exactly how he feels about the situation and, if you ask me, I think you're worried for no reason."

"I don't want to hurt Keaton, and I'm sorry for getting involved with him in the first place. No man wants a woman who can't give him a family."

"Meridan, that's not always true."

"I see how he is with MaLeah and Fredrick. He adores them and they adore him," she whispered as she blew her nose.

Cupping her face, Zenora said, "They're his niece and nephew, Meridan. It's not the same. Honey, you are Keaton's match; no matter what you think. You two are good for each other. Don't you see it? Feel it?"

Shaking her head, she solemnly said, "I don't know anymore."

"Ahh, Meridan."

Meridan turned to her. "I need to get going and, Zenora, I would appreciate it if you would keep what I've told you between us right now."

Patting her on the leg, she said, "I will, Meridan, and I'm here if you ever want to talk. Okay? Don't be so hard on yourself and give my son a little credit. He's a reasonable man, if you'd just explain everything to him."

Opening her car door, she said, "I'll think about it, Zenora."

"Okay, my dear. Now, let's get you to your plane. I pray that your friend will be okay."

"So do I."

They exited the car and walked into the airport together. After checking in, Zenora hugged and kissed Meridan and watched her walk down the tunnel to her plane.

Keaton couldn't concentrate. He was concerned that Meridan had to hurry back to Philadelphia without him by her side to protect her. It had also gotten to the point where he couldn't sleep peacefully without her. He knew sleep wouldn't come easy to him because holding her body against his as they slept felt right. The warmth of her body and the rhythm of her breathing were more soothing than he could've ever imagined and he was going to miss her. Her sensual body fit like the piece of a puzzle to his tall frame, a one-of-a-kind piece at that. As he shuffled the employee applications on his desk, he knew he had to clear the rest of his paperwork and join her in Philly as soon as possible.

CHAPTER 50

Meridan's taxi ride to the hospital wasn't fast enough for her. She had no idea what to expect when she saw Nikki. She prayed that everything would be okay. Her heart was beating wildly when the car pulled in front of the hospital. The taxi driver set her bags down and asked, "Will there be anything else, Ma'am?"

Still looking around, she removed her jacket, and said, "No thank you."

Reaching inside her purse, she tipped him and walked into the hospital.

When he got on the floor of Nikki's room, she met Deacon in the hallway. He approached her with a worried look on his face.

"Deacon, what happened?"

He hugged her. "I'm still not sure. All I know is she was checking on your house and one of your neighbors called the police after hearing a gunshot. Nikki was found unconscious on your kitchen floor."

Trembling, she asked, "How is she?"

Shaking his head, he said, "It's touch and go right now. The next twenty-four hours are crucial."

She hugged his neck. "Was it Sam?"

"I'm pretty sure it was. I have some detectives working on the case."

"Oh my God," she whispered.

"Meridan, you have to be careful. I'll be here as much as possible and, when I'm not here, I'll have an officer posted outside her room. Did Keaton come back with you?"

Wiping her eyes, she said, "He wanted to but I couldn't wait on him. He said he'd be here as soon as he could."

"Good, because you can't be walking around here all alone."

Meridan gnawed on her nail in despair. She knew in her gut that Sam was the one who shot Nikki.

"I'll be fine, Deacon," she responded.

"This is nothing to play with, Meridan. You've already seen what Sam can do." She nodded.

"Are you ready to go see Nikki?"

"Yes," she reluctantly answered.

They walked into Nikki's room and Meridan's heart immediately broke. She looked so helpless. Turning to Deacon, she hugged him and sobbed loudly.

"It's okay, Meridan. She'll be fine," he assured her. "She's just sleeping right now."

"It's all my fault," Meridan said.

He kissed her on the forehead. "No, it's not your fault."

Releasing him, she said, "Excuse me for a second, Deacon. I need to go to the ladies room to get myself together."

"Take your time. I know this is a shock, seeing her like this."

"I'll be back in a second, Deacon."

Meridan walked down the hallway to the bathroom. She took a breath and leaned over the sink. She felt nauseated, lightheaded, and weak. Turning on the faucet, she closed her eyes and sprinkled her face with cool water. A few seconds later, she felt the presence of someone else in the room. When she looked up into the mirror, she found Sam standing behind her.

Meridan gasped and before she could react, Sam had her pinned against the wall. A muscular hand covered her mouth, preventing her from screaming.

"Hey, baby. Long time, no see. Have you missed me?"

Meridan shook with fear. Sam's body gyrated into her sexually. Tears streamed down Meridan's face as a wicked grin appeared on Sam's face.

Seconds later, Sam stopped and said, "You still feel and smell just as sweet as you did back in college. I'm going to remove my hand and, if you scream, I'll kill you where you stand."

Meridan nodded and Sam's hand lowered.

Meridan swallowed hard and asked, "Why are you doing this? Why did you have to hurt Nikki?"

Sam laughed. "I told you I was going to pay that bitch back. Enough about Nichole. Let's talk about us."

Sam pulled Meridan over in front of the mirror and hugged her from behind. Meridan flinched in fear when she noticed the gun.

Sam tightened the grip and said, "We really do make the perfect couple, don't we?"

Angry, Meridan yelled, "How can we make a couple? We're both women for God's sake! For the last time, Samantha, I'm not gay, never have been gay, and will never be gay!"

Sam just looked in the mirror and smiled. She kissed Meridan on the back of the neck and said, "You know, from the time I was a little girl, the name Samantha never suited me. I'm so glad you guys started calling me Sam in college. It suits me much better, don't you think?"

Trying to get out of Sam's grip, Meridan said, "All I know is what you did to me was foul. You deserved everything you got and more."

Sam turned Meridan around and put her finger in her face in anger.

"Let me tell you something. You're not going to stand there and act like you didn't like that loving I gave you. I love you, Meridan. Why can't you understand that?"

"You tried to kill me, Samantha," Meridan whispered.

"I figured if I couldn't have you, no one would. That bitch, Nichole, ruined everything, and don't call me Samantha again."

Pushing away, Meridan said, "It was Nikki who saved my life!"

"Well, she's paying for that now, isn't she? Who's going to save her?"

Silence surrounded them.

Meridan gritted her teeth. "If anything happens to Nikki, I will see to it that you don't see the light of another day."

Sam grabbed Meridan by the throat and pushed her hard against the wall.

"You can't threaten me, sweetheart. Nichole put herself in this hospital and until I have my way with you, I will not stop at getting what I want…you."

Meridan struggled to breathe as Samantha leaned down and kissed her hard on the lips. She released her grip and turned to walk away. She stopped halfway to the door. She was dressed in baggy jeans, a Chicago Bears throwback jersey, and a black scarf tied around her head. She was every bit of six-three, very tall for a woman, and could easily be mistaken for a man by her muscular build.

She turned slowly and said, "By the way, whoever that tall dude is that I've seen you hanging around with…get rid of him before he has an accident worse than Nikki's. See you soon."

Meridan's heart jumped up into her throat. She now realized that Sam had been stalking her. The last thing she wanted was for Keaton to get hurt. Before she could respond, Sam laughed and disappeared through the door.

Returning to Nikki's room in a daze, reality had set in. When she walked in, Deacon looked up and said, "Damn, Meridan, you look like you've seen a ghost."

It was at that moment she started to have trouble breathing. Deacon ran over to her and caught her before she slid to the floor.

He yelled, "Nurse! I need some help in here!"

A nurse ran in and saw Meridan struggling to breathe.

Deacon was frantic trying to find out what was wrong with her. "Meridan, what's wrong? Talk to me! Nurse! Help her!"

The nurse attended to Meridan as quickly as she could. She tried to talk to Meridan in as calmly as possible.

Deacon looked at the nurse. "What's going on?"

"She's hyperventilating, Sir."

The nurse called for assistance and after a few tense moments, Meridan's breathing was back to normal.

Deacon held her hand and tried to soothe her as best he could. Minutes later the nurse removed the items covering her mouth and nose and asked, "Are you feeling better?"

Meridan nodded and whispered, "Yes. Thank you."

The nurse took her vital signs. "She'll be fine, Sir. Just give her a few more minutes. If anything changes, give me a call."

"Thank you, Nurse."

"You're welcome," she said before leaving the room.

Meridan lay back in the chair and Deacon gave her a cup of water. She gulped the water down and looked up at him with tears in her eyes.

He softly asked, "What happened, Meridan? You scared the shit out of me."

She swallowed hard. "It was Sam. Sam did this to Nikki."

"How do you know?"

"She cornered me in the bathroom and made all kinds of threats."

"This is getting out of hand, Meridan," he said as he checked his .9mm. "When I see her, I might have to take justice into my own hands. I'll be right back."

"I'm sure she's long gone by now," she said with sadness as she looked over at Nichole.

Putting the gun back into his holster, he yelled, "I'm still going to look for the bitch!"

Touching his hand softly, Meridan said, "Deacon, please don't do anything to ruin your career. Samantha's luck will run out in due time. She needs to be stopped before she hurts anyone else. Now she's threatening to hurt Keaton if I don't stay away from him."

"Don't worry. I'll make sure she's dealt with. Stay here with Nikki. I'm going out for a while. The policeman I ordered is on his way upstairs. I'm going out to find that heifer and bring her in."

Meridan kissed him on the cheek. "Be careful and thanks, Deacon."

"I will."

CHAPTER 51

Hours later, Meridan realized she hadn't called Keaton to give him a report on Nikki. Looking at her watch, she noticed it was late, but she really needed to hear his voice. She nervously waited for him to answer.

"Hello?"

"Hey, Keaton," she answered softly.

"I've been calling you and all I got was your voicemail. What's up? What happened to Nikki?"

"I'm sorry, Keaton. My cell phone doesn't pick up in here."

"Are you still at the hospital?"

Sighing, she said, "Unfortunately, I am. Keaton, Nikki's still in a coma and it looks like Sam shot her."

Keaton still had no clue of the situation Meridan was in the middle of. He ran his hand over his head. "Shot? I knew I shouldn't have let you go back there by yourself."

"I'm okay, Keaton. Deacon is coming in and out, and he posted a policeman outside Nikki's room."

"That's not good enough."

"Keaton—"

"No! If that idiot shot Nikki, what do think will happen to you?"

"Keaton—"

"No! You listen to me! I'm on the next plane!" he yelled.

"Please, Keaton! There's nothing you can do here. I'm safe here with Nikki."

He stood and paced the room. "You know, what I can't understand is why you don't want me there with you."

"I miss you, Keaton; believe me. But it's not a good idea for you to be in the middle of this right now. I don't want anything to happen to you," she pleaded.

He sat down on the side of his bed. "I can take care of myself, Meridan."

"I know you can, but please do this for me. I don't know what Sam will do next and, the less people in the equation, the quicker it will be to put a stop to all this madness."

Keaton held the phone in silence feeling defeated. "Do you need anything?"

"I need you to pray that Nikki wakes up soon."

"I will, and Meridan?"

"Yes?"

"I won't sit here long. Do you understand what I'm saying?"

In a whisper, she said, "I understand. Look, Keaton, I've been thinking and maybe we should chill for a while. I mean, at least until all of this is over."

"What?"

She stuttered and said, "I'm under a lot of stress right now with Sam, Jacob, and Nikki, so I think it's best if we try not to have a relationship right now. It's not fair to you because I really don't have time to deal with all of this right now. Maybe once this thing with Sam is over, we can look at it again."

Silence engulfed the telephone and pain shot through Keaton's head. He couldn't believe what he was hearing.

He calmly asked, "Are you breaking up with me, Meridan?"

"Keaton, don't say it like that. I just think—"

"Oh, you just think, huh? You're crazy if you think you can call me up and dismiss me without sitting down and discussing it. Where is this coming from? I know you're worried about Nikki and the situation, but that should pull us closer, not pull us apart."

"Keaton, don't make this any harder than it is. I'm trying to discuss it with you now," she explained.

"It doesn't sound like a discussion to me! It seems like you have all the answers!" he yelled in anger.

Silence engulfed the telephone once again. Meridan was about to lose control of the conversation.

"Keaton, can't you respect my wishes? I still love you. I simply can't be anything more than a friend to you right now."

"What about what I want?"

"I'm sorry."

Becoming angry he said, "I'm coming up there to find out what's really going on."

"No! Please don't! I need some time to get some things in my life in perspective. If you come here, it'll only make things worse."

"What things? Are you seeing someone else?"

Meridan couldn't believe Keaton thought there was another man in her life. No one could ever take his place. She was trying to protect him because she wouldn't be able to live with herself if something happened to him.

After a long pause, she said, "There's no one else, Keaton. I told you why. Can't you respect my wishes?"

"Damn! I didn't know I was that much of a problem. Look, if you're that adamant about it…forget it. Forget everything. I'll talk to you some other time. Take care of yourself. Goodbye."

Before she could say another word, he hung up the telephone.

Keaton placed the telephone back on the cradle and climbed out of bed. He looked over at the airline ticket on his dresser. Today was the day he had planned to fly to Philadelphia to be by Meridan's side. What he got instead was the air sucked out of his lungs. Picking up a small paperweight, he threw it across the room, breaking a framed picture hanging on the wall.

CHAPTER 52

Over the next week and a half, Nikki came out of her coma, recovered from her injuries, and was released from the hospital. Meridan stayed with her at her house so she could take care of her until she felt better. It was then they told each other everything Sam had said and done. The strange thing was that they hadn't seen or heard from her since that night in the hospital.

"You know she told me that if I didn't get rid of Keaton, she was going to hurt him."

Nikki looked at her and said, "I hope you're not seriously thinking about doing it."

"It's too late. I've already done it," Meridan admitted.

"Tell me you're teasing because I know you didn't really break up with him."

"I had to, Nikki. You and I both know firsthand what Sam is capable of, and I can't risk Keaton getting hurt or worse."

Holding Meridan's hands, Nikki said, "Don't let Sam dictate your life because you and Keaton belong together."

"I can't take that chance," Meridan said as tears dropped from her eyes.

"What did you tell Keaton?"

"I told him I couldn't juggle a relationship while dealing with all this drama right now. He was so pissed."

Nikki said, "He has a right to be, Dee."

She sighed. "I never did tell him that I couldn't have children. I tried, but I just couldn't do it. Besides, he deserves to be with a woman who can give him children."

Nikki asked, "So you gonna go ahead and let him walk away?"

"I have to," she whispered.

"Damn, Dee. How can you just let him go like that?"

Wiping away her tears, she said, "I have no choice."

"Yes, you do. Let this thing play out, Dee. Keaton can take care of himself."

Meridan hugged her. "Nikki, you almost died and I'm not going to give Sam a chance to hurt Keaton. Look, I'm tired of talking about it. I'm going to bed. Is there anything you need before I turn in?"

Looking out the window at the policeman stationed outside the house, she solemnly said, "Nah, Deacon's coming over later. Go ahead and get some rest. Goodnight."

"Goodnight. I love you, girl."

"I love you."

"Come get me if you need anything. I'll see you in the morning."

Meridan disappeared up the stairs. When she was out of earshot, Nichole picked up the telephone and made a call.

"Detective Miles speaking."

"Hey, babe," she said with a smile.

Deacon's sexy, bass voice said, "Hey, babe. How are you feeling?"

"I'm still sore, but I'll live," she answered. "Have you found out anything?"

"Nothing concrete, but I'm still working on a few leads. That chick is really off da hook."

Nikki poured herself a glass of wine to calm her nerves.

"When we were in college she was always aggressive in everything she did. I don't know what made her click like she did."

Deacon said, "Well, whatever it was, she's on the rampage now and she's dangerous. Do you need me to pick up anything before I come over?"

"Just you," she said with a smile.

"I think I can arrange that. I'll see you shortly."

"Thanks for everything, sweetheart."

"You're my woman. I'm supposed to take care of you."

"I know, babe. See you soon."

"Good and just know I'm doing everything I can to track that chick down. I don't know what I'll do once I get my hands on her."

Nikki swallowed hard. "I know and thank you for taking care of me."

"How's Meridan holding up?"

"Scared, confused, etc... You name it," she whispered.

"Well, let her know I'm working hard to get Sam off the streets."

"Thanks, Deacon. I'll see you later."

"No doubt and I love you."

"I love you, Deacon. Goodbye."

"Goodbye."

Hours later, Nichole wondered if Meridan was doing the right thing by breaking up with Keaton. She couldn't sleep so she decided to do a little cooking while she waited for Deacon to arrive.

As she stood there in deep thought, the officer's voice came in over the radio Deacon gave them.

"This is Samurai One calling, over."

"Yes?"

"We have a gentleman outside identified as Keaton Lapahie who said he's a friend of Miss St. John, over."

Nichole peeped out the window and saw Keaton detained by officers. She smiled and said, "He's okay, officer. Thank you."

"Ten-four."

Relief swept over her as she swung the door open with excitement. "Keaton! What are you doing here?"

He hugged her. "I see Deacon is doing a good job to protect you."

"Yes, he is." She pulled him by the hand into the house. "I'm glad you came."

"I came here to see how you were doing and to hopefully talk some sense into Meridan."

Pulling him further inside, she said, "Well, I'm doing much better and I hope you can talk some sense into her. She's miserable, Keaton."

Looking toward the stairs, he said, "Really? So am I. Nikki, what's really going on with Meridan? We had a conversation in Texas that leads me to believe she's really struggling with something from her past with this Sam person."

"I can't get in the middle of this, Keaton. Maybe now that you're here, you two can work things out."

He knew something else was going on and he was determined to finally get to the bottom of it. Looking around the room, he asked, "Where is she?"

Motioning for him to follow her into the kitchen, she said, "She went upstairs to go to bed a little while ago." Hugging him again, she said, "I'm so glad you're here."

Sampling the food Nichole was cooking, he said, "We'll see."

Sitting his glass on the counter, he smiled. "Well, I guess I'd better go on up and let her know I'm here. Wish me luck."

"Good luck, Keaton."

Nichole watched as he slowly disappeared upstairs. She prayed that tonight Meridan would finally tell Keaton everything.

Once upstairs, Keaton made his way toward Meridan's bedroom. He took a deep breath as he stood outside the door and immediately picked up her scent. He wasn't going back to Texas without knowing what was really going on with her and if she really didn't want him in her life anymore. He had to look into her eyes to accept the fact that their relationship was over. He opened the door and noticed her curled up in bed. She was sound asleep so he gently closed the door so he wouldn't wake her. Walking closer, he stood over her and watched the rhythm of her breathing. He removed his jacket and gently placed it in the chair. He sat down and removed his shoes, then climbed into bed, embracing her. Meridan shifted her position slightly as she continued to sleep. He gently kissed her neck and caressed her body. She moaned and scooted back against him. Keaton could tell she was still in a deep state of sleep when she turned to face him. She threw her arm around his waist and snuggled even closer. The urge to kiss her was too strong so he didn't fight it. He gently kissed her and ran his hands over the satin material covering her body. She responded naturally by sprinkling his neck with kisses. Keaton's body immediately responded. He never could control himself around her.

"Meridan, Baby, wake up," he whispered.

She slowly opened her eyes and, in surprise, she whispered his name. "Keaton. What are you doing here?"

He caressed her cheek. "I came to see you, sweetheart. I couldn't just let you walk away from me, now could I? I love you too much. Don't you still love me?"

Meridan ran her hands over his jean-clad body and caressed his hips. "Is it really you?"

"It's really me, Baby."

"Oh, Keaton, I'm so sorry I messed up everything. I'm so glad you're here. Hold me. I need you to hold me."

He had no problem holding her, but what he did next was even better. He removed his jeans and sweater, then climbed back into her bed. Meridan couldn't wait to feel him. Her lower body was already throbbing just from the sight of him. She squirmed closer as he positioned himself over her.

She cupped his face and breathlessly said, "Damn, I missed you."

He kissed her hungrily, neither of them caring that Nichole was downstairs. He sampled every inch of her body and then some.

"Meridan?"

"Yes?"

"I know we have a lot to talk about, but it's going to have to wait until morning. Tonight, it's about us and what we have between us."

Cuddling closer, she said, "I'm happy you're here."

Climbing on top of her body, he said, "So am I."

CHAPTER 53

I n the wee hours of the morning, Meridan woke up to find Keaton in the bathroom running a hot bath. He was still in his birthday suit and didn't see her standing there in all her glory. He turned off the water and tested the temperature. She smiled and asked, "Is it ready?"

"Did I wake you?" he asked with a smile.

"No, you didn't wake me. I guess I missed you."

He took her by the hand and led her over to the mirror. Embracing her from behind, he said, "We look good together, don't you think?"

This scene was oddly similar to the one she'd had with Sam in the hospital bathroom and it saddened her.

Meridan swallowed hard and solemnly said, "We're naked, Keaton."

Laughing, he said, "That's even better."

"I look a mess," she said as she tried to smooth down her braids.

Caressing the scar on her abdomen, he said, "You look beautiful, as always."

They stared at themselves in the mirror in silence. Keaton continued to caress her abdomen with a smile on his face.

"What are you grinning about?"

He kissed her cheek. "We've been making love most of the night and I still haven't had my fill of you. There's also another chance that I've knocked you up."

She looked away. "Is that what you want?"

"I wouldn't mind," he admitted.

She turned to him and asked seriously, "Well, do you or don't you want children? It's a simple question, Keaton. Can't you answer it?"

"Are you getting angry with me?" he asked curiously.

She closed her eyes and said, "I just need to know."

"Well, regardless of what I want, it's probably too late anyway, since we haven't used any protection at all tonight."

Meridan gave him a frustrated look and before she could speak he threw up his hands and said, "Meridan, listen to me. It doesn't matter to me one way or the other. I never planned on falling in love with anyone so I never really gave the subject of having children much thought. That was until I met you. It's you I want to marry. If you want children, we'll have children. If you don't want children, that's fine with me, too. But I will tell you this. I'll never want children with anyone except you."

Without commenting, she tried to walk away.

He pulled her back into his arms and asked, "What's wrong, Meridan? Why are you always trying to run away from me? Was it something I said?"

She couldn't look at him, but she could feel her eyes filling with tears.

He tilted her chin upward so he could see her warm eyes. He immediately noticed the tears.

"Meridan, please. For the last time, talk to me," he pleaded.

She wrapped her arms around his neck and softly said, "Because of what Sam did to me, I can't have children, Keaton, and I want children so bad. I want your babies."

Meridan had to see his reaction when she finally broke the news to him so she didn't break eye contact. The funny thing was that Keaton didn't even blink when she told him. He just continued to hold her.

Seconds later, he smiled. "Is that the real reason you've been acting so strange?"

"Yes," she admitted with sadness.

Kissing her, he said, "Well, you've wasted a lot of time and energy over nothing. I love you, Meridan, and it doesn't matter to me. If we can't have children, we can't have children. If you want a family, we can adopt. All I want is for you...no, I want *us* to be happy together. Do you understand where I'm coming from?"

"Yes, but—"

"No buts, Meridan. I need to know if you want to be my wife because I'm not planning on taking your ring back to the jewelry store, and I'm tired of carrying it around in my pocket."

Feeling somewhat relieved, she asked, "You got me a ring?"

"Stay right here."

Meridan nervously watched Keaton go back into the bedroom. He was so handsome and sexy. Walking around naked didn't seem to bother him at all; even though she was still a little self-conscious.

Keaton returned to the bathroom with a small gray velvet box. "Meridan, I've been carrying this around with me for quite sometime. I've been trying to find the right moment to propose to you. I had planned to do it on my yacht, but you changed my mind."

"Wait a minute. You mean you own that yacht?"

Grinning, he said, "Sort of. Gerald and I bought it together. I guess I'm busted, huh?"

"Why didn't you want me to know?"

"I planned to tell you, but it seemed like something kept interrupting me. Anyway, I bought this ring for you before I left Philly. When I saw it, I knew it was the one for you."

Meridan swallowed hard. "Well, can I see it?"

Keaton opened the box and Meridan gasped at the sparkling diamonds shining before her. She was frozen in her spot because she had never seen anything so beautiful and he had chosen it for her. Fighting back her emotions, she watched as he took it out of the box and reached for her hand.

Looking her in the eyes, he asked, "Meridan Gabrielle St. John, will you please marry me?"

He slid the ring onto her left hand and she said, "Perfect! Now...kiss!"

Keaton pulled her into his arms and kissed her deeper, touching her soul.

"Keaton, there's one more thing I need to tell you about my past," she said after taking a deep breath.

Confused he asked, "Talk to me! What is it, babe?"

She buried her head against his warm neck. "Keaton, remember when I told you Sam sexually assaulted me in college?"

"Yes."

She looked up into his eyes and said, "Keaton, Sam is short for Samantha. I was sexually assaulted by a woman and she can't seem to understand that I'm not gay. She had everyone on campus believing I was part of their gay lifestyle. Now she's threatening to hurt you if I continue a relationship with you."

He shook his head. "Why didn't you tell me?"

"I was afraid you would look at me differently. That you might think I really was gay; just like everyone did on campus."

"Meridan, you should've told me all of this weeks ago," he argued.

She held onto him tightly and sobbed.

"I just want this to be over, Keaton. I want Sam to stop hurting the people I love and leave me alone."

Keaton kissed her tenderly on the lips. "Meridan, I will make sure that woman never lays another hand on you. Do you understand?"

She nodded in agreement.

Minutes later, Deacon and Nichole arrived and they all met in the living room to talk about the situation and how they were going to handle it. Keaton wanted Meridan to go back to Texas with him so he could protect her.

"Keaton, I'm not going to let Sam follow me right to your house so she can hurt you. It's me she wants and it's only a matter of time before she makes a mistake. It's best I stay here," Meridan explained.

Keaton disagreed, but saw that she was not going to budge. Nichole explained how scary her ordeal was with Sam, but agreed with Meridan. They were not going to let Sam run them out of town.

Deacon calmed everyone down and told them he had a plan that would allow him to bring Sam in. Keaton reluctantly agreed to hear him out. Once they finished discussing the plan, Keaton announced that he was not going to hang around town for a few days. His hope was to bring this situation to a close for once and for all.

Keaton and Meridan made it a point to spend several days together in seclusion. They enjoyed intimate dinners out on the town and quality time around the city under very watchful eyes.

One afternoon, they even took in one of the local high school basketball games. Keaton was amazed at the number of kids who recognized him and asked for his autograph.

After they left the gymnasium, one child in particular was stopped in the hallway by a stranger.

"Hey, kid!"

The young boy looked up and said, "Yes?"

"May I see that autograph you have there?"

The young man held the piece of paper out to show the stranger.

"Thank you, Lil Man. You can go on back inside and enjoy the game now."

As the young man walked off, Samantha turned and mumbled, "Well, well, well, Meridan. Now I see why you're fighting me so hard. It's too bad you won't be able to enjoy Mr. Keaton 'The Chief' Lapahie much longer."

The next day, Keaton and Meridan said their regretful goodbyes. It hurt him deeply to go back to Texas without her, after vowing their love for each other. This trip was the turning point in their relationship. He would continue to worry about her safety until Sam was arrested, but one thing comforted him on his journey: the fact that Meridan was his and Deacon was close to catching Sam. He boarded the plane to Texas, leaving all his trust in Deacon to protect the love of his life.

CHAPTER 54

A week had passed since Keaton had reluctantly returned to Texas alone and Sam was still on the loose. As he gave the evening crew at his restaurant their instructions, he said goodnight to Trenton, then walked out into the warm evening air to his car. Keaton loved his car, but not as much as he loved Meridan. He had recently had his Mercedes detailed and it looked good.

Today, he decided to go by his yacht to make preparations to stay there the night of the fund-raiser. In the morning, he would call Winston and let him know that he would go ahead and sign the deed for their new summer home after all. First, he would go by his house to get a change of clothes. He might just stay on the yacht tonight instead of returning home because he needed some time to reflect on the recent changes in his life.

Daydreaming, he drove toward his house with a slight smile on his face when "Reasons" by Earth, Wind and Fire boomed through the speakers. That was the song he had danced with Meridan on at her father's birthday celebration. He recalled how heavenly it felt holding her and he missed that feeling.

As he crested a large hill and descended, he noticed something different about his car. Pressing on the brakes, the car seemed to accelerate even more. He tried pumping the pedal, then realized he didn't have any brakes. His stomach turned upside-down as he tried to concentrate on steering the vehicle. Maneuvering the car wasn't easy; especially at this high rate of speed. Cars blasted their horns at him as he crossed the center line to maintain control. Coming up was a three-way intersection and he prayed he would escape death as he neared it. He finally saw something up ahead that could possibly save his life. All he had to do was get to it without getting broadsided.

Keaton pressed his horn, hopefully to alert drivers that he was coming through. After saying a short prayer he barreled through the intersection. A pickup truck narrowly missed him as his Mercedes plowed into a large row of neatly rolled hay. The force of the crash immediately released the airbags. Keaton sat stunned and dazed from his ordeal. He opened the door and slowly got out of the car, shaken, but okay.

An hour or so later, he watched as the tow truck pulled his car out of the field. Paramedics were called to the scene by witnesses to his crash, but he refused to go to the hospital. Instead he was treated for a small bump on the head, which could've been worse had it not been for the airbags.

Turning toward the tow truck driver, he said, "Bobby, if you don't mind, I would appreciate it if you could drop me off at my house down the road."

"No problem, Mr. Lapahie."

Keaton climbed into the tow truck and pulled out his cell phone. He called the car dealership that would be working on his car. He explained to them what happened and told them if anything showed up suspicious to call him immediately. Keaton hung up the telephone and gazed out the window of the truck. His head was throbbing so under the instructions of the paramedics, he would take some pain medicine and call it a night. He didn't want to worry his parents or Meridan until he knew what was wrong with his car. Until then, he would only tell him the vehicle was being serviced.

Later that evening, Meridan sat alone in her house severely distraught. If she didn't love Keaton so much, he would never be in danger.

The telephone startled her out of her daze. When she answered, Mr. St. John said, "Hey, Baby Girl! How are you doing?"

"I'm doing fine, Daddy."

"Have you decided if you're going to Texas for the fund-raiser?"

"I don't think so," she answered solemnly.

With concern in his voice, he asked, "Why not?"

Sighing, she said, "I have a lot of work to catch up on, Daddy."

"Well, you told his parents you were coming so you need to stick to your word. Do you understand?" She did not respond. "Meridan?"

In a whisper, she answered, "I'm here, Daddy."

The tears started flowing heavily. Actually, she started sobbing. Mr. St. John felt sorry for his daughter. He tried to console her the best way he could from so far away.

"Meridan, I wish there was something I could say or do to make things better for you. You know I love you and I'm sure everything will work out fine. Hang in there, kid, and, in the meantime, be careful."

Her voice was cracking. "Thanks, Daddy. I'll talk to you later."

"Goodbye, sweetheart."

Another called beeped in on the line. "I have to go, Daddy. I have another call."

"Okay, Meridan. I'll call you tomorrow."

"Goodbye, Daddy." Meridan clicked over and said, "Hello?"

There was a brief silence before she heard, "What's up, babe?"

Disgusted, she yelled, "I'm getting sick of you!"

Laughing, she said, "Meridan, my love, you might feel like that right now, but I'm going to make you so happy. Did you get rid of your little boyfriend like I told you to?"

"Yes!"

"You're lying! I saw his punk ass with you last week! Did you sleep with him?"

"That is none of your goddamn business! You need to stop spying on me and my house, and who I sleep with is none of your business!"

"Oh, but it is! You will be mine one way or the other!"

"You're dreaming, you bitch!"

"If you think I'm playing, Meridan, you'd better think again! If you don't believe me, you'd better check with your little boyfriend. He went on the ride of his life today. Hee…hee…hee!"

Meridan slammed the telephone down and noticed her hands were trembling. She worriedly picked up the telephone to call Keaton.

"Hello?"

"Keaton? Are you okay? Did something happen to you today?"

"Calm down, babe. I'm okay, but my car isn't doing so good. I believe someone tampered with my brakes and I suspect it could've been Sam."

She covered her mouth and cried, "Oh, my God! Baby, I'm sorry."

He stood and walked around the room. "It's not your fault, Meridan."

She whispered, "Are you okay?"

"Besides a bump on the head, I'll be fine, but I'll be better once I have you back here with me."

She let out a breath. "You know, Keaton, I feel the same way. I'm tired of being afraid and putting my life on hold. I want Sam to come after me so I can look her in the eyes right before I—"

"Hold on, Meridan! Don't go trying to be a hero. Let Deacon keep doing what he's doing. I don't believe we have much longer to wait before Sam is caught," he begged.

"I guess you're right," she answered. "Have you called Deacon and told him what happened?"

"Yes, he's waiting for the inspection report from my brakes."

Silence surrounded them.

"Keaton, please be careful. If Sam did this to your car, then it means she's in Texas."

"I will and you do the same. I love you."

"I love you, too. I'll call you in the morning."

Sam sat in the hotel room flicking the channels on the TV. Her conversation with Meridan earlier had finally sunk in. There was no way in hell Meridan was going to stay away from Keaton with a little incentive from her.

She sat there surfing the channels until she came upon CNN. The reporters were talking about all the upcoming elections. One in particular that caught her eye was of a tight race in Texas. Sam sat up after she recognized Keaton in a photograph standing next to Judge Lapahie. He turned up the volume and listened to every detail.

One close race in San Antonio, Texas is between Judge Herbert Lapahie and Alonzo Alvarez. Judge Lapahie has sat on the bench in San Antonio for several years. He is seen here with his family on victory night of the primaries. Judge Lapahie will end his campaign with a huge fund-raiser at the Montrose Hotel next month. Doctor Alonzo Alvarez, the incumbent, expects Judge Lapahie to give him a run for his money. Now, over in South Carolina, we have another close race—

Laughing, she said, "Well, I'll be damned."

She bent down and took a sniff of a white powdery substance, sat back, and closed her eyes with a huge smile on her face.

Nichole was in deep thought as she twirled around in her chair. She was back at work, but she couldn't concentrate. Putting her ink pen down, she picked up the telephone and dialed.

"Deacon Miles speaking."

"Hey, babe. Have you had any luck yet?"

"Not yet. Sam is being very careful, but I've got a feeling her luck is about to run out."

She smiled. "It has to. Meridan's miserable being away from Keaton, and I'm tired over looking of my shoulder."

"I know, babe. I'm working as hard as I can," he responded.

"I'm sorry, Deacon. I'm just on edge," she said with a smile. "Are you still cooking dinner for me tonight?"

"You bet! I'll have it ready by the time you get there."

"Thanks, boo."

"No problem, sweetheart. I'll see you later."

CHAPTER 55

K eaton sat in his office going over paperwork. It was just numbers on paper to him. He wasn't mentally deciphering any of the figures, because his mind was elsewhere. He picked up the telephone and dialed Mr. St. John. Things were beginning to get serious and some extra precautions needed to be taken. Since he was going to Meridan's father's wedding, he needed to be even more careful so he decided to call William.

Mr. St. John answered, "Hello?"

"Hello, William. It's Keaton."

"Keaton! I'm so glad you called. I was just getting ready to call you and make sure you were still coming to my wedding this Saturday."

"I wouldn't miss it for the world, William."

Satisfied, William said, "Good! The ceremony starts at four o'clock and it's at the church down the street from the house."

"I'll be there," he acknowledged. "Oh, William, there's one more thing. The reason I called was to tell you that someone tampered with the brakes on my car. I can't help but suspect this Sam person but, then again, Jacob's not too happy with me either."

Alarmed, William asked, "What happened? Were you injured?"

"I crashed my car, but luckily I only got a bump on the head. The mechanic said the lines were definitely cut and I've reported it to the police."

"Does Meridan know?"

"Yes, I told her even though I didn't want to worry her any more than she already was. That's why I think we need to talk about security for the wedding.

I don't put anything past Sam, and she might be looking for an event like this to make a move on Meridan."

William St. John was at his rope's end. Clearing his throat, William said, "You're right, Keaton. Be careful and I'll pick you up from the airport. Just call me back later with your flight information."

"Will do. Thanks, William."

"No, thank you for caring about my daughter so much."

"It's my honor," he responded before hanging up the telephone.

Keaton hung up and placed a call to Jacob's office in Atlanta. The receptionist told him that Jacob had taken an indefinite leave of absence due to health reasons. Hanging up, Keaton pondered on this new information. If Jacob was on medical leave, it was looking more and more like Sam was the culprit for tampering with his brakes. Right now, there was no telling where Samantha was and what she was up to. Looking at his watch, he called Deacon to get an update on his search for Sam. Hopefully he would have some new leads.

A few days later, Meridan and Nichole woke up in Meridan's Mississippi bedroom. After eating breakfast, they hurriedly dressed so they could get to the church to help Gwendolyn decorate the sanctuary for their father's wedding. It was their father's wedding day so they wanted everything perfect. Meridan didn't want to damper anyone's spirits with her problems.

It was going to be a unique wedding because Ms. Leona wanted everyone to dress in white for the wedding. She was going to be wearing pink and thought it would be a nice contrast. Meridan chose a strapless gown that fit snug to her figure. Gwendolyn would wear a beautiful white suit that had a long skirt and a slit up the back. Nichole bought a conservative white linen pantsuit.

Later that afternoon as they dressed quietly, Gwendolyn asked Meridan, "Are you okay, sis?"

"I'm fine, Gwendolyn. I haven't been getting much sleep lately," she admitted.

She held her hand and said, "Meridan, we all love you and I know you've been a little stressed, but things will be okay sooner than you think."

Smiling, Meridan said, "That's what I'm hoping for, Gwendolyn. Now we'd better get over to the church. The ceremony will be starting in thirty minutes."

Gwendolyn picked up her purse and asked, "Is Keaton coming to the wedding?"

"I don't know. So much has been going on that we never did talk about it."

Checking her makeup one last time, Gwendolyn said, "Well, I hope he makes it. Hey! I heard that Jacob was sick. Have you talked to him?"

Frowning, Meridan said, "No, I haven't talked to him in a while. Jacob knows he's burned his bridges with me, but I hope he's okay."

Fluffing her hair, Gwendolyn said, "Me, too. On that note, I guess we'd better get going, ladies. You look beautiful."

In unison, Nichole and Meridan said, "So do you."

Meridan wrapped her arm around Gwendolyn's waist and said, "Girl, I'm surprised Thomas is letting you wear that skirt."

Smiling, Gwendolyn said, "I don't know what you're talking about. He was the one who bought it."

They all laughed together and headed out the door to the church.

At the church, family and close friends gathered to witness the joining of William St. John and Leona Gilbert. Gwendolyn, Meridan, and the rest of the immediate family took their seats at the front of the church. They hadn't seen their father since earlier that morning and they were anxious to see him. As they sat there, an usher walked down the aisle and handed Meridan a note.

Meridan,
I need to see you in the minister's office before the ceremony.
Love,
Daddy

She eyed it suspiciously as she read it. Confused, she showed the note to

Gwendolyn, then excused herself from the sanctuary. When Meridan opened the door to the minister's office, she saw William dressed handsomely in his black tuxedo. At his side was his brother, Conrad St. John. Meridan looked at her father in confusion and when she walked in, a chill ran over her body as she came face to face with Keaton.

She gasped.

"Keaton! You made it!"

Keaton stood there looking unbelievably handsome in his black suit. He smiled and walked over to her.

Leaning down, he kissed her softly on the lips. "Hello, beautiful. I've missed you and I wouldn't miss this wedding for anything."

She smiled with joy. "I was hoping you'd make it."

William said, "Honey, I asked you in here so Keaton could assure you that everything is going to be okay. I know you've been under a lot of stress, Baby, and you know we wouldn't let anything happen to you."

Tears formed in her eyes as she listened to her father's words.

"I'll leave you two alone for a moment." Looking at his watch, he said, "You guys have five minutes."

Finally alone, Keaton said, "Meridan, you look absolutely breathtaking."

Blushing, she replied, "Thank you. You look handsome yourself."

"Thank you."

Caressing her arm, he continued saying, "Your father told me you've been stressing since you've been here, and I want you to know that we went through great lengths to make sure you would feel safe. We hired security guards to be here to protect everyone, in case Sam tries to show up."

Shocked, she said, "Really? I didn't see any security guards."

"You won't see them. They're blending in with the guests so relax and enjoy. Okay?"

Meridan took a deep breath and said, "I'll try."

They kissed each other passionately one last time before William tapped on the door. "Hurry up in there, you two. You're holding up our wedding."

Meridan yelled, "We're coming in just a minute!"

Before leaving the room, Meridan said, "I love you, Keaton."

"I love you, Meridan."

"I guess we need to get out of here before Daddy comes in here after us."

Taking her hand into his, he said, "Let's go, beautiful."

They returned to the sanctuary and witnessed the marital joining of William and Leona St. John.

Thankfully, Sam stayed away and the wedding went off without any problems.

CHAPTER 56

A couple of weeks later, Meridan received an urgent message that Jacob was very ill in a Florida hospital. Her mind told her not to go visit him, but her heart told her she couldn't let their friendship end this way; especially since he was ill. Against her better judgment, she caught a flight to Miami to visit him.

Upon arriving, she caught a cab and made her way to the hospital. As soon as she stepped off the elevator, she knew how sick Jacob was.

As she entered his room, she walked over to his bed and whispered, "You're always trying to get attention, aren't you?"

He forced a grin. "Thanks for coming, Meridan."

Meridan sat down. "You know, this was hard for me; especially after what you did."

He looked up toward the ceiling. "I'm so sorry I tripped out on you like that. It was the drugs, Meridan. You know that wasn't me."

She tried to swallow the lump in her throat but it wouldn't go down. "Why are you messing with drugs anyway?"

He turned away. "I don't know. Stupid, I guess."

Looking around his room, she asked, "How long are you going to be in here?"

"I don't know. I hope not long. They want me to get a little stronger first."

"I see," she answered with sadness.

Curious, he asked, "So, are you still with that guy?"

She folded her arms. "I'm trying to be and, if you're asking me if I love him, the answer is yes."

"Then why the long face?"

She sighed. "Do you remember that girl, Samantha, who stabbed me?"

He sat up and frowned. "How can I forget that crazy Amazon? What has she done now?"

Meridan stood and walked over to the window. "She's out of jail and she's after me. She's trying to force me into a homosexual affair with her."

Jacob laughed and said, "You're shitting me!"

"It's not funny, Jacob. She's threatening to kill me. She already shot and nearly killed my friend, Nikki. Thank God, she's okay now."

Jacob sat up in bed. "You're serious, aren't you?"

Meridan sat back down. "I wouldn't joke about something like this. She told me to stay away from Keaton or she's going to hurt him. I think she tampered with the brakes on his car. It nearly killed him."

Jacob couldn't believe what he was hearing. He wiped his eyes and said, "You know that chick did look a little scary in court. You be careful because it sounds to me that she's not playing."

"You don't have to tell me," she responded.

"Damn, Meridan!"

She laid her head down on the side of his bed and said, "I'm scared, Jacob."

"What is that dude, Keaton, doing about it?"

Mumbling, Meridan said, "He's mad as hell. I told him to stay away from me until the police find her so he won't get hurt."

"Now you know that man's not going to do that," Jacob added.

She looked up at him and said, "He doesn't have a choice. He came to Philly to get me but I told him things would be better if he stayed in San Antonio."

"He's a fool!"

"No, he's not. He doesn't know what she looks like, Jacob. It would be easy for Sam to hurt or kill him. You know if she tried to kill me, she wouldn't think twice about doing something to Keaton," she said in frustration.

Taking a sip of water, he said, "I guess you're right."

She walked over to the window and softly said, "I'm supposed to go to San Antonio to his dad's fund-raising dinner that's coming up, but I don't know."

"You should go," he urged.

"Why?"

Jacob sighed. "Well, you say he's your man so, if that's true, you should be by his side. This campaign thing is a big deal. I saw his father on CNN a while back. He's in a tough race."

Toying with her hair, she said, "I don't know."

"You have nothing to worry about. I'll tell you what. I'll be your guardian angel looking out for you while you're there."

She laughed and said, "Yeah, right!"

He looked at her seriously and said, "I'm dead serious, Meridan. I won't let anything happen to you. Okay? I owe you that after what I did."

Humoring him, she said, "Okay, Jacob, you can be my guardian angel."

He clasped his hands together and said, "With that settled, I want to thank you for coming down to see me and I want to apologize again for everything that happened between us. You're my only friend, Meridan, and if there's anything I can do to help, you just say the word."

Meridan smiled. "You hurry up and get out of this hospital."

Solemnly, he asked, "Can you find it in your heart to forgive me, Meridan?"

She held his hand. Squeezing it, she smiled and said, "Yes, Jacob, I forgive you."

He laid his head back against the pillow and whispered, "Thank you, Meridan. Now tell me about your dad's wedding. Mom says everyone's talking about it. I know he's pissed off at me right now."

"That's an understatement. He's not happy with you at all," she admitted. "He was ready to give you a beat down."

Staring across the room, he thought about the night he shot at Devon and Keyshaun. He turned to Meridan and said, "Babe, I've done a lot of foul things over the past few months. Some that I'm very ashamed of, but I promise you, from this day forward, I'm going to do right."

She hugged him. "Good!"

A heavy burden had been lifted off his heart with Meridan's forgiveness. He also thought of the perfect way he could redeem himself in this lifetime. He would make sure Sam never hurt Meridan again.

Meridan's plane landed in Philly right on time. She'd spent two days with Jacob and mended their bruised friendship. As she walked through the airport, her cell phone rang.

"Hello?"

"Meridan, I admire what you did, but I can't say I agree with you."

"Keaton, try to understand. Jacob and I go way back. Yes, he acted like an ass, but I decided to forgive him and put it behind me. He's sick. Can't you understand that?"

He was quiet for a moment on the other end. Meridan grabbed her luggage and headed out the door.

"Keaton?"

"I'm here. Look, Meridan, this thing is getting ridiculous and we're not getting anywhere. I want you here with me."

Climbing into the cab, she said, "I know, babe. I wish things could be different right now, but they can't and I'm sorry."

"You're still not coming to Daddy's fund-raiser?"

"I'm not sure, but just in case, give my love to your parents and the rest of your family. I love you."

Hurt and feeling abandoned, he said, "Look, I'll talk to you later. I love you, Meridan."

"Bye, babe."

"Goodbye, Meridan, and stay safe."

"I will."

She hung up the telephone and rode the rest of the way in deep thought.

CHAPTER 57

Days later, it was the night of the big fund-raiser and Keaton didn't know why he let Gerald talk him into picking him up. Gerald had always been a party guy and he knew tonight would be no different. He wasn't in the party mood, but could use some cheering up. He missed Meridan terribly since he'd seen her in Mississippi. He wanted to hold her. He knew he was going to have to do a lot of acting tonight since the media would be focusing on his family. It was going to be hard to smile without Meridan by his side.

Eyeing himself in his tuxedo, he took one last glance in the mirror. The doorbell rang and he knew Gerald was downstairs waiting. Opening the door, he found Gerald and two women dressed in formal gowns standing there.

Shocked, he asked, "What have you done?"

"Keaton, I would like you to meet Amelia Monroe. Amelia, this is my best friend, Keaton Lapahie. You know Keisha already."

Keaton reluctantly extended his hand and said, "It's nice to meet you, Amelia." He then turned to Keisha. "Hello, Keisha."

Keisha hugged Keaton and said, "It's about time you came back to Texas."

Keaton smiled. "Thanks. Come in and have a seat. Ladies, please excuse us for a minute."

The ladies sat down and Keaton hustled Gerald out of the room. Inside the kitchen, he said, "Gerald, why'd you bring that woman here?"

Smiling, he said, "I figured you didn't really want to go without a date tonight, so I thought I'd hook you up."

"Gerald, I'm able to get my own date if I want one. Damn! You know the press is going to be there tonight! What if Meridan sees me in the paper with this woman?"

Gerald grabbed some bottled water from the refrigerator and said, "I'm sorry. Man, I didn't know. I thought you and Meridan haven't been able to make this thing work and you've been so down lately. I thought you could use some cheering up and some company. Amelia's nice and she's fine, too."

Keaton looked at Gerald, then his watch. "Don't do this shit again. Let's go before we're late."

Opening the door, Keaton saw the limo outside. Gerald smiled and said, "You know I only travel in style. Come on, man! We're going to have fun tonight."

At the hotel, Keaton greeted some of his family members. He was also happy to see Mr. St. John and Ms. Leona in attendance. He walked up to Mr. St. John and extended his hand. Instead of shaking it, he pulled Keaton into a warm embrace. In his ear, he said, "It's so nice to see you again, Keaton."

Releasing him, Keaton said, "Same to you, William. You look beautiful, Leona."

"Why thank you, Keaton. You look dashing yourself."

Taking a deep breath, he asked, "Thank you."

They made eye contact in silence for a moment, then William said, "Well, let me go thank your parents for inviting us. I'll talk to you a little later. Okay?"

"Okay. I hope you enjoy your evening."

"I'm sure we will. See you later."

Keaton finally found Arnelle and Winston. They were there along with the children. Winston walked over and put his arm around Keaton's neck. "How are you holding up, my man?"

Shoving his hands in his pockets, he said, "I'll live."

"You know I'm not going to hold you to that bet," Winston said as he sipped champagne.

"Nah, bro. I have no problem buying the house with you. Besides, it'll be a nice getaway for me."

"Thanks, brother-in-law. Hang in there," he said as he patted him on the shoulder. "Aight?"

"I'll try," Keaton answered.

Winston turned Keaton in the opposite direction and asked, "Who's the runway model you walked in with?"

Frowning, he said, "Some woman Gerald set me up with."

Grinning, Winston said, "Not bad."

Rolling his eyes, Keaton said, "Yeah, whatever. Look, I'm going over to see Arnelle and the kids. I'll meet you over at the table."

"Okay. Take care of yourself."

Winston watched a broken Keaton weed his way through the crowd, shaking hands with business and personal friends of his father's.

The moment had come for everyone to take their seats. Judge Lapahie went to the microphone and began to welcome everyone to the event. Keaton took his seat at the table with his mother, his sister and her family, along with Mr. St. John and Ms. Leona. Keaton couldn't help but stare at the empty seat next to him and feel sad.

After Judge Lapahie's speech, the waiters and waitresses started bringing out the dinner.

MaLeah looked at Arnelle and loudly said, "Momma! I have to tee tee!"

Arnelle looked at MaLeah and said, "Shh, MaLeah, not so loud. Come with Momma."

Keaton didn't really have an appetite. He looked at Arnelle and said, "I need some air. I'll walk you guys to the restroom."

Walking alongside Arnelle, he swung MaLeah up into his arms and kissed her chubby cheek. There were people coming and going throughout the hotel. He kind of felt bad that he hadn't spent any time getting to know Amelia. The fact was, he wasn't in the mood to be sociable and he couldn't wait until the night was over.

Once they reached the restroom, he sat down in the hallway on a sofa and rested his elbows on his legs. Holding his head in his hands, he sat there in silence and in deep thought. Out of nowhere, a soft hand rested on his shoulder.

In his ear, an angelic voice whispered, "Are you out here waiting for me?"

Keaton knew he had to be dreaming. He slowly looked up and found Meridan standing over him. He didn't want to get too excited; even though his heart was about to jump out of his chest.

He stood and said, "Hello, sweetheart."

"Hello, Keaton."

"I didn't expect you here," he said with a smile.

"Neither did I."

Turning to look over her shoulder, she said, "I had some help getting here."

Keaton looked up and saw Nichole and Gwendolyn waving at him. Both were dressed beautifully in their gowns, but neither could shine a light to the dress Meridan wore.

She looked so beautiful and her burgundy, beaded gown hugged her curves and sparkled in the soft lighting from the hotel. She was wearing her hair layered, which fell lovingly to her shoulders. Keaton took in every detail of her body. Her eyes shimmered and he could tell she was a little nervous.

He stood slowly and pulled her into his arms. He softly said, "Well, I'm glad you decided to come."

Looking into his eyes, she said, "So am I."

"Are you hungry?"

"Just a little bit."

"Your father's here with Ms. Leona."

Taking his arm, she said, "He told me they were coming."

Keaton couldn't stand it any longer. He cupped her face and lowered his mouth to hers. He didn't care who saw them, and if photographers were going to take any pictures of him, this was the one he wanted on the front page.

Burying his face against her neck, he whispered, "Damn! I've missed you."

She nuzzled his neck and said, "I've missed you, too."

Keaton escorted Meridan to the table to join his family. He also found seats for Nichole and Gwendolyn. Winston and the rest of the family looked up in surprise as Keaton and Meridan joined them. Mr. St. John smiled as he stood to greet his daughters.

He hugged and kissed Meridan and said, "I'm glad you made it, baby girl."

"Me too, Daddy."

Keaton held out her seat for her as she sat down. She made eye contact with Ms. Leona, who winked at her.

Meridan smiled and said, "Good evening, everyone."

They all acknowledged her, returning the greeting. Arnelle and MaLeah returned to the table. She looked over, noticing Meridan. She ran around the table and hugged her neck. "I'm so glad you made it, Meridan. You look stunning," Arnelle said excitedly.

"Thank you, Arnelle. So do you."

MaLeah stood behind her mother, waiting for her turn.

"Dr. MeMe!"

Meridan stretched out her arms to give MaLeah a hug and kiss. She stood to give Fredrick a kiss also. Judge Lapahie and Zenora exchanged hugs with Meridan before starting dinner. When she made it back to her seat, Keaton spontanoeously took her hand and stroked it lovingly. She looked into his eyes, leaned over, and kissed him tenderly. Meridan's cell phone rang, causing them to break their kiss.

"Excuse me, everyone. I meant to turn this off," she said as she switched off her telephone. "Hello? Hello? Is anyone there?"

Keaton looked at her and asked, "Is everything okay?"

"Everything's fine."

Keaton frowned and asked, "Are you sure?"

"I'm sure; now stop worrying."

He leaned closer and said, "Just so you know, we have security guards here. I left specific instructions for them not to take their eyes off you, but not to stare too hard."

She smiled, gave his hand a loving squeeze, and said, "Thanks for telling me."

CHAPTER 58

The Lapahie family ate dinner and enjoyed each other's company. Judge Lapahie made a brief speech to his supporters, which was answered by a thunderous applause.

It wasn't until later that Keaton remembered he had another date at the dinner. He explained Amelia to Meridan, then asked her to excuse him so he could bid the young woman goodnight. He made his way over to the table where Gerald and the ladies were sitting.

He sat down and said, "Amelia, I'm sorry about my distance this evening. You see...Gerald was trying to help by getting me a date for tonight. Unfortunately, my date was able to make it after all. I apologize for any inconvenience this may have caused you and I'm sure you are a remarkable woman."

"Thank you, Keaton. I guess I'm a little too late, huh?"

Smiling, he said, "I'm sorry. Please feel free to stay and enjoy the rest of the evening."

Shaking his hand she said, "Thank you, I will. Your lady friend is a lucky woman."

"Thank you, but I feel like I'm the lucky one," he said as he stood up. Keaton looked over at Gerald, winked, and said, "I'll holler at you later."

"No problem. Thanks for the invite. Go handle your business."

Once dinner was over, Judge Lapahie had interviews with members of the media. Keaton and Meridan strolled through the ballroom together thanking the guests for coming.

After the interviews, Judge Lapahie came over and announced, "Everyone, come over here. I want to get a family picture."

Keaton grabbed Meridan's hand and followed his dad. Chairs were being positioned for the ladies to sit in near a beautiful floral arrangement.

Meridan said, "I'll wait for you here. Go take your picture."

"What? You're going to be in it with me."

Shaking her head, she said, "No, Keaton, your father said 'family.'"

He looked at her seriously and said, "I know what he said. Now, come on."

Judge Lapahie was helping to get his grandchildren in position with Arnelle and Winston. He looked over, seeing Meridan's reluctance. Smiling, he went over and said, "Meridan, I want you, your sister, your best friend, William and Leona all in the picture."

"Are you sure?"

Kissing her cheek, he said, "Most definitely. Keaton, you and Meridan go stand next to your mother. William! You and Leona and the young ladies stand next to Winston."

Posing, Meridan said, "I don't believe this."

Keaton kissed her neck. "What? That this picture will probably be on the front page of the paper tomorrow? Or that you're in it?"

Looking up at him, she said, "All of the above."

The photographer aimed his camera and said, "Okay, everyone. On three, so get ready. Here we go...One, two, three."

The camera clicked, taking the picture.

Zenora pulled Meridan over to meet a major client of hers after several pictures were made. While Meridan was talking to the gentleman, she tried to find Nichole and Gwendolyn in the crowd. Her conversation with Zenora's client ended when he was summoned by another guest. As she worked her way through the crowd, Keaton met her halfway.

He took her hand and asked, "Meridan, are you ready to get out of here?"

Sighing, she said, "More than you can imagine. It's been a long day."

"Before we leave, I need to get some things from the suite upstairs. Hold my jacket and I'll be right down," he said as he kissed her quickly on the lips.

She blushed. "I'll be right here."

Meridan watched as Keaton and an undercover security guard made their way toward the elevator. He waved back at her as the doors closed.

She walked over to the table and sat down. When she laid Keaton's jacket across her lap, the hotel key fell out of his pocket and onto the floor. She reached down and picked up the key. She looked around and spotted Arnelle. She walked over to her and said, "Arnelle, Keaton went up to the suite to get his things, but he forgot the key. What room is it?"

Arnelle shook her head and said, "That sounds just like him. It's room 614 and when you see him, tell him—"

At that moment there was a loud commotion at one of the ballroom doors, interrupting their conversation. It was a large group of protesters chanting their opposition to Judge Lapahie.

"What the hell?" Arnelle searched the crowd for her family. "I'll be back, Meridan. I've got to find Winston and the kids."

Meridan grabbed Arnelle's hand. "If I miss Keaton on the way up, let him know I'm looking for him."

Arnelle nervously looked around and said, "Meridan, why don't you wait until he comes back down. You don't need to go up there by yourself and I don't know who the guards are."

At that moment, they heard a scream. Meridan had to get out of there. Arnelle ran toward the stage so she could spot her family members easier.

Meridan noticed people gathering to see what was going on while organizers were trying to get the protesters out of the room. Meridan saw this as an opportunity to get to the elevators to find Keaton.

Upstairs Keaton and his security guard arrived at the door. Keaton reached inside his pants pocket and yelled, "Damn!"

"What is it, sir?"

"I left the key downstairs in my jacket."

The guard looked down the hallway and noticed a maid pushing a linen cart. He motioned for her to come assist them. Keaton was somewhat embarrassed that he had left his key downstairs.

The maid approached and asked, "How may I help you?"

The guard showed her his identification and Keaton did the same.

"Ma'am, if you would be so kind to let Mr. Lapahie into his room. He mistakenly left his key downstairs in his jacket."

The maid looked at their identification, then at her clipboard to verify the information. Satisfied she said, "Sure, Sir."

Keaton and the guard stepped aside so the maid could unlock the door. They walked in and the maid closed the door behind them.

Meridan's heart was beating wildly as she rode up the elevator in silence. Once she reached the designated floor, she stepped out and headed toward the suite. As she got closer to the room she heard angry voices. When she slid the card key into the slot and opened the door, she gasped.

"Oh my God!"

Meridan looked down and saw the bloody body of the guard on the floor.

"Meridan! Get out of here!" Keaton yelled.

She was frozen in fear when she looked up and saw Sam dressed in a maid's uniform holding a gun on Keaton. Sam motioned for her to go move over next to Keaton, which she hurriedly did.

"Meridan, you're trembling," Sam said sarcastically. "What's wrong? Cat got your tongue? Hmm, and I must say you have a delicious tongue."

Keaton gritted his teeth and said, "You bitch!"

Laughing, Sam said, "What's wrong, playboy? You're just mad because I've had a taste of your girl here?"

Meridan was angry and scared. "Why are you doing this, Sam? Why don't you leave me alone?"

"No can do, babe," Sam boasted. "I'm going to have you right here, right now, and I'm going to let your boy here have a ringside seat."

Meridan began to cry.

"Get into the bedroom!" Sam yelled angrily.

Keaton said, "You must be crazy if you think I'm going to stand here and let you do anything to her!"

She pointed the gun directly at Keaton and asked, "Oh! Do you want to be a hero tonight? Huh, playboy?"

"I don't care what you do to me, but you're not going to hurt Meridan!" he screamed.

Sam yelled, "I said, get into the goddamn bedroom!"

Keaton took a step toward Sam, but Meridan grabbed his arm, stopping him. It was obvious Samantha was unstable.

Staring at the gun, Meridan asked, "Sam, haven't you ruined my life enough? Put the gun down!" she begged.

"No! I'm tired of people coming between us!" she yelled.

Crying, Meridan said, "Why can't you understand that I'm not like you?"

Sam shook the gun at Keaton. "You're not supposed to be standing here anyway. I loved the way your car zoomed down that hill. I wasn't counting on that truck missing you though."

Making fists, Keaton said, "I knew it was you who tampered with my brakes!"

Meridan yelled, "You're going to end up back in that horrible place you just got out of, or dead!"

Keaton stood there trying to think of something to do to distract Sam and his wait wasn't long.

Aiming the gun at Keaton, she said, "You know what? Maybe I should go ahead and get rid of you. Say goodbye to your lover boy, Meridan, because starting tonight, it's going to be just you and me."

Meridan's eyes widened as she watched Sam's finger squeeze the trigger. At that moment, Jacob burst through the door and yelled, "Sam!"

She turned and fired, missing Jacob. He shot back, striking her in the neck.

Keaton shielded Meridan from the gunfire as he knocked her to the floor. As Sam lay bleeding, Jacob walked over and stood over them. He asked, "Are you guys okay?"

Keaton looked up at Jacob in disbelief. As he helped Meridan up off the floor, he said, "Thank you, Jacob."

He blew his breath across the nozzle of the gun and said, "Don't mention it. I had to do something to help out my homegirl."

Meridan hugged Jacob tightly and whispered, "Thank you, Jacob. You saved our lives."

Jacob smiled. "I told you I'd be your guardian angel, didn't I? That Amazon got what she deserved for hurting you."

Before Meridan could respond, another shot rang out in the room. Keaton turned and realized that Sam still had her weapon in her hand. The bullet struck Jacob in the back and, since Meridan was still holding onto him, they both fell to the floor. Keaton picked up Jacob's gun, but before he could shoot, security guards and several police officers stormed the room. As they apprehended Sam, they realized she had expired and she was quickly pronounced dead at the scene. The officers went over to assist Jacob and he also was pronounced dead at the scene, as well as the guard who was with Keaton.

Everything was moving so fast and what Keaton hadn't realized was that the bullet that struck Jacob had passed through his body into Meridan. Keaton looked down and yelled, "No!"

A policeman yelled, "Is she breathing?"

Another officer yelled, "I think so! Get some help in here!"

A guard checked Meridan's pulse and yelled in the radio, "I need LifeFlight here, now!"

Keaton cradled her lifeless body in his arms in total hysterics as she lay bleeding. Officers tried their best to comfort him.

"She's going to be all right, man. Talk to her," one of them urged.

Keaton leaned down and whispered the depth of his love in her ear. Luckily, there were paramedics onsite and, within minutes, they were on the scene. They rushed in to give medical attention to her and, at the same time, Arnelle walked through the door. She screamed when she saw Meridan bleeding on the floor.

An officer comforted her and said, "It's okay, we're taking care of her."

She ran over to Keaton and frantically asked, "Keaton! Are you okay?"

He mumbled, "I'm fine, but Meridan's hurt bad."

"Oh my God!"

The paramedics were working frantically to save Meridan's life.

A plainclothes detective walked into the room and asked, "Sir, can you identify this gentleman?"

With sadness, Keaton explained, "That's Jacob Richardson, her childhood friend. He saved our lives." Keaton looked up at a guard and asked, "How did this happen?"

The guard said, "I'm sorry, Sir, but some protesters stormed the ballroom, distracting everyone. We lost sight of Miss St. John in the crowd. You have my deepest apology."

Watching the paramedics work on her, Keaton mumbled incoherently, "How am I going to tell her father? He's downstairs and has to know something has happened!"

Arnelle tearfully said, "I'll get him, Keaton. You ride along with Meridan and we'll meet you at the hospital."

Keaton stood there in a daze, unable to tear his eyes away from Meridan as they put her on the stretcher.

Arnelle hugged Keaton and yelled, "Keaton, she'll be okay…go! I got this."

Keaton followed the paramedics out of room and up to the roof for air transport to the hospital.

CHAPTER 59

At the hospital, Keaton and all the rest of the family paced the floor as they waited for Meridan to get out of surgery. William had been in the hospital chapel for a while praying. Keaton slowly made his way to the chapel to join him.

He sat down next to him in the serene room and sighed. With his head hanging, he said, "William, I don't know what I'll do if—"

"Don't even think like that, Keaton. Meridan's going to make it. She has to. She's my baby girl. I lost Eleanor and that was painful enough."

"Yes, Sir."

Keaton sat there looking down at Meridan's blood that still stained his shirt. He cradled his head in his hands. "I wish she'd never come back here," he cursed himself. "I was being selfish by wanting her here."

William put his hand on Keaton's shoulder. "You weren't being selfish, son. We all knew this thing had to eventually come to an end. I just hate that my daughter and Jacob ended up this way."

Keaton openly sobbed.

Angry, William said, "That girl was out of her mind! The police found a couple of vials of cocaine in her jacket. I don't know how I'm going to break the news to Jacob's parents. I've known that boy all his life."

Keaton cleared his throat and softly said, "Jacob saved our lives."

William closed his eyes and continued to pray. Keaton sat there in silence as he said his own special prayer for Meridan.

Moments later, Leona came to tell them Meridan was finally out of surgery. They hurried upstairs and stood in complete attention as they listened to the surgeon explain the extent of Meridan's injuries.

The surgeon said, "We've repaired all the damage and removed the bullet fragments. Meridan's a lucky woman because had it been a few more inches either way, she would've been in serious trouble. But even better news is that the baby is just fine."

The whole family stood there in shock and silence staring at him. Gwendolyn's and Nichole's mouths hung open as tears dropped from Keaton's eyes.

Zenora yelled, "Praise God!"

William asked, "What did you say?"

The doctor said, "I said, Meridan's unborn child is doing just fine."

They all continued to stare at him.

William asked, "What baby? Are you telling me my daughter is pregnant?"

"I'm sorry. I assumed you already knew," the surgeon answered.

"No, we didn't know," William explained. "My daughter can't have children!"

The doctor tucked the clipboard under his arm. "I don't know Meridan's medical history, but I know at the present, she is pregnant. We'll need to keep a close eye on her for a few days, but her prognosis looks very good."

Gwendolyn and Nichole hugged each other and cried openly after hearing the news. William turned and looked at Keaton. He asked, "Did you know about this?"

Wiping his tears away, he said, "No, Sir, I didn't know."

William also teared up as he pulled Keaton into a warm embrace. The two men hugged each other tightly. They were both thankful that their prayers had been answered, in more ways than one.

Releasing Keaton, William turned to the surgeon and asked, "Excuse me, doctor, when can I see my daughter?"

The doctor looked at his watch. "She's being moved into Intensive Care. You can see her in about thirty minutes, but only for about five minutes. She's been through a lot tonight so it might be best to wait until morning."

Keaton shook the surgeon's hand and said, "No, Sir. I have to see her tonight."

Smiling, he said, "I understand, but remember only for about five minutes."

William turned to Keaton and asked, "I wonder if Meridan knows she's pregnant?"

Nikki stepped up and said, "I doubt it, Mr. St. John. She would've told me."

Keaton looked seriously at everyone and said, "If all of you don't mind, I would like to be the one to tell Meridan about our child, but I want to wait until we get home. Agreed?"

The family nodded in agreement as well as the doctor.

Nichole walked over and hugged Keaton. "Keaton, I'm so happy for you guys and I'm so glad this nightmare is over. I'm so sorry about Jacob, but I'm glad he was there to save you guys."

Keaton hugged her. "I know, Nikki. I can't believe I'm going to be a father. I told Meridan it didn't matter whether we had children or not."

William walked over and said, "I guess God had a different plan for you two."

"I believe he did," Keaton said as he hugged William again.

They walked side by side down the hallway to the Intensive Care Unit.

CHAPTER 60

Meridan recovered after spending two weeks in the hospital. Now she was ready to go home so she could fully recover. Keaton hardly ever left her side unless William or his parents stopped by to relieve him. When William told her that Jacob was dead, she was devastated and cried hysterically for him. He had been a good friend over the years, but thankfully they settled their differences before his untimely end.

When Keaton pulled up to his house, everyone was on the porch to welcome Meridan home. There were balloons and a huge sign welcoming her.

Blushing, she looked up at Keaton. "You did all this?"

"Nah, the family did it. Let me get you inside."

Opening the door, he helped her out of the car and picked her up into his arms. He carried her up the stairs and into the family room. He sat her in the chair and she looked around at all the food and decorations.

Becoming emotional, she said, "Thanks, you guys. This is so sweet."

Hugs and kisses were showered upon Meridan until she eventually sobbed with joy. While everyone was mingling, Keaton tapped on his glass to get everyone's attention.

"First, I would like to thank all of you for your prayers and help during Meridan's hospital stay. If it hadn't been for you guys, I don't know if I would've made it." Everyone smiled as Keaton's voice cracked as he spoke. He held Meridan's hand and continued. Turning to William, he said, "William, I love your daughter will all my heart and it's because of that love that Meridan and I would like to let you and the rest of the family know that we decided to make it official."

Everyone in the room was silent as they watched Keaton help Meridan up out of her seat. They knew it was inevitable for him to propose to her and it seemed the time was now.

Meridan kissed him. "What Keaton is trying to say is that we are officially Mr. and Mrs. Keaton Lapahie and have been for some time now."

William yelled out, "What the hell? When?"

Zenora folded her arms and said, "I know you two didn't!"

The whole room immediately filled with noisy chatter as everyone tried to get an understanding of what they had just heard.

Keaton looked at Meridan and said, "I told you they would be upset."

"They'll get over it," she said with a smile.

Keaton tapped on the glass again and said, "We're sorry for breaking the news to you like this, but we wanted to wait until we could tell you all together."

Nikki, Gerald, Gwendolyn, and Arnelle all clapped loudly upon hearing the news. Winston walked over nonchalantly, kissed Meridan on the cheek, and said, "Congrats, you two."

Keaton smiled back at him and said, "Thanks, bro."

Winston hugged Keaton and said, "I'm really happy for you guys."

"Thanks, Winston."

He stared at Keaton once more and said, "I'll give you a call later, bro. We do have some unfinished business to discuss."

Laughing, he answered, "That we do. I look forward to talking to you."

William was still stunned. Meridan walked over to him and asked, "Daddy? Are you okay?"

He hugged her and said, "I'm more than okay. You just don't know how blessed I feel right now. He's a good man, Meridan, and you two deserve each other."

She hugged his neck and said, "Thank you, Daddy."

Turning to Keaton, William yelled, "Keaton! You do know my daughter will get a proper wedding?"

Zenora agreed, saying, "I know that's right!"

Keaton smiled and said, "Whatever Meridan wants is fine with me, William, and again, I'm sorry we didn't tell you. Momma, don't be upset."

She hugged them both and said, "Don't mind me. That's just my motherly selfishness kicking in. I do want you two to let us give you a proper wedding, like William said."

"We'll think about it, Momma."

Zenora put her hands on her hips and asked, "Now, when did you two get married?"

"We did it when I visited Philly a few weeks ago. Meridan told me everything about Sam as well as some other things. She thought it was best we kept our marriage a secret until we could relax a little easier."

William smiled, took a sip of punch, and said, "Well, I'll be damned! You guys pulled a fast one over on us, but as they say…the best is yet to come."

William winked at Keaton before walking over to talk to other family members.

The family only stayed for about an hour before they started cleaning up. After saying goodbye to everyone, Keaton picked Meridan up and carried her upstairs.

She held onto him and said, "There's nothing wrong with my legs, Keaton."

"I know. I just like having you in my arms," he said before kissing her. He smiled mischievously and said, "I have another surprise for you."

"You do? What is it?"

He sat her down and took her hand into his and said, "Close your eyes." They walked down the hallway and Keaton swung the door open. He softly said, "You can open your eyes now."

Meridan opened her eyes and immediately became speechless. Keaton had transformed one of the bedrooms into a nursery. She couldn't control her tears as they fell from her eyes. Keaton had decorated the room with the Noah's Ark theme. He had everything from the crib to the changing table to the baby bed, all in shining gold. A huge rocking chair sat near the crib and soft lighting radiated throughout the room. She turned to him and solemnly asked, "Why did you do this?"

"I did it because our baby has to have somewhere to sleep."

She turned to him in confusion and asked, "So does this mean you want to adopt?"

He laughed out loud, unable to contain his excitement.

Meridan turned to him and folded her arms. "What's so funny, chief?"

Hugging her, he said, "Oh, nothing much."

"Then why are you laughing? All I did was ask you if this meant you were ready to adopt?"

He leaned in close to her ear and whispered, "No, sweetheart, I'm not interested in adopting because we're having a baby of our own."

Meridan looked up into his eyes in shock and asked, "What did you say?"

"I said…we…are…having…a…child…of…our…own."

Meridan's legs turned to jelly as she fought to maintain her balance. Keaton quickly steadied her. She put her hand over her mouth momentarily, then asked, "Keaton, what are you talking about? If this is your way of playing a joke on me, it's not funny."

He sat down in the plush chair, pulling her into his lap. He caressed her back and said, "Babe, I wouldn't joke about something that means so much to you."

"You're not making any sense. I told you I can't have children," she said, clearly agitated.

Making direct eye contact with her, he touched her stomach. "Listen to me very carefully, sweetheart. We're pregnant and we're going to have a baby of our own in about seven and a half months."

She screamed out loud and yelled, "No! It can't be true! The doctors told me that I can't have children!"

"Well, they were wrong. We *are* having a baby. So, do you like the nursery or not?"

Meridan burst into tears as she hugged his neck. She cried so hard, Keaton was worried that she might aggravate her injury.

"Meridan, it's okay. Please, don't make yourself sick," he urged her.

She did her best to stifle her tears, but it was difficult. She eventually calmed herself and laughed openly. "I still can't believe it's true. I had no idea. I mean, my cycle has always been irregular. I would've never suspected."

He nuzzled her neck. "I'm so thankful you're safe."

"So am I."

They held each other in silence for several minutes.

"So, does this mean you like the nursery?"

"I love it and I love you," she admitted with sincerity.

Standing, he picked her up into his arms and carried her back to their bedroom.

"Good, little momma; now come to bed because my two favorite people need to rest."

"Are you going to continue to pamper me, Keaton?" she asked as he lowered her to the floor.

Without looking into her eyes, he said, "Yes, Mrs. Lapahie, as much as possible; especially now that I have two people to take care of."

She giggled, then turned her back to him. "You know you're amazing, don't you?"

He unzipped her dress and said, "I'm just a man who loves his wife."

Meridan let the dress fall to the floor, then looked up at him mischievously. Keaton blinked, then walked slowly toward the bathroom to run her bath.

"Stop teasing me, Meridan. You know I can't touch you for a few more days," he warned.

She lay across the bed and said, "I'll be waiting, Big Daddy."

Later that night, Keaton built a fire and made them a pallet in front of it. It was there Meridan rested securely in his arms.

"Keaton, I'm sorry for causing you so much stress with all my drama," she apologized.

Stroking her hair, he said, "Thanks for reminding me. You are due a spanking, but I'll wait until you're feeling better first."

She caressed his arm and said, "I knew I had to do something to get Sam out of my life. I had no idea Jacob would show up to help. He told me he would be my guardian angel."

"We could've been killed," he whispered.

Sighing, she said, "I know."

He played in her hair, then said, "Let's not talk about it anymore. It's in the past and all I want to think about is our future."

Cuddling up to him, she answered, "Me, too."

At that moment, the telephone rang, interrupting them. Keaton answered, "Hello?"

"What's up, Bro?"

"Hey, Winston. What's up?"

"I was just checking on Meridan. How's she doing?"

"She's sore and tired," Keaton answered as he caressed her cheek.

"Well, tell me this. How cold do you think it is in Hell right now?"

Smiling, Keaton said, "You don't forget anything, do you?"

"No, I don't and since I didn't get to attend this secret wedding of yours, there's another little matter you haven't taken care of."

"You never quit, do you?"

Laughing hysterically, Winston asked, "No, I don't. Where's Meridan?"

"She's lying right here. Why?"

"You know why. Let me speak to her."

Keaton had no idea what Winston was up to. Meridan took the telephone and answered, "Hello?"

Keaton watched her facial expressions as Winston said God knows what to her. She would be smiling one minute, then the next minute she had a serious look on her face. Finally she said, "Okay. Goodbye and thanks for calling. Tell Arnelle and the kids I said goodnight."

Holding out the telephone, she smiled and said, "Here you go, Keaton."

Taking the telephone, he asked, "Yeah, man?"

Winston started laughing, then said, "Start singing, brother-in-law, right now, to your lovely wife."

Keaton swallowed hard, then closed his eyes and started softly singing a love ballad by Luther Vandross to Meridan. She smiled, then closed her eyes and listened to him rip Luther's song into shreds, but it was the message she listened closest to. She knew what he was doing was some sort of dare between him and Winston, but him going through with it made it special.

Once he finished singing, he asked, "Are you happy now, Winston?"

"I'm very happy. I'm also happy for you, Bro. Congratulations! Now, I still get to name your first born, right?"

Keaton laughed. "When hell freezes over! Goodnight, Winston!"

CHAPTER 61

onths later, Meridan delivered Jeremiah Mathew Lapahie, who weighed in at nine pounds, two ounces. Meridan and Keaton didn't have a preference on whether they had a boy or girl, but he knew if it was a girl, MaLeah might be very jealous. He had spoiled her like she was his own daughter and the adjustment would've been difficult. Luckily, they didn't have to deal with it.

Six weeks after the birth of Jeremiah, Keaton threw a party to celebrate the birth of his son and his baptism. The whole family was in attendance as well as Nichole, Craig, Venice, and their children. William wanted as many family members as possible to be there for the celebration, so he chartered a bus for their transportation. Meridan's sister, Gwendolyn, and her family flew in to be a part of the joyous celebration as well. Meridan never thought she would ever be a part of a family like she had found with Keaton and their son.

All in all, over one hundred family members and friends were in attendance, even Aunt Glo. Deacon wasn't able to come, but he sent his regards to the family. He had an important case he was in the middle of and couldn't get away. Keaton's best friend Gerald was there to support him. Keaton also invited the guys on the basketball team, even Malik. Arnelle invited Damon Kirkpatrick, a dear friend and coach of the Philadelphia Eagles football team who just happened to be in Texas looking at a prospective ballplayer. Damon had Winston losing his mind when he was dating Arnelle, and it was Damon who caused Winston come to his senses when they were having problems. Winston saw Damon as a serious threat to his relationship with Arnelle, but later found out they really were just friends.

After the baptism at the church, everyone joined back up at Keaton's house for food and fun that lasted another five hours. It was a day-long event, which eventually wound down. Meridan took Jeremiah up for his bath and bedtime while Keaton said goodnight to their guests.

Keaton joined her in the nursery later. He found Meridan in the rocking chair burping his son.

He kissed her on the cheek and whispered, "Are you happy, Meridan?"

Meridan smiled as she put their sleeping son in his crib. Keaton turned off the lights and they walked out into the hallway arm in arm.

She looked up at him and she answered, "Keaton, I can't believe you asked me that. I'm happy here with you and Jeremiah. I've decided to put my career on hold for a while. I want to enjoy being your wife and a full-time mother. If I get bored, I'll go out on the court and shoot a few hoops or help your mom with her catering business or something."

Laughing, he said, "I want to make sure. Promise me, you'll let me know the moment you're ready to open a practice or whatever."

She kissed him. "My love, you'll be the first to know."

"Good! Oh, a letter came for you today from a law office in Atlanta."

Frowning, she asked, "I wonder what it could be?"

Walking around the bed, he said, "I bet it has something to do with Jacob."

Meridan's hands trembled as she picked the envelope up from the dresser. Keaton looked at her and asked, "Do you want me to open it for you?"

She swallowed and said, "No, I can do it."

They were silent as she opened the letter and began to read it. Keaton went back into the bathroom to run her bath. When he returned to the bedroom, Meridan sat there with a blank look on her face.

"What's wrong, sweetheart?"

Meridan was speechless. She held the letter out to Keaton. He cautiously took it from her hand and began to read it. It was a letter forwarded to Meridan in the event of Jacob's death.

Dear Meridan,

If you're reading this, it means that I am no longer on this earth. After all that happened between us, I hope this letter finds you in good spirits. After I left Mississippi and moved to Atlanta, I got caught up in the fast lane of the city. Being raised in a small country town, I felt like a prisoner who was experiencing real life for the first time. Unfortunately, my adventures came back to haunt me and I turned to drugs because I was a man in pain. There is another envelope enclosed, which is my Will and Testament. Within it, I made provisions for my family and you. You might be wondering 'why you.' Well, Meridan, you were the only person in my life that never judged me or looked down on me no matter what I did or said. For that, I have always loved you and been grateful to you. My behavior towards you in Atlanta was the beginning of my end. It was around that time that I found out my time on this earth was limited when I tested positive with HIV. No, I'm not gay. Yes, I had a hunger for fast women and I paid for it with my life. When you visited me in the hospital, it hurt for you to see me like that. Even then, you didn't question or judge me. As a doctor, I knew the risks, but somewhere along the line, I got careless. I never intended to hurt you or anyone around you, but it was hard to see you so happy with Keaton when I was going through my own hell. I'm glad you forgave me. It meant everything to me and I didn't want you to pity me. I just wanted my old friend back. I don't know when or how my life will end, but I want you to know that I'll love you forever.

Jacob

Keaton opened the other envelope and saw that Jacob left Meridan around seven hundred and fifty thousand dollars. His heart sank, then went out to her. She looked up with tears in her eyes.

He pulled her into his arms and said, "I know. I'm so sorry, Meridan."

"I can't believe it. I wish I could've done something to help him."

"His pride wouldn't let him so don't feel guilty, Meridan."

"Should I keep the money?"

"You do what you want to with it. He wanted you to have it. It's a gift."

Standing, she walked across the room and said, "I think I'm going to donate it to the high school back home. This money can send a lot of kids to college. I'd hate for Jacob to be remembered the wrong way. Maybe setting up a scholarship fund will somehow overshadow the issues he had. You know?"

Smiling, Keaton said, "That sounds like a great idea, babe."

"Thanks, sweetheart. I love you, Keaton."

"I love you more, Meridan Lapahie."

EPILOGUE

At the hotel where the guests were staying, Nichole relaxed in the lounge with an apple martini. After the party at Keaton's house, she couldn't wait to change into some comfortable jeans and T-shirt.

Damon Kilpatrick was bored and tired of looking at football film. Relaxing at Keaton's house had been a welcome distraction from his job. Finding Nichole sitting at the bar also rejuvenated him.

He walked over and said, "Nichole, it's so nice seeing you again."

She turned and smiled at the baritone voice greeting her. "It's nice seeing you again, too, Damon. That was a nice party today, huh?"

He shoved his hands in his pockets and said, "Yes, it was."

He stood by the stool next to her and asked, "Do you mind if I join you?"

Motioning toward the seat, she said, "Not at all. Actually, I'm glad you came in. I was beginning to look pathetic sitting here in this beautiful hotel all by myself."

Damon laughed and stared at her. "A woman like you could never look pathetic, Nichole."

Arnelle had introduced them earlier at the party and they seemed to hit it off immediately. They discussed politics, the stock market and surprisingly sports. Nichole found Damon handsome and charming, but the reality was, she was already dating someone and would never cheat on Deacon.

She blushed and said, "Why, thank you, Damon."

Turning away, he asked, "What are you drinking?

Holding up her glass, she answered, "Apple martinis."

"It looks like you're out. Let me get you another one."

She touched his arm and said, "You don't have to do that."

Showing her his dimples, he smiled and said, "I know, but I want to."

Damon motioned for the bartender to bring Nichole another drink.

"Thank you, Damon."

"You're welcome," he politely replied. "So, what are you doing here all by yourself?"

The bartender sat her glass in front of her.

"I could ask you the same thing."

He laughed. "I guess I deserve that, huh?"

They laughed together. Nichole couldn't believe a handsome man like him wouldn't have a woman traveling with him. He was working the black ·jeans he had on, and the tan, starched shirt he wore showed just how fine he was. Now she was curious to know why there was no woman by his side.

She tilted her head and asked, "So, Damon, how is it that your woman let you travel all over the country without her?"

He stared at her and said, "Who said I had a woman?"

Nichole took a sip of her drink and nervously said, "I just assumed—"

"While you're all up in my kool-aid, why is it that your policeman friend let you out all by yourself?"

Nichole's face became hot with embarrassment. She swallowed and asked, "Have you been checking up on me, Damon?"

With sincerity, he said, "What can I say? You caught my eye. You're a very beautiful woman, Nichole, and if you were my lady, you wouldn't be here alone."

"It's so sweet of you to say that, but my friend had to work. Thanks for the compliment," she responded with appreciation.

"You're welcome," he said as the bartender sat a soda in front of him.

She sipped her martini, then asked, "Aren't you going to order something?"

"I already have." He showed her his glass.

"Soda?"

"I don't drink alcohol," he informed her.

Amazed, Nichole asked, "For real?"

"For real."

It was then her cell phone rang. She pulled it from her purse and said, "Excuse me for a second, Damon."

Damon nodded and took a sip of his soda as he watched the news showing on the TV monitors above the bar. Nichole turned her back to him so she could talk privately on the phone. It was noisy in the lounge, but it didn't stop Damon from hearing a muffled scream come out of her mouth. He looked over at her and noticed she was trembling. Concerned, he jumped up from the bar stool and came around in front of her.

Her head was lowered and she was sobbing uncontrollably. Damon pulled her up out of her seat and asked with concern, "What's wrong, Nichole?"

"It's Deacon, my boyfriend. He's...he's...he's been shot."

Hugging her, he asked, "Is he okay?"

"I don't know. All they said was he's been shot."

Hugging her, he said, "I'm sorry, Nichole. What can I do to help?"

"Nothing. I'm sorry; I have to get back to Philly," she said, still trembling with fear.

Damon was worried that she was going into shock. He looked at his watch and said, "Don't worry, I know someone that could get us back to Philly."

"What do you mean, us?"

He looked down at her and said, "Unless there's someone else who can go with you, I'm not going to let you travel alone under these circumstances. You don't need to be by yourself right now."

Damon was a stranger to her, but he was a friend of the Lapahies so she figured he had to be okay. Unable to object, she collapsed against his large body and cried hysterically. He embraced her and his heart melted as he wondered what awful tragedy she would face when she stepped off the plane.

AUTHOR BIO

Darrien Lee, a native of Columbia, Tennessee, resides in LaVergne, Tennessee with her husband and two young daughters. Darrien picked up her love for writing while attending college at Tennessee State University, and it was that experience which inspired her debut novel, *All That and a Bag of Chips*. Later she released the sequels, *Been There Done That* and *What Goes Around Comes Around*. Both were *Essence* bestselling titles.

She is a member of A Place of Our Own Bookclub, Women of Color Bookclub, and Authors Supporting Authors Positively.

Please visit her web site http://www.darrienlee.com/ for upcoming appearances and events.
You can email the author at: DarrienLeeAuthor@ aol.com.